I0533750

# No Easy Way

S.R. Claridge

Global Publishing Group

Global Publishing Group LLC

Printed in the United States of America

First trade edition: October 2010

10 9 8 7 6 5 4 3 2 1

ISBN 978-0-9898467-6-9

The author would like to offer special thanks to her brilliant team of editors, whose expertise is invaluable: Cash, Jerrye, Gary, Matt and Beth

She would like to thank her family for their love and support, and thank God for every blessing.

~

A complete list of books by S.R.Claridge is located at the back of this book.

For previews and information about the author, visit AuthorSRClaridge.com or find her on Facebook.

**Prologue**

Remorse beat a deep ache into his chest. Lou Miller wasn't a man who cried easily, but the tears flowed freely now. Turning onto the freeway, flashbacks of the past year flood his brain as he drove. He squinted and blinked to see through the tears, then wiped them with the back of his hand. *What have I done?* He thought. For sixty years he was a man of integrity, dependable and faithful. Sure, he'd made the usual bone-head choices as a teenager, told a few harmless white lies in his day, made some poor financial decisions as a young adult, but never anything close to this. What he did was just plain wrong and he knew it. He pondered how one moment of weakness could dismantle his entire ethical code, knowing all the while it wasn't merely a moment of weakness that led him here, but two years of secret indiscretions. From the first night he succumbed to her, he had been trying to cover it up, to conceal what he'd done, and it changed him.

"Why?" His wife, Madeline, demanded after learning of his affair.

"I don't know," was the only truthful answer.

Madeline screamed, "She's too young for you!" He knew she was right. Arianna was young enough to be his daughter and a part of him was repulsed by the age difference, but she made him feel youthful and alive. After that first night he couldn't stop. He never planned to take her as a lover. He never planned for any of this to happen.

Slumping further into the driver's seat, and deeper into the throes of regret, he let the steering wheel bear the weight of both arms. He felt demoralized. Letting Arianna go was the right thing to do but that awareness did little to ease his

4

guilt.   He knew the decision he made tonight would torture him the rest of his life.

Twisting the handle on the driver door, Lou rolled down the window and let the cool night air slap against his skin.  Each mile marker passed slowly as the heaviness in his spirit bore down on him.  He wondered if Madeline would leave him after forty years of marriage.  He wondered if she was right about Arianna wanting him only for his money.  He wondered if either woman would ever forgive him for the brokenness he caused.  Not ready to face the certain reality of another brutal conversation at home, Lou veered off the freeway three exits early and drove along a two lane gravel road winding through the Kansas countryside.  He knew these roads well, as many a night he drove them alone, stopping for a smoke.  Tonight felt unusually dark.  A deep orange moon sat overhead rendering little brightness below, as Lou pulled his olive green Oldsmobile to the side of the road and stepped out, letting the door creak closed behind him.  He stood staring up at the night sky, unable to peel his eyes away.  Ordinarily the moon brought a feeling of serenity and comfort, but tonight its eerie hue sent a shiver through him. Taking a deep breath, he inhaled the aroma of corn and the distinct odor of cow manure that had baked all day in the afternoon sun.  He leaned against the car, pulled a cigar from his blazer pocket and lit it with a match.  The smoke circled his head, and he squinted for a moment until it cleared.   In the silence of his mind he prayed, *forgive me*, and closing his eyes, felt a momentary peace.

Lou had been too deep in his own thoughts to notice the black pick-up trailing behind him for several miles. The driver killed the lights half a mile from where Lou pulled over and sat quietly watching.  Straining to see his silhouette in the moonlight, Lou's cigar smoke gave proof of his precise location.  The driver took a deep breath, gripped the wheel with white-knuckled rage and floored the gas.  By the time Lou heard the sound of the engine and turned his stare in the direction of the truck, it was too late.  The driver hit the lights, blinding him as the pick-up swerved toward him with the kind of precision only blind rage can empower.  Lou's muscles tensed and his eyes widened seconds before impact.  The pick-up slammed against his body, smashing him between his driver door and the grill of the truck.  He heard the sound of the collision, the crumbling of metal and breaking of glass, then his body went numb and dropped in a heap to the gravel.  His right cheek slammed to the ground with gravel digging deeply into his skin.  Somehow he managed to open his left eye, only to see the pick-up reverse, stop, and then barrel toward him again.  Piercing pain shot down his spine, then darkness.

Throwing the truck into reverse a second time, the driver backed up, straightened the wheels and sped off, checking the rearview mirror only once to make sure there was no movement on the ground.   All that could be seen was the tiny glowing ember of the cigar still clenched between the fingers of Lou's left hand.

A teary eyed Madeline clipped the obituary from the newspaper and taped it into her journal next to the photograph of Lou.  She kissed the picture one last time, then closed the book and held it tightly to her chest.  She never imagined it would end like this.

## Chapter One

Kate sat in the reception area with her stomach in knots. Tom was late. Again. After eighteen years of marriage, she should be used to it, but it still infuriated her. Tucking her shoulder length dark brown hair behind her ears, she pulled a small spiral notebook from her purse and began to jot down thoughts. She found it helped her stay calm and focused when dealing with emotional situations. Her therapist encouraged her to journal as often as needed. "Getting your thoughts on paper," he told her, "makes them clearer to understand and assign emotion to." She didn't know if that was true, but it did pass the time. Fifteen minutes passed. Twenty. Thirty. Kate set the notebook on the chair next to her and began to fiddle with her wedding band. Another nervous tick she had, twisting her ring counterclockwise around her finger. It had been Tom's grandmother, Madeline's band. Kate grinned as she pictured Madeline, with her white hair tied tightly in a bun and her bright pink lipstick.

"Pulling my hair back real tight," she would say, "is like getting a face lift for free." Kate thought this was true, but it also made her big blue eyes sort of bulge out of her head like a Chihuahua.

Madeline gave Kate the wedding band the same year Tom's grandfather, Lou, died in a tragic hit and run accident. The driver who killed him was never found and the case was labeled "unsolved." Though rumors about Lou circulated around the small town of Stilwell, Kansas, Grandmother Madeline assured everyone she believed there was no foul play. "It was a terrible accident," she told Tom and Kate, "but accidents happen and life goes on." After the funeral, Madeline pulled Kate aside and gave her the wedding ring. "It is time," she said, taking Kate's hand in hers and patting it. Madeline's eyes always had a discerning twinkle, but that day they beamed with kid-like excitement.

Kate often wondered why Madeline wanted her to have the ring instead of saving it for Tom's brother Martin to give a future bride. After all, Martin was the older grandson. Madeline dismissed the question with a quick shrug of her boney shoulders and a roll of her bulging eyes. "This ring," she said, "embodies a promise." Kate was puzzled. "This ring," she whispered, squeezing Kate's hand, "covers a multitude of sins." She said it as if it were something magical. Something that would ensure a marriage would last forever.

"What does that mean; it covers a multitude of sins?" Kate asked.

Madeline's answer came swiftly, "forgiveness." Kate studied her eyes as they sparkled with wisdom and truth she hoped would one day be hers. "God joins spouses in marriage. He created marriage. What He joins let no man," Madeline paused and drew in a deep breath, "and no woman separate." She pointed her long, skinny finger in the air for effect. Then placing Kate's hand between hers she emphasized, "Forgiveness is the key and you are strong enough to carry its burden." Replaying more of the conversation in her mind, Kate felt she could almost hear Madeline's voice telling her marriage was both a mountainous journey and a joyous adventure.

"Never give up," she said, patting Kate's hand, "never give up."

Now, staring at the band, Kate fought back tears as a feeling of guilt rushed through her. She knew Madeline would be ashamed of what she and Tom were about to do. They had given up and this was the last step to make it final. Kate kicked Tom out of their home six months ago, shortly after her fortieth birthday. She knew Tom blamed her behavior on mid-life crisis, but Kate knew it was more than that. Maybe she and Tom were both going through a change of life in some regard, but what tore their marriage apart was deeper than any physical change or hormonal imbalance. For ten years they tried to get pregnant and the four times they did ended in miscarriage. The cost of in vitro fertilization put financial strain on Tom, while the fertility drugs took their toll on Kate. Each time they lost a baby, a piece of Kate shut down. She couldn't handle the guilt, knowing it was her fault they couldn't conceive. Tom's sperm was doing its job. He was perfect and she was not. She was failing. Kate's depression became all encompassing and it drove Tom toward the one stable part of his world, work. He became a workaholic and Kate grew resentful of what she viewed as his inability to help her cope. Ten years later, they had not only grown distant, but had fallen apart.

"Mrs. Miller?" The young woman's voice jolted Kate from her thoughts. "Your attorney has another hearing to go to now. Since Mr. Miller hasn't arrived yet, we're going to have to reschedule your appointment."

Kate starred blankly. She felt disappointed, yet not completely deflated. Maybe this meant Tom had the same reservations she did about preceding down this path. Maybe it meant there was still some hope left in them, somewhere deep down. Maybe it merely meant he was too irresponsible to show up. She rescheduled the appointment and left.

~

Tom's office was buzzing with people. Vendors in from all over the country, new product lines on the floor, sales goals, and corporate initiatives in play. You name it, it was happening today. As the VP of Sales & Marketing at his grandfather's company, LouLineCo, Tom was usually in the mix on everything, but today was different. Today he sat at his desk, door closed, blinds drawn shut, and his phone held closely to his ear. He was soaking in every word that came through the receiver.

"If this is what she wants just go and get it over with," came the advice of a long trusted friend.

"I don't think I can," said Tom, running his hand through his light brown hair, which was now speckled with more gray than brown. He rubbed his eyes and exhaled a sigh of discouragement.

"It doesn't sound like you've got a choice. At least go and see if you can talk her out of it." Tom knew Jace was right. Jace was on his third marriage, so he had some experience in the department of divorce etiquette. Much as he didn't want to, Tom knew he had to show up or things would get worse, though he couldn't help but wonder how much worse. The ending of an eighteen year marriage felt like bottom of the barrel to him. He couldn't believe it had come to this and that Kate actually wanted a divorce. His mind stalled each time he tried to pinpoint what went wrong. Sure he wanted a baby, but more than that, he wanted his wife back. He wanted the Kate he knew before they ever embarked on the pregnancy quest. He missed her laugh and the glow of her smile. He longed for her touch, something he hadn't felt in almost a year. The problem was he didn't know how to reach her anymore. Everything he tried was wrong. Either he said the wrong thing or the right thing at the wrong time. A part of him wanted to breakdown and sob, but the reality of divorce numbed him to the point where he couldn't even cry. It was as if the aching in his heart was so deep even tears couldn't release it. He was mourning the loss of the woman he loved and the marriage he treasured.

A quick glance at his watch confirmed he was late and he abruptly ended his conversation with Jace. Tom sat for a moment with his hands to his face, trying to muster the will to get up and head to the divorce attorney's office.

Tapping on Tom's door, Rita opened it slightly and poked her head inside. He whirled around in his chair to meet her gaze, aggravated by the interruption.

"What do you need?" He blurted coldly, lowering his eyes to the paperwork on his desk, as a signal he did not want to be bothered.

Rita slipped inside and closed the door. Her expression told him she didn't appreciate the frigidity of his tone, especially when she hadn't said anything to deserve it. She and Tom had known each other practically their whole lives. Her family lived in Stillwell, Kansas, two mile markers from Tom's grandparents and Rita's folks worked at LouLineCo until retirement. Rita joined the company right out of high school, working her way through college and into a management position after graduation. She was later promoted to the position of Controller, which fit her personality well. It was apparent she wanted to control everything, but mostly Tom.  Over the years, Rita made her affection for Tom known.  Each time he shut her down she grew more hostile with a competitive rage even people outside the company could sense.  Tom often remembered the warning from Jace, "hell hath no fury as Rita scorned." Though his gut said she was harmless, merely after him for the inheritance she knew would one day be his, Tom didn't trust her.  Maybe it was that she resembled the wicked witch in the Wizard of Oz, with her high cheekbones and pointy nose. Maybe it was her cut-throat business sense that often spilled into her personal life, leaving her with few friendships.  Tom couldn't put his finger on it, but his hair stood on end whenever Rita came close.

They butted corporate heads plenty of times, mostly over money, and the whole company could feel the tension whenever Rita and Tom were in the same room.  A tension Rita wanted to link to one brief sexual encounter they shared after high school graduation.  It was a night of fumbling innocence in the back of Tom's pick-up brought on by too many Purple Passions.  A night Tom would have long forgotten if Rita didn't bring it up every chance she got.  Tom knew if she had her way, he would be married to her instead of Kate and they would be running LouLineCo in wedded bliss. What Rita didn't know was that merely working with her was hard enough and he would rather be strung up by his balls than imagine one moment married to her.

Sliding into the chair across from his desk, Rita folded her hands on her lap and pursed her narrow lips.  "It's awfully dark in here."

Tom glanced around the room, realizing for the first time how dark it was.  Dark brown paneling covered two walls, and a floor to ceiling dark wooden bookshelf was built into the far wall, so when the blinds were shut and the door was shut there was no outside light coming in. A small lamp illumed his desk area, but the overhead lights were turned off. "I like it dark."

"It seems to fit your mood lately."

Tom glared at her. "What do you need Rita?" His jaw tightened, as the very sight of her made him irritable.

Rita narrowed her hazel eyes and wrinkled her pointy nose at him. "You're in a foul mood."

Tom shook his head and held up his hands in disgust. "If you don't need something right away, I'd like to be alone."

Leaning up out of the chair and over the desk, Rita flipped her dark auburn hair to one side. "Listen you son-of-a-bitch, I came in here to see if you were doing okay." Tom raised his eyebrows. "Rumor has it you're on the verge of a breakdown and if my VP of Sales is about to go off the deep end I need to know about it."

"I'm not on the edge," he lied, "just a lot going on at home. Nothing for you to worry about."

"Cut the crap Tom," Rita blurted, plunking back down in the chair, and swinging one leg across the other. "We both know you've been living in a rental apartment for six months and Kate has filed for divorce." Tom looked at her as if to ask how she knew, but before he could ask, she spattered arrogantly, "it's my business to know."

Tom wanted to leap across the desk and smash his fist into her snide little smirk. For a brief second he imagined reaching over, gripping her boney little neck and shaking the life out of her. Instead he shot out of his chair and shoved one arm into his coal gray sport coat. Rita stood, ran her hands over her black skirt, straightened the sleeves on her white blouse and stared deliberately at Tom. She crossed her arms and pursed her lips as she spoke and Tom thought she looked like she had a beak.

"Your grandfather put me in charge of this company from a financial perspective."

"And?" Tom belted, cutting her off.

"And," she continued, sarcasm oozing from her pores, "if your personal life interferes with your professional abilities I won't be able to justify the financial liability of your salary."

Tom seethed at her. Talk about kicking someone when they're down. This was low even for her. Tom packed up his laptop and headed for the door with his briefcase in tow. He stopped in the doorway and glared at Rita. "You better watch yourself," he warned, "if grandmother's Will leaves me the sole heir of this company, I guarantee there will be changes around here."

"Who are you kidding," Rita snapped, "everyone knows you can't touch the Will until both you and your brother are present, and nobody's been able to locate him for years."

"Until now," winked Tom.

Rita's mouth fell agape. "That's impossible."

"Now if you'll excuse me," Tom sneered, "I have an appointment with my grandmother's attorney."

He wasn't really meeting with Madeline's attorney. He lied and chuckled to himself as he walked to his car, leaving a stunned Rita standing in his office. Rita was right about the Will. It couldn't be opened until both Tom and his brother, Martin were present, or unless a death certificate was filed should one of the brothers be deceased. Tom felt confident per grandfather's instructions that LouLineCo had been left to him. All he had to do was find Martin to prove it, but he was beginning to think Martin had fallen off the face of the Earth. Madeline died six months ago and still no sign of him. It wasn't completely out of character for Martin to disappear for months on end. He'd always been a loose canon, but Tom would have bet his life on the fact that Martin would show up once Madeline died, for the inheritance money alone.

Despite his frustration over Martin, Tom enjoyed being able to dangle the Will in front of Rita's bird-like face and watch her squirm.

Pulling into the lot, Tom took a deep breath, feeling the oxygen make a feeble attempt to push the dread from his chest. He read the sign on the front of the building, *MI & BI, Attorneys at Law*, and wondered if that stood for "Make It & Break It." Every part of him fought walking into the office. He knew Kate would be angry at his tardiness and a fight would ensue. He also knew the tension he felt deep down stemmed from the fact that he did not believe in divorce. Marriage was supposed to last a lifetime. Through thick and thin, good and bad, ups and downs, it was supposed to last. Tom hesitantly opened the office door and braced himself for the verbal lashing he anticipated, but silence was his only greeting. His eyes darted around the room as he approached the check in desk. When he found out Kate already left, he breathed a sigh of relief.

"Boy I bet she was pissed," he joked with the receptionist who offered a half-witted smirk, letting him know she didn't find him at all amusing.

"Your wife left this in the reception area," she said, holding up the spiral notebook. "I'm certain it's hers because she was the only one sitting here long enough to have time to journal."

Tom acknowledged the underhanded dig with a closed lip grin. "I'll see to it she gets this back."

Once in his car he couldn't resist the temptation to take a peek at Kate's writing. A lump entered his throat as his eyes drank in the emotion she never shared with him. Thoughts she'd never put into verbal patterns. Frustrations she never vented out loud. Tears he never saw her cry and secrets she never disclosed. For the past ten years he hadn't felt the deep, raw emotional honesty in his wife that he felt now, leaping off the pages of her notebook. For the first time in years Tom couldn't stop the flood of emotion. He gripped the steering wheel and wept.

~

Kate drove toward home in a daze. The rhythmic drumming of rain drops against the windshield mesmerized her mind with the irony of how well the storm fit her mood. She was angry at Tom for not showing up nor bothering to call. She could have phoned him from the attorney's office, but she was tired of being the responsible one. Tired of being dependable Kate, reliable Kate, and punctual Kate. She felt drained from years of nagging Tom to be on time and vowed not to be his walking reminder any longer.

Rain pounded on the windshield with such ferocity even the wipers set to high couldn't keep it clear enough to see. Kate tapped her breaks to slow down; afraid she would hydroplane if she kept going the speed limit. The wipers methodically swished side-to-side doing their best to provide a sense of visual security, but failed against the strength of the downpour. Cautiously, Kate pulled to the side of road and stopped to wait out the storm. The Kansas wind whirled and shook the car with an intensity that made Kate fear she was in the midst of a tornado. Turning on the radio and repeatedly pushing the scan button, she searched for a weather update. Unable to hear anything but static, Kate hit the off button, leaned her head back and let tears of exhaustion and emptiness stream down her cheeks. This was not the way she envisioned her life. She didn't have unrealistic expectations. She knew marriage came with challenges and everything wouldn't come easy, but where did it all go wrong? When had they stopped communicating? When had their hearts grown numb?

"Damn it!" she blurted aloud, as mascara seeped into her right eye and burned. She fumbled with her seatbelt, unhooked it and reached for her purse in the passenger seat. Looking down, digging for a tissue, Kate never saw what happened next. The squealing of tires was the last sound she heard before impact.

## Chapter 2

Tom knocked on the front door, but no one answered. He wasn't supposed to use his key out of respect for the boundaries they set upon being officially separated, but after a good ten seconds in the rain, he breezed past those boundaries and let himself in. A wave of sadness filled him as he entered. It had been their home for what seemed like forever. It literally housed all the memories he held most dear, and his heart ached at the very thought of letting it go. Divorce meant splitting assets, ripping apart everything they had built. It sickened him. He walked past the family room and his favorite, brown leather chair, making a bee line to the den. It had been turned into a home office with built in book cases along the back wall and a large mahogany desk. He sat down in the leather swivel chair, contemplating whether he should dig through Kate's files. It was wrong to invade her privacy, but he felt driven by the need to understand her heart. For the first time in a long time he saw a side of his wife that left him wanting.

Opening each drawer, he skimmed the file labels until he found one that read "ILYWAMH." It took only a moment to recognize and remember the acronym, meaning I Love You With All My Heart. He made it up when they were in college and that was how he signed all the cards and letters he sent to Kate when they were first engaged. Kate was in her last semester at the University of Missouri in Columbia when Tom proposed. He had already graduated and returned to his grandparent's house

in Stillwell, Kansas to begin his career at
LouLineCo. It was the same year Grandpa Lou
was killed.

Tom leaned his head back against the
leather chair and surrendered his mind to the
flashback.

It all began when he was eight years old
and his mom died of cancer. His dad dropped Tom
and his older brother, Martin, at Madeline and
Lou's house one summer and never came back.
Tom could still see his dad speed off down the
gravel road and disappear behind the row of trees
that marked the start of Madeline and Lou's
property.

Through the years Tom tried to squash the
agony, but he'd never forget that moment on
Madeline and Lou's porch. He stood there,
clutching a paper bag that housed all his
belongings, staring at the dust from the road and
trying not to cry. His brother, Martin, chased up
the road after their dad, yelling things a twelve
year old boy shouldn't say and throwing rocks.

"He'll be back, right Grandpa?" Tom's eyes
searched Lou's face for reassurance, but found
only a truth he didn't want to face. His dad was
never coming back.

Tom sunk to the step and buried his face
between his kneecaps.

"Walk with me Tommy." Grandpa Lou said,
then stepped off the porch and headed for the open
field. Tom leapt to his feet, catching up quickly
and trying to match grandpa's stride. Lighting a
cigar, and tucking the matchbook back into his
pocket, Grandpa Lou showed Tom the fields and
the barn and the big tractor. In his own gruff
manner, he told Tom he was going to raise him and
Martin as his own.

"This is your home now Tommy," he said, draping his strong arm around Tom's shoulder, "it will always be your home." Tom soaked in every word.

It was the first of many talks he and Lou would come to share in the open field. Conversations about the responsibility of raising a family and running a business, which were two things Lou did well.   He never outright said LouLineCo would be left to Tom, but it was implied and Tom understood the expectations and the unspoken commitment he and Lou shared.

Back from memory lane, Tom opened his eyes and swiveled around in the chair, reaching the phone and dialing Jace.

"How'd it go man?" Jace answered.

"I was late and she was already gone.  I'm sure she's pissed." Tom's voice sounded as hollow as he felt.

"Where are you now?  You wanta grab a beer?" That was the good thing about Jace.  No matter what time of day it was, if you needed him, he was there.

"I'm at the house.  Thought maybe I'd wait here and talk to Kate when she gets home."

"You're not digging through old photos and shit like that are ya?" Jace didn't sugarcoat things and his blunt approach gave Tom a chuckle.

"You know me well," Tom admitted.

"Man, don't put yourself through that." Jace moaned in the phone.  "It'll only make it worse."

Tom nodded his head and sighed.  "Yeah, you're probably right.  I just keep thinking about what went wrong and how we let it get this bad."

"Speaking of bad, I got a call from the wicked witch today."

"Rita?"

"Yep. She wanted to know if you found Martin yet."

Tom was stunned that Rita would go as far as to contact Jace about his brother. "She is unbelievable."

"Not only that, she's scary as hell. That woman makes my balls shrink up and quiver."

Tom laughed out loud at the visual Jace painted.

"So any luck finding Martin yet?"

"Nope." Tom tapped a pencil against the desk. "I don't know where else to look either. It's like he's just disappeared."

"He's always been that way though, right?" Jace reminded Tom how volatile Martin's relationship with Lou was and how, as a teenager, Martin would disappear for months on end, showing up only when he needed money.

"True." Tom agreed, but something stuck in his gut and gnawed at him. He would have bet his life that Martin would come to Madeline's funeral. It was true Martin went off the deep end, dropped out of high school, spent time in prison for possession of narcotics and an unconcealed weapon, but Tom believed all those things were a product of their dad's abandonment and not that Martin was a bad person. Even if he was wrong and Martin was corrupt to the core, Tom still thought he'd have shown up by now to collect his share of the inheritance.

"You checked all the prisons right? And the morgues?"

"Madeline's attorney has done a nationwide search and I've contacted everyone I can think of." Tom was tired and hope of finding Martin was running out.

"Maybe you should hire a private investigator?" Tom could hear Jace's voice elevate with excitement at having what he considered a great idea. "I hired this PI when I suspected my second wife was cheating. He got me the dirt I needed and was reasonably priced."

Tom grinned. Hiring a PI was such a Jace thing to do. "I'll think about it. Send me your guy's information."

"My guy doesn't do the PI thing anymore. Got the shit kicked out of him and called it quits. But I'll dig around and find out who's the best in town."

"Thanks." Tom sighed loudly.

"Seriously man, don't get lost in the past. It'll only keep you from moving forward."

Jace always had good advice and somehow remained sanely grounded in situations where other people would easily crack. Tom wished he could be more like Jace, roll with the punches better, and not sweat the small stuff. The problem was it all felt like big stuff and Tom was wearing thin.

Turning back to the file, Tom opened every card, reading what he wrote to Kate and letting the flood of memories rush over him. He must have sent her a card every week in college, and now he wished he had sent more.

The next file folder was labeled "Journal Entries." Tom took it out and began his journey. He felt like a knight on a quest to storm the castle of his wife's heart and somehow save their marriage. He read page after page, wondering how he had been so blind to the pain she felt. He knew the answer. Work. After the first couple miscarriages he started burying himself in work to hide from his own pain. Somewhere along the line he stopped feeling anything at all and started going through the motions. For years he felt resentment toward Kate for pulling away from him, but now in the pages of her journal, he began to see the truth.

"I left you," he whispered aloud as the realization sent chills up his back. "I left you when it got too hard."

A lump of shame formed in his throat and stayed there as he read page after page. Every sentence bore more of Kate's soul. Each word lingered in his psyche and chipped away at the calloused corners of his heart.

He read:

*"Tom used to make me laugh so hard my sides would ache. I miss laughing. I miss him. Where is the man I married?"*

Tom responded aloud, "I'm right here Kate and I still love you. I do still love you."

Two hours passed and Tom put a sizeable dent in the folder. There was still more to read, but his eyes were burning and his heart needed a break. He glanced at his watch, 3:30pm. *That means its five o'clock somewhere and time for a much needed drink,* he thought.

"And a stiff one at that," he muttered aloud.

He took the long way to the kitchen so he could look at pictures in the hallway. An outsider would admire these photos and even comment what a happy couple they were, but now all Tom saw was the emptiness in Kate's eyes. He witnessed the clenching behind her smile and the heartache in her gaze. He deflated, as it all seemed like a façade now. Loneliness encompassed him and he bent to his knees and cried out, "God, please don't let me lose her. Please."

He didn't realize how much weight his prayer carried at that very moment.

## Chapter 3

"The doctor would like to run more tests," explained the nurse as she scribbled something onto her clipboard.

Kate closed her eyes for a split-second. "Is it really necessary? I feel fine other than a headache and that's probably more from stress than the accident."

"I understand Mrs. Miller, but the doctor needs to take a closer look before we can send you home." Irritation showed on Kate's face. "According to the EMT report you were unconscious when they arrived at the scene, which indicates head trauma, and a head injury is nothing to take lightly." She patted Kate's arm. "Now, is there someone we can call for you?"

Kate stared and shook her head no.

"Your husband?" The nurse asked, pointing to the wedding band on Kate's finger.

Kate shook her head.

"What about a friend?"

Kate stared blankly. The truth was she didn't have many friendships left. She had been so absorbed in trying to get pregnant the past decade that she let her friendships go by the wayside. When her friends started having babies and embarking on the adventure of raising a family, Kate felt like she no longer fit. She wanted to feel joy for them and yet her emotions were clouded with her own despair. Eventually depression kept her from even desiring to venture out of the house or talk on the phone. She had stopped going to church altogether and dropped out of her monthly book club. Distance had grown between her and almost everyone in her life.

"Think about it. When it's time for you to be released someone will have to pick you up."

Kate was so irritated with Tom the mere thought of phoning him made her stomach knot. She had one close friend named Kimberly, but Kate didn't want to call her unless it was a last resort. She knew Kimberly would come get her, but she wasn't sure she was up for a big rant on the way home. Kimberly was sort of overbearing at times, with her pro-feministic, woman-are-stronger-than-men attitude. She would probably waltz into the hospital and tell Kate to get her sorry ass out of bed and stop being a baby. She was great to have around when you needed a pep talk, but not very good at compassion.

When the nurse left the room big tears rolled down Kate's face. The bright white hospital walls did nothing to help ease her pounding headache. She put her hands up to her face and quickly realized her bangs were matted and sticky with blood. She ran her fingers over the top of her head and could feel more dried blood. *Gross*, she thought. At least her hair was dark brown which made the blood harder to notice. A small gash on her forehead had been bandaged but dry blood still clung to the side of her cheek and she tried to scrape it off with her fingernails. There was no mirror to confirm, but Kate was certain she looked awful, probably as awful as she felt. She closed her eyes and let her head sink back into the crisply clean white pillow. Thunder rumbled outside as Kate succumbed to exhaustion and dozed off.

~

As Tom perused the files of Kate's heart, he found himself enthralled by the ups and emotionally drained by the downs of their marital journey. The excitement danced from the pages and he laughed out loud at her written renditions of the good times they'd shared. When they were up there was no one higher. And when they were down, there was no greater loneliness. He reached in the folder and pulled out a small white envelope addressed to Kate. Knowing he shouldn't, but realizing he had already violated her privacy on so many levels, he retrieved the letter and unfolded it. His eyes drank in his grandmother, Madeline's, handwriting as he read a note he never knew existed.

*"My Dearest Kate,"* Tom read. *"If you are reading this letter it is because I have gone to join my eternal Lord and Savior Jesus Christ in the Heavens. Don't be sad for me dear, as I am in a body that is in better condition than yours right now."* Tom laughed, recalling how grandma always bragged about the new body she was going to have in Heaven. She told him she was going to be one of those "heavenly hotties." She'd wiggle her hips and dance in a circle with a boney finger up in the air and Tom would shake his head and chuckle. The memory brought a grin to his face as he pictured that always-present twinkle in grandma's eyes. He read on. *"Kate, you have been chosen because you remind me of myself. I see the strength in you that is needed to carry this burden of forgiveness, to protect our legacy and to hold our family together. So young and naïve are you and so treacherous is the world upon young hearts. Tom, bless his soul, is a Miller boy and he's bound to screw this marriage up. The Miller boys always do dear."*

Tom picked up his bourbon and water, shook the ice a bit and slurped the rest of it down. "Thanks a lot Grams," he said aloud. "I appreciate the vote of confidence." He went back to reading.

*"Tommy has a good heart and he loves you, so be patient with him. Never give up on him Kate. You must always remember that marriage is a combination of love and friendship and a life long trek. It will be wonderful and awful. It will be beautiful and boring. The important thing is that it will be... and continue to be... despite the hardship you encounter along the way. Look at every change as a potential for growth. Look to God for guidance and strength. You can overcome even the greatest of obstacles as I have done, if you forgive. Remember Kate, forgiveness is KEY. The ring is your covenant, your inheritance of strength, your unbreakable code of love."*

Tom leaned back in the desk chair, locked his fingers behind his head and closed his eyes. He exhaled deeply letting the significance of Gram's words sink into his heart. In the silence of his mind he traveled back to the first time he met Kate and how beautiful she was with her long, dark brown, wavy hair and big brown eyes. He was speechless in the presence of her beauty. She had a smile that took his breath away and a laugh that was contagious. What he wouldn't give to see that smile and hear that laugh now.

"I miss you Kate," he whispered into the empty room.

Leaning forward in his chair, Tom reached into the folder and pulled out a sticky note. Written on it was *"Martin. September 5th."* His mind raced to assign meaning but failed. Did this have something to do with his brother Martin? Or was there another man in Kate's life named Martin? What happened on September 5th? Did

27

she meet this Martin person somewhere? Was she having an affair? Even if she was, he knew he had no right to judge her. Still, he found his heart trapped between curiosity, jealousy and remorse.

Tom was deep in thought when the phone jarred him from his chair. "Hello?" He answered only to hear a gasp of stunned silence on the other end. "Hello?" He repeated.

"Tom?" Kimberly said, with surprise in her tone. She was undoubtedly surprised he was at the house. She made it no secret how anti-Tom she was. The last several times he'd seen her she showered him in snide comments about being a typical non-attentive, self-absorbed man. Tom was no Kimberly fan either, as he felt certain she played a large role in convincing Kate to file for divorce.

"Kimberly," he mused, with a sarcastically upbeat inflection, "so good to hear from you."

"What are you doing there?" she asked flatly. "Where's Kate?"

"I don't know. She hasn't been here all afternoon."

"Right." Kimberly's tone alluded to the fact that she thought Tom was lying.

"Honestly, she's not here."

"Then why are YOU there?" She spewed with a spiteful tone. "It's not your house anymore."

Tom felt anger rising in his throat. He could hear the smirk in her voice and he wanted to reach through the phone and smack it off her face. He pursed his lips together and swallowed hard to control his temper. "You're mistaken. It IS my house and Kate is not here right now. If I see her I'll let her know you called."

"Where is she?" Kimberly demanded.

"She's probably out shopping. You know how you ladies are. Get a little upset and go buy four pairs of shoes."

There was an awkward pause and Tom guessed Kimberly didn't appreciate his feeble attempt at female shoe humor. "She was supposed to meet me at 6:00pm."

Tom thought he heard an actual hint of concern in Kimberly's voice and he glanced at the clock across the room. 6:43pm. This was strange. Kate is never late. Everyone knows if Kate is anything she is punctual. "Like I said, she's probably shopping, but if I see her I'll have her give you a jingle." Tom's speech quickened as he was trying to get off the phone and clean up the office. He hadn't realized it was so late and now felt anxious that Kate might walk through the door at any moment and find him reading her journals. He knew damn good and well that would send her through the roof.

"You know Tom," said Kimberly, "if you wanted to save your marriage you'd make an attempt to win Kate's heart back, not sit idly by and watch it wither."

Tom was speechless, pissed by the implication that he wasn't trying. Clearly he was trying. The mess in the office indicated he was trying. He hung up the phone and began to gather all the papers and place them back in the file folders. He hoped she didn't have them in any particular order because he hadn't paid attention to those details when he took them out.

Once the office was put back together, Tom fixed himself another drink and decided to wait for Kate to return. He was curious to see if she would arrive home with another man, though the very notion nauseated him. He hoped at the very least they could talk. He sat down in his favorite chair and turned on the family room television. He felt the chair form around his body, like a baseball glove broken in to fit perfectly. It had been a while since he sat here and he couldn't deny it felt good to be home. He surfed channels, but mentally exhausted and emotionally drained, it wasn't long before Tom was snoring.

~

The nurse came back in and slid open the curtain surrounding Kate's bed, revealing two men with a gurney. "We're going to go ahead and move you upstairs to a room for the night," she explained.

"What?" Kate sat up groggily. "Why can't I go home now?"

"You have a level three concussion," the nurse explained, "and since there is no one at your home, the doctor wants to keep you here tonight and monitor your progress."

Reluctantly, Kate explained there was someone she could call. "I can have my soon-to-be ex-husband pick me up and stay with me." The nurse handed Kate her bag of personal belongings, including her cell phone.

Kate dialed Kimberly first but it went straight to voicemail. She left a brief message that she was at the hospital and to call her back. Then she sat up in bed and slowly dialed Tom's number. No answer.

Once settled into her hospital gown and bed, Kate grabbed the phone to try Kimberly and Tom once more. At this point she didn't care who came to pick her up, she just wanted to go home. Before she could finish dialing there was a knock on the door and a policeman poked his head in. He stood six foot four inches with dark brown hair, hazel eyes and a handsomely rugged face. Kate guessed him to be in his late-thirties since his hair showed signs of graying, and his slightly tanned skin portrayed little smile lines around his eyes.

"Mrs. Miller?" he asked.  "I'm sorry to bother you ma'am, but we'd like to ask you a few questions about the accident you were in earlier today.  May we come in?"

Kate nodded and two officers entered quickly, one taking a seat on the window sill and the other pulling a chair right up next to Kate's bed.  "I'm Officer Dale Gordon, Special Investigations."  He pulled out his badge and ID for Kate to view.  Motioning to the officer sitting on the window sill, he said, "This is my partner, Officer Emily Cross."  Emily raised her eyebrows and nodded a silent hello.

"Did I do something illegal?" Kate joked with a half-witted smile, feeling a bit nervous by all the attention.

"No ma'am," blurted Emily, "we'd just like to know what you remember about the accident." Officer Gordon shot Emily a glance, as if to imply he would handle the talking, and Emily lowered her eyes, surrendering the floor.

Feeling uncomfortable, Kate stammered, "Well, I, um, don't really know what happened because I was trying to get a Kleenex from my purse..."

"So you weren't watching the road," Emily interrupted.

"I was on the side of the road, due to the rain, and I looked away for a split second."

Emily jotted something down in a tiny notepad she pulled from her front pocket.  Kate could feel a lump rising in her throat.  "I'm sorry," she said quietly, "I don't know what's going on or why you're here."

31

The officers exchanged a quick glance before diverting their eyes back to Kate, but before either of them could speak Kate belted out, "oh my God, did I hit someone when I pulled over?" She sat up straight in the bed and nervously ranted, "I pulled over because it was raining so hard I couldn't see the road anymore and I got scared. The rain was so loud and hard and it was coming so fast, and the wind was blowing so hard I just quickly pulled to the side." She cupped her hands over her mouth, wide-eyed, "omigod, did I hit someone?" Her eyes filled with terror at the possibility. "Did I kill someone?"

Emily scooted abruptly from the window sill to her feet, sending her red pony tail bouncing in the air. Her green eyes shone compassion as she held her hands up and shook her head, "oh, no, no, no, no Mrs. Miller, you haven't hit anyone. Someone hit you."

Officer Gordon held his hand up toward Emily motioning her to be quiet, and then he leaned in closer to Kate. "Mrs. Miller, we have reason to believe the vehicle that hit you was used in another crime. We were hoping you could describe the vehicle and possibly the driver to us." He stared intently in her eyes.

Kate felt relief encompass her. "I'm sorry, but I didn't see anything. I was looking down at my purse, reaching for a Kleenex."

"Are you positive?" Emily blurted.

Kate closed her eyes and tried to force a memory but there was nothing. "I'm sorry," she said, "I don't remember seeing anyone. I don't even remember being hit."

"Okay, Mrs. Miller," said Officer Gordon as they both stood and moved toward the door. "Thank you for your time and if you remember anything later please give us a call." He laid his business card on the table at the foot of her bed and motioned for Emily to open the door. Just as they were about to leave the reality of what happened seeped into Kate's brain and she jolted up in the bed and hollered, "Officer Gordon wait!"

"Yes?" He spun around, inching closer.

"Are you telling me that someone hit me and didn't stop?" Kate studied their faces as their quick glance to each other spelled out volumes. "Why didn't they stop?" She searched their eyes for an explanation.

Emily closed the door while Officer Gordon walked back over and sat down next to Kate's bed. He drew in a deep breath and narrowed his hazel eyes as he spoke. Kate could tell he was trying to form his words carefully so not to cause fear or panic. "Mrs. Miller," he began, "we have reason to believe the individual who hit you was trying to hit you."

Kate felt sick in the pit of her stomach. "Why would someone want to hit me?"

"To kill you." Emily's blunt tone was not appreciated nor approved of by Officer Gordon who leapt to his feet and escorted her outside. Emily nodded with cowering eyes as she left the room, acknowledging her enthusiasm had once again overridden her ability for tact. It happened a lot.

Sitting back down next to Kate, Officer Gordon explained that the conversation they were about to have needed to remain confidential for her own protection and the protection of anyone else that could be in danger. Kate's mind was spinning.

"Mrs. Miller," Officer Gordon began, "on September 5th a man was killed in a car accident, a hit and run accident similar to yours." He shifted in his chair. "The car was hit by an oncoming vehicle in the other lane, just like what happened in your accident," he explained.

Kate interrupted, "but it's easy for a car to accidentally veer over into on coming traffic. I mean, you only have to look away for a second."

Officer Gordon nodded, "yes, but when cars accidentally veer over they hit side to side or head to head, they don't typically hit head to side."

Kate cocked her head to the right and narrowed her brow, staring at Officer Gordon but really looking almost through him as she tried to picture what he was describing. "Head to side?"

"And," he continued, "cars that accidentally veer into one another, both stop." He studied Kate's face for a sign of comprehension. "When people are in accidents, especially accidents substantial enough to total cars and require ambulance care, all vehicles involved are typically there when the police arrive."

Kate admitted, "I don't understand what this means."

"The accident on September 5th was a collision where the driver hit the victim from the oncoming lane head on into the driver's side panel." He shuffled in his chair. "Just like his accident, you were hit head to side with an angle of impact that implies there was no accidental veering." Kate sat very still, finding it hard to catch her breath, as he continued. "Whoever hit you was trying to hit you which is why they drove off after the collision."

Kate's eyes were wide with innocence. "Did that victim give you a description of the car or the driver?"

"He was pronounced dead at the scene."

"Why do you think this driver is the same person from the September accident?" Kate's mind was grinding out questions.

"A hunch. Mainly because the driver didn't stop after the hit."

"Who was the victim from the first accident? Does he have any connection to me? Kate could see Officer Gordon was impressed by her thinking, as his lips curled up into a slight grin.

"He's labeled John Doe. We haven't been able to find proof of identity."

"What about fingerprints?"

"Do you watch cop shows?" Officer Gordon grinned.

"Guilty," Kate dropped her head and blushed. "Sorry."

"Don't be. Questions are always good." He leaned back in the chair. "Fingerprints were inconclusive."

"So why do you think there's a connection between his accident and mine?"

"I don't know ma'am," he said, shaking his head, "a hunch at best." He stood up. "It's my job to find out any and all connections, which is why I need to know anything you saw, heard or remember before or after the collision."

Kate bit her lip. "I didn't see anything."

Officer Gordon moved toward the door and paused, "Mrs. Miller, is there anyone you can think of who would want to hurt you?" Kate shook her head. "Is there anyone who would benefit from your demise?"

"What do you mean benefit?" It seemed harsh to even imply anyone would benefit from another person's death.

Officer Gordon fixed his gaze on her eyes, "does your husband have a girlfriend that wants you out of the way? Is there a relative that stands to inherit a large sum of money when you die? Did you do something in the past to cause someone to seek revenge?" The questions came rapid fire and Kate knew they were rhetorical, but her defenses jolted alive and she felt compelled to answer. Before she could speak, he added, "If you think of anything, anything at all, please give us a call." The door closed behind him and Kate sat motionless.

Once in the hallway, Officer Gordon shot Emily an irritated glare. "I'm sorry," she mumbled.

Grabbing her arm he scolded, "We've got to find out what she knows without raising suspicions." Emily lowered her eyes. She knew he was right and she knew how much was riding on it.

~

Mrs. Netbaum opened the passenger door and helped Kate out. "Look," she said, "Tom is still here." Kate paused and stared in disbelief at Tom's car in the driveway. "He's been here all night. I just assumed he had to work early this morning, which was why you called me to come get you from the hospital, but he's still here."

"He's been here all night?" Kate felt her face flush with anger, though she tried to conceal it from Mrs. Netbaum. She was livid Tom had the nerve to spend the night, but even more angry that he didn't answer any of her calls.

"Sure has." Mrs. Netbaum nodded, closing the door behind Kate and helping her walk to the front porch. Kate didn't really need help walking, but Mrs. Netbaum insisted on looping her arm around Kate's waist and nudging her along. "He got here yesterday afternoon and he's been here ever since." She drew her eyebrows in and twisted her mouth to the side. "I thought it was strange he was here but then I thought maybe you were making up, or maybe he was here to pack up some more of his stuff. I never saw him take anything out of the house though, and I was watching real good."

That wasn't hard to believe. Mrs. Netbaum was always watching real good. She took the concept of a Neighborhood Watch program to a whole different level. As the neighborhood gossip, if you wanted to know anything about anyone on the street, Mrs. Netbaum was your gal.

Kate put her key in the door and opened the lock. "You sure you're okay now?" Mrs. Netbaum asked for the umpteenth time, "Because I can stay awhile if you need me. I can make you some soup, run a hot bath, whatever you need."

Kate shook her head no and thanked Mrs. Netbaum for picking her up and bringing her home. She was a sweet enough woman, short, plump, with white blond hair styled in a sixties flip. But Nosey Netbaum, as she and Tom privately called her, was not a person you wanted to have in your home. Any sign of weakness, dirty dishes piled in the sink or dust on shelves, would be broadcast to the entire street and Kate wasn't in the mood to deal with being the center of neighborhood attention. Not only that, but her head was pounding and Mrs. Netbaum had a habit of talking non-stop. She didn't even take a breath in between sentences. Kate feared if she stayed she might actually talk her head right off.

When Kate stepped inside and saw Tom sleeping in the chair, she slammed the front door as hard and loud as she could. The noise made Tom levitate about six inches above the chair and mumble something incoherent. He squint his eyes at Kate's image. Kate stood staring at him, arms crossed with a big white brace around her neck. He jumped to his feet and realized for the first time, it was daylight. "What time is it?"

"Time for you to go," she answered flatly, breezing by him on the way to the kitchen.

"Wait a second," he blurted, "you stayed out all night, Lord knows where and with God knows who and you're mad at me?"

The implication in his tone was more than Kate could take. After all, she'd just been in an accident, had a sixteen hour hospital stay, her car was totaled, she spent the last hour with Mrs. Netbaum's constant chatter, and was trying not to think about what the police had told her. She whirled around and pointed to the neck brace. "I was at the hospital." She glared at Tom. "Typical. I'm right in front of you and you're so self-absorbed you don't even notice me." Kate stormed off into the kitchen.

Tom walked closer, noticing the blood caked in her hair, and the gash on her head. He silently reprimanded himself for coming on so strong and tried a tender approach. "Honey, what happened? Why were you at the hospital?" He made every attempt at eye contact but Kate looked away. He reached for her arms but she turned from his grip and busied herself making coffee.

"Kate, please talk to me."

Kate rolled her eyes and walked from the kitchen into the den. She could see Tom wasn't planning on giving up anytime soon. He followed behind her until she abruptly stopped, and bent down to pick up a small piece of paper lying on the floor next to the desk. She saw him swallow hard as she turned around and for the first time met his gaze with an icy stare. Her heart pound faster as she read: "Martin. September 5th."

Tom could see her mind working to recall when she wrote that and how long it had been since she had pulled it from her file. He could see her brain calculating the possibility, or rather the impossibility that it could have leapt from the file onto the floor by itself. She backed up to the desk and sat down, immediately opening the file drawer and looking at her files. She never spoke, but Tom could see the disappointment and anger welling inside her as she shook her head from side to side. There was no denying he had invaded her privacy.

"I was looking for...I was making sure there were no outstanding bills we needed to pay," he stammered.

Kate's eyes met his in an abrasive stare that spoke volumes. Why? How could you? She didn't ask. She slammed the sticky note onto the desk and hollered, "Get out."

Tom couldn't speak. His mouth went suddenly dry and a lump of agony crept into his throat. "I'm sorry," was the only thing he was able to muster.

In the driveway he stood for a moment, letting regret envelope him. "You really are an ass," he mumbled to himself, while grabbing the handle and thrusting the driver's door open. On the passenger seat was his cell phone and Kate's spiral notebook the receptionist had given him. He picked up the phone and realized Kate called him eight times throughout the night. Eight times! He slammed his forehead against the steering wheel, "you idiot" he yelled.

## Chapter 4

After Tom left, Kate locked the front door and made sure the backdoor and garage door were locked as well. The conversation at the hospital made her feel uneasy about being home alone, but she was too mad at Tom to ask him to stay. After a quick walk-thru of the house, she headed to her closet to retrieve a hat box from the top shelf. It was a walk-in closet and the hat box sat in the middle of the shelf on the right hand side. Standing on a step stool she scooted the box to the front of the shelf to get a better grip on it, and then slowly lifted it down. A manila envelope came sliding off the shelf with the box and bounced off her forehead, making Kate jump and lose her balance. She let out a shriek as the step stool overturned and threw her into the back of the closet atop a pile of sweaters. "Good thing I'm already on pain killers," she thought, "or this might have really hurt."

Kate scrambled to her knees and picked up the envelope she had placed on the shelf six months ago, and forgotten it existed. Now, pulling back the tabs she opened the envelope and viewed the contents inside. He didn't say why, but Martin told her keeping it hidden was a matter of life and death. Staring at it, she now wondered if it had something to do with why someone would try to kill her. Kate shrugged. Martin was the only one who might have that answer and there was no way of finding him. She'd have to wait until he showed back up as promised.  Kate closed the envelope and placed it back on the shelf in the closet.  Then she picked up the hat box and moved to the edge of the bed.

Opening the box unleashed the strong scent of leather and brought back memories of a time when life felt easier.  She lifted Grandmother Madeline's brown leather journal from the box, then she reached back in and pulled out a 9mm Smith & Wesson.  It had been Grandpa Lou's gun and was handed down to Tom.  Thankfully they'd never had cause to use it and Kate hoped she wasn't going to need it now.  Making sure it was loaded and the safety was on, Kate slid the gun into the nightstand drawer.

Her body ached even with the heavy medication and she longed for a hot shower.  She sat for a moment thinking about it, but couldn't muster the energy, so she grabbed Grandmother's journal, pulled off the stuffy neck brace and gently propped herself up in bed.  Despite good intentions to read the journal, there had been so much on her mind over the past six months that Kate had forgotten about it altogether.  The front cover was stiff with age and made a crinkle sound as it opened.  Madeline's handwriting swirled from the pages right into Kate's heart and she spent the next several hours basking in the wisdom of grandmother's offerings.  She got up only to get more coffee and take another pain pill when the throbbing in her head returned.

~

Jace slapped Tom on the back and nodded to the bartender for another round.  Tom sat with his shoulders slumped, leaning on the bar.  "It's not the end of the world," consoled Jace.

"It's the end of mine," Tom moaned, picking at the corner of the label on his beer bottle.

Jace shook his head, "c'mon man, it just feels that way right now, but you'll bounce back. Trust me." He was on his third marriage. Jace was independently wealthy, had deep brown puppy dog eyes, Italian olive skin, dark brown hair that showed little signs of graying, a body that told the world he worked out every day and a dynamite smile. He was what you would call a chick-magnet. Tom knew Jace could bounce back, but he wasn't sure about himself.

"You know what you need," Jace said, grinning ear to ear. But Tom shook his head no before Jace could say it. "C'mon man," Jace urged, "how long has it been since you've gotten some?"

Tom frowned and slowly blinked.

"That long?" Jace wrinkled his nose and wrenched his mouth. "That's not healthy."

"Tell me about it." Tom slumped listlessly against the bar.

"You're officially separated right?" Jace asked with the implication that a little on the side action would be understandable, even justifiable.

Tom nodded. "We're officially separated."

"Then what are you waiting for man," Jace pushed. "Get you some action and it'll clear your head and give you a new perspective on life. A guy can't think straight when his juices are backed up. You don't wanna permanently end up with LDS do you?"

Tom squished up his face. "What's LDS?"

"Limp Dick Syndrome," wailed Jace. "Not enough action makes poppy floppy. You get what I'm saying?"

Jace made it sound so easy and so vulgar at the same time. Tom chuckled and shook his head while Jace slurped down the rest of his beer.

"Seriously man, if you don't let him bat, your homerun hitter will get in a permanent slump." Jace motioned to the bartender for another beer. "Then you gotta use drugs to get a stiffy."

Tom assured Jace his batter was still perfectly capable of hitting a homerun. "Good," said Jace, "because a store bought taut just ain't the same."

"Good to know," said Tom, chuckling aloud.

They sat in silence for a few minutes. "I miss her," Tom confessed.

"Do you miss her or do you miss your home?" Jace explained, "With my first divorce I thought I was missing Sheila but I was really missing the comfort of our home and lifestyle I was accustomed to." Jace took a swig of his beer. "You know what I mean? It's like you have your favorite chair, your remote control, all your stuff. You're used to the sounds of the house and the smell as you walk in the door. You're senses are accustomed to that place and that triggers the emotional missing feeling you have." Tom stared blankly.   Jace added, "That's what three thousand dollars of therapy taught me anyway."

They both chuckled, but the conversation made Tom begin to analyze what it was he missed. Was it just the familiarity of their lifestyle or was he really missing Kate? He didn't ponder long. The answer was evident: Kate.

Later that evening Tom lay in bed and thought about the unsettling in his spirit. He thought about his childhood, his parents and his grandparents. He remembered the time that grandmother said he would one day find a beautiful princess, marry her and live happily ever after. *Where was that happily ever after now*, he wondered.

43

He smiled at the memory of pretending to be a brave knight, adorned with a long tin foil sword grandpa Lou made for him. Grandmother was pretending to be the princess. She tied a bath towel on her head to make it look like long flowing hair, and stood up on the arm of the couch to pretend she was high in a castle. Suddenly, Tom sat up straight in bed, his heart racing as the reality of the memory came alive in him. He remembered calling out, "princess, I will save you!"

Grandmother hollered back, "dear prince, I am your true love, call me Kate."

Chills ran up his spine. Call me Kate she had said, as if she knew his true love's name years before he ever met her. He felt a tug at his heart. An unexplainable sensation, he could neither define nor shake, as if grandmother were there in the room beckoning him to not give up.

His cell phone buzzed on the nightstand jerking him back to reality. It was a text from Jace.

"Call P.I. Stephen Braznovich. Best in town. Happy hunting."

~

Madeline labeled every entry in her journal by subject matter and shared personal stories throughout. Kate found herself laughing and crying at the same time, as she related to some of the challenges Madeline and Lou faced in their marriage. Lou was Mr. Logic and a workaholic, just like Tom. Madeline was creative and dramatic, more like Kate. Tom was so non-emotional Kate often referred to him as a Vulcan. As she read what Madeline wrote about Lou, she felt closer to Tom, as if stories from his family's past somehow granted clarity into his character. The clarity didn't excuse his shortcomings but it did explain some of them.

Kate reached for the phone on the second ring. It was Kimberly, calling to apologize for not getting her message sooner and being at the hospital with her.

"It's okay," said Kate, "Mrs. Netbaum picked me up."

"Nosey Netbaum?" Kimberly wailed, "Now you're probably the talk of the street."

"I know. I'm not going outside for a long time because I'll be bombarded with questions."

"Speaking of questions," Kimberly added, "you want to go grab a late supper?"

Kate explained that she hadn't showered, her hair was matted with blood, she was in a neck brace and she felt like crap. "Besides, I'm snuggled up with Madeline's journal for the night."

There was a long pause. "Who's journal?"

"Tom's grandmother, Madeline."

"Why do you have her journal?"

Kate thought for a moment. Why did she have Madeline's journal? She had it because it was left to her, but she never quite understood why it was left to her. The day Madeline passed away, her attorney came to the house and announced that her Will couldn't be opened unless both grandsons were present. Then he sat on the sofa next to Kate and handed her the journal.

"This is for you," he said. Kate ran her fingers over the soft leather and listened as he explained. "I was given explicit instructions that this journal was to be given only to you." He looked at Kate with compassionate eyes and did his best Madeline impression. He pointed his finger in the air, like she used to, and spoke deliberately, emphasizing each syllable. "This is for my Kate's eyes only. No one else."

"Hellooooo?" Kimberly ambled into the phone. "Are you still there?"

Kimberly's voice jolted Kate from her flashback. "I don't know why she gave me her journal."

"She never told you why?"

Kate thought back. "Actually, the day she died her attorney gave me the journal with a letter she had written. I haven't read it in a long time, but basically she said I reminded her of herself and I was strong enough to hold the family together."

"So what does the journal say?"

Kate laughed. "It says a bunch of stuff. It talks about her life and her marriage to Lou, and a lot about forgiveness. She was such an insightful woman."

"Whatever." Kimberly sneered. "It doesn't sound like an exciting read to me."

"Madeline was spunky. I think you would have liked her."

"I'm sure."

"And she was a great judge of character."

"What do you mean?" Kimberly asked. "Who's character?"

"A lot of people, though most of the names in here I don't recognize." Kate paged through the tabs at the top of the journal. "Here's a tab labeled Rita."

"What does it say about her? Total bitch?'

Kate laughed out loud. "It says, 'controlled by greed, aroused by power.'

Kimberly snorted, "She sure nailed that one."

~

After she got off the phone with Kimberly, Kate popped another pain pill, slipped into her jammies and crawled into bed. Knowing the medicine would kick in soon and she would get sleepy, she elected to read one more section from Madeline's journal. It was a poem entitled, "The Broken Log." Kate wasn't much for poetry, but she noticed her name scribbled in cursive next to the poem, so she assumed it was a message Madeline wrote just for her. Kate read aloud:

*One day you took a path where a log crossed a stream*
*You stepped upon that log and it cracked; then you screamed*
*Before you hit the ground you saw my grandson's face*
*And knew he was the one to share true love's embrace.*
*Despite the hands of time, despite the year's decay*
*The truth that log holds will never fade away.*

Grandmother had the uncanny ability to speak to Kate's heart, even from beyond the grave. What struck Kate as unique about this particular poem was that it was a true story. When Kate and Tom were dating he took her on walk through the woods by Madeline and Lou's home. It had rained a lot that spring so the creek was more like a babbling brook, with tiny rapids chasing over rocks and racing toward their final destination of a small lake in the break of the trees. Kate spotted a fallen log just as they approached the mouth of the creek, where it dumped into the lake. The log created a bridge across the creek, and Kate, excited to prove herself daring and spontaneous, let go of Tom's hand and ran toward the log. Despite his warning, she jumped atop the log and began to dance her way across.

It wasn't very high so the fall wouldn't have killed her, though it would have hurt. Getting hurt wasn't Kate's concern when her ears met with the undeniable sound of splintering wood. Her first thought was of snakes. There were probably snakes in the water and they would get her if she fell. Kate's eyes widened with panic as the log continued to crack. She let out a shriek that echoed through the trees and Tom dove for her arms. Kate felt his muscular form wrap around her as they hurled through the air and rolled to safety on the ground. They laughed hard that afternoon and despite her embarrassment, Tom told Madeline and Lou what happened.

Madeline gleaned proudly at her Tommy. "He's your knight in shining armor," she said to Kate with a knowing wink of her bulging blue eyes.

Kate read the poem again and wondered why Grandmother wrote it? She never realized Madeline was such a poet, though it didn't surprise her. Madeline used to rhyme things all the time. She said it made life more exciting. "I can make a rhyme, any place, any time," she used to say, and then she'd giggle to herself. Tom used to tell her she had a knack for cracking herself up, which Grandpa Lou found amusing. Madeline would pat Tom's cheek with the palm of her hand and say, "yes I do, Tommy, and I always get the last laugh. Remember that. I always get the last laugh."

Kate kept thinking how ironic it felt, like the broken log was a metaphor for their broken marriage. As she drifted to sleep, she pondered in her heart whether Tom could be her knight in shining armor once again?

## Chapter 5

Kimberly rang the doorbell. She waited ten seconds and rang again. Then again. She pulled out her cell phone and called the house. The phone jolted Kate from a deep sleep and she fumbled for the receiver. "Hello?" she said trying to sound awake and nonchalant.

"Get your lazy ass up and let me in!" Kimberly waited for no one. She was always on time and always impatient.

Kate jumped out of bed, despite the stiffness in her back and neck, hurried down the hall and unlocked the front door. Kimberly rolled her eyes at Kate's dis-shelved appearance. "That's not a good look for you," she teased.

Kate sighed, "I was up late."

"Ooh," smirked Kimberly, "anyone I know?"

Kate playfully nudged her arm as she walked by to go to the bathroom. "Like you're one to talk," she said, "you evidentially had some fun the other night."

"What are you talking about?" She squint her light brown eyes at Kate. "What night?"

"The other night when you left me at the hospital. Remember, I called you a bunch of times and finally had to have Mrs. Netbaum pick me up."

"I said I was sorry." Kimberly defended. "I didn't have my phone on me."

"I left you a message," Kate pouted.

"I'm sorry sweetie, but you know I would have been there to get you if I would have known."

49

Kimberly grabbed a blood-clotted chunk of Kate's hair and held it up. "Maybe you should shower."

"I know, I know, I look awful and because of you and Tom, Mrs. Netbaum probably told the whole world how awful I look!" Kate shuffled down the hall, through her bedroom and into the bathroom.

Kimberly frowned, "because of me and Tom?"

"Neither one of you answered your phones that night, so I was stuck at the hospital."

Kimberly rolled her eyes and plunked down on the bed. "So," she teased, "is your hot guy from last night still here because I only brought two coffees."

Kate played along with dramatic sarcasm, "why yes, he's in here with me right now, doing wildly sexual things to pleasure me."

Kimberly chuckled, "you wish." She took a sip of her coffee and noticed the leather bound journal on the bed. "Is this the journal you were telling me about?"

Kate flew out of the bathroom, hurled herself across the room and dove onto the bed. "Don't read it!" she screamed.

Kimberly jumped up trying to keep the coffee from spilling.

"Don't read it," Kate yelled again, clutching the book.

Kimberly stared with stunned awe. After several seconds she broke the silence, "sweetie, you're a little freaky about that book."

Kate burst into laughter. She knew how insane she must have looked, diving across the bed in her towel. She laughed until her cheeks hurt and though Kimberly giggled, Kate was certain Kimberly wondered if she was on the verge of an emotional breakdown.

When the laughter ran out Kimberly said, "Why don't you and your book go back in the bathroom and get dressed. Me and my coffee are going to wait for you in the kitchen." She widened her eyes and raised her eyebrows at Kate, exhaling a fake cough that said "crazy."

Kate threw a towel at her.

~

"Tom," came the voice of his administrative assistant Cindy. "Tom!" He had been zoning at his desk. He jumped and looked at Cindy with a blank stare. "Your twelve o'clock," she said, pointing to her watch.

"Oh, right," he stammered, "my twelve o'clock. Are they here?"

Cindy shook her head. "Your twelve o'clock is at Murrays on Providence. It's with the Executive of the Halloway retail chain."

Tom sat motionless.

Cindy came closer and leaned against his desk, her long, thin blonde hair hanging to her waist. She spoke tenderly. "I know you're going through a rough time. We all know it. But you've got to pull yourself together." Tom looked in Cindy's round, blue eyes. He couldn't help but think she looked more like Malibu Barbie then what you'd expect to see sitting behind a desk in a stuffy oil company office. He never imagined his right-out-of-high school assistant would be giving him a pep talk. Nonetheless, it was needed and he was grateful.

He smiled at her. "Thank you."

Her face lit up and she beamed, "any time."

Tom grabbed his sport coat, brief case and cell phone and headed out. He stopped abruptly at Cindy's desk, "did you say Murrays?" he asked.

Cindy nodded.

"Why is the meeting at Murrays?"

She shrugged. "I don't know. The Halloway Executive chose the location." Cindy twirled a piece of her blonde hair around her finger and narrowed her big blue eyes. "Now that you mention it, she was pretty emphatic about it being at Murrays."

"What's the name of the executive?"

Cindy's expression was blank and her mouth curled into a frown. "I don't know."

"You don't know who I'm supposed to meet at Murrays? Didn't they give you a name?"

"No," Cindy shook her head and Tom could see by her widened eyes that she was worried she would be in trouble for not getting a name.

"Oh, okay then." Tom started to head for the door.

Cindy added, "Is that a problem?"

"No, no problem." Tom forced a smile and gave a quick wave. There wasn't a problem, but Tom was concerned how he might feel walking into Murrays. It was his and Kate's special place, the place where they got engaged, the place where they went to celebrate their anniversary each year, and Tom hadn't been there since the separation.

On his way to Murrays he dialed private investigator, Stephen Braznovich from his cell. His call went into voicemail and Tom left a detailed message, emphasizing the urgency for finding his brother.

Within minutes of leaving the message, a text came through that read: "Meet me at 3:00pm today at the Backrow Tavern on 163rd and Metcalf to discuss your case."

~

Kate sat in the front seat of Kimberly's silver Cadillac. She was blowing on her newly manicured nails. "Where are we going NOW?" Kate moaned, feeling more than ready to go home.

"I thought we could do lunch before heading back." Kimberly was a do- lunch, shop all day, mani-pedi sort of girl, and Kate was more a do-lunch, go home and take a nap sort of girl.

Kate couldn't deny she was hungry but her head was starting to pound and she longed to lie down. She and Kimberly had been shopping all morning. Kate hated shopping. Most of all, she hated crowded malls and dirty bathrooms and the constant disappointment of finding something she liked but not in her size. Shopping with Kimberly was like running a marathon, constantly darting in and out of stores, putting things on hold to go find it a dollar cheaper somewhere else, then back to the first store to take it off hold. At one point Kate offered to pay Kimberly the extra two dollars if she'd just buy the damn skirt so they wouldn't have to schlep back to the store that had it marked down. Kimberly was the queen bargain hunter. "I don't have a man taking care of me," she explained to Kate, "and when you have expensive taste and no man, you have to find the bargains."

The sun beamed through the Cadillac windows and warmed the car. It made Kate feel cozy and sleepy. "I'm not all that hungry," Kate lied.

"Yes you are," demanded Kimberly, "we haven't eaten all morning."

Kimberly studied Kate's face. "You just want to go home and read that stupid book and sulk and I'm not going to let you." Kate knew Kimberly was right but it irritated her nonetheless.

"It's not a stupid book," retorted Kate. "It's a journal. It's better than any old random book. And I'm not sulking. Madeline's journal actually makes me feel better."

"Ooh, a journal," mused Kimberly. "Anything juicy in it, like affairs, revenge, murder?" Kimberly was her typical, over-dramatic self, prying for information.

Kate rolled her eyes, "no, nothing like that. It's more like a diary."

"How come she left it to you instead of Tom? I mean, he's her actual flesh and blood right?"

Kate shrugged. "I dunno."

"Has Tom read it?"

"No. I haven't even read all of it yet." Kate couldn't imagine Tom ever wanting to read it. He only took interest in things that were sports related or stock related.

Kimberly stopped at a red light and looked at Kate. "You didn't just get it right? I thought you said the lawyer gave it to you when she died."

Kate closed her eyes and turned toward the passenger window so the sun would shine on her face. She told Kimberly how she stuck the journal in the hat box and forgot it was there until the other night when she opened the box to get out the gun.

"A gun?" Kimberly gasped. "Why do you need a gun?"

Kate shrugged. "I just feel safer having it in the nightstand, especially now that Tom has moved out and I'm alone all the time." She didn't feel like explaining everything the police had told her at the hospital. The more she thought about the possibility of someone trying to kill her, the more freaked out she got, and she didn't need Kimberly's drama added to her own fear. They rode for a moment in silence then Kate conceded to Kimberly's wishes. "Fine, I'm hungry, let's go eat."

Kimberly gloated, "I knew you'd come around."

~

As soon as Tom left the office, Cindy pulled out the envelope that had been delivered earlier and tore it open. Her pulse beat hard as her eyes darted across the document, scanning for pertinent information.

Birth name:  Cynthia Miller Borgman
Birth mother:  Arianna Borgman
Birth father:    N/A

"Yes!" She said quietly, knowing her mother would be pleased to see the name Miller was legally listed as part of her birth name. Cindy didn't have the full story, but understood the monetary importance of proving she was a Miller. From what her mother said, whoever Cindy's father was, he promised Cindy would be given a substantial inheritance. All she needed to do was prove she was biologically a Miller, which her birth certificate did, and then find her father, which was not easy considering Miller is a common last name.

Cindy didn't just want the money for herself, but for her mother who sacrificed a lot to raise her on her own. She wanted to repay her mom by finding her father and demanding he give her mother the respect and recognition she deserved. From what her mother said, Cindy's father walked out on them a year after she was born and never came back.

Now that she had the birth certificate showing the Miller name, it was time to find out what happened between her mother and father all those years ago. She already searched online using every genealogy site she could find, and paid to run background checks on several men with the last name Miller, but none of them fit the bill. Now that she had a steady job at LouLineCo, she could afford to hire a private investigator. She Googled private investigators and called the first one on the list. A man named Stephen Braznovich.

~

Walking into the restaurant Kate felt her stomach knot. "Why did we have to come here again?" She asked.

"I told you, therapists say the best way to get through a failing marriage is to confront it, starting with a look at where it began. This is where it began for you and Tom, so this is where you need to start." Kimberly's voice sounded harsh, but in all fairness she had explained it to Kate three times already.

Half way through her Cobb salad Kate excused herself to the ladies room. Her head was throbbing. Kimberly sat alone, looking at her watch and reminding herself that bringing Kate here was a good thing. They'd spent the first half of their lunch talking about what she was going to do after the divorce. She told Kimberly she'd have to sell the house because she'd need the money and wouldn't want to live with the memories day in and day out.

"You'll be okay with money once Tom gets his inheritance right?"

Kate shrugged. "I don't know what kind of money is in the inheritance."

"I bet it's a lot." Kimberly grinned.

"I don't know. Anyway it doesn't matter because the inheritance can't be paid out until Tom and Martin are both there and nobody can find Martin."

Kimberly narrowed her eyes in a manner that told Kate she was skeptical about something. "I'm not so sure I'm buying that story."

"What do you mean? It's the truth."

"I mean maybe Tom is just waiting until after the divorce so you don't get any money." Kimberly raised her eyebrows at Kate. "Men are like that you know."

"No. I heard the attorney explain it to him right after Madeline died."

"What I'm saying is, maybe Tom knows where Martin is but is just waiting until the divorce is final so you don't get half of what is left to him."

This had never even entered Kate's mind. Now that she thought about it, it made some sense. Maybe that was the reason Tom didn't show up at the attorney's office this week to sign the papers. Maybe he really was stalling on purpose.

"I'm just saying. Tom's always been more about work and money than he has been about you and your marriage."

Kate deflated. What Kimberly said made sense. Tom was all about work and money.

Tears filled Kate's eyes and Kimberly reached across the table. "Oh, sweetie, I'm not trying to hurt you. I just want you to be realistic about this divorce and protect yourself because that's what he's going to do."

A part of her knew Kimberly was probably right, but the other part wanted to believe Tom still loved her and would protect her and treat her fairly, even in a divorce.

Kate fought back tears as she excused herself to the bathroom. She chose the last stall and searched for the carving she and Tom made in the wall eighteen years ago. It read: "KATA." And stood for "Kate And Tom Always." They carved it in the wall the night they got engaged. Murrays was their hang-out in college because it served the best chicken wings and every Saturday night Murrays ran specials on wings and pitchers of beer. One night, after Kate and Tom devoured a plate of wings and pitcher of beer, Tom pretended to drop his napkin on the floor. He slid out of his chair and onto his knees, taking Kate's hand in his. A brief moment to muster up courage, Tom swallowed hard and asked her if she would marry him. Kate giggled and threw her arms around his neck, getting hot sauce all over his shirt. She repeated, "Yes, yes, yes, yes, yes" almost a hundred times. Another pitcher of beer later and Kate and Tom ended up in this bathroom stall together, doing things that made her blush to this day. *Wild, wonderful things*, thought Kate. They shared a sexual intensity that gave her chills just thinking about. Her face flushed as she leaned against the stall door and evoked the memory of his hands gripping her waist, pulling her closer, then sliding up and fondling her breasts with strokes of undeniable eagerness. She could feel the heat as if it was happening now, and though it was only a memory, her body felt the craving. She opened her eyes, suddenly drenched in loneliness, realizing how much she missed the wanting, the heat, the sweaty thrusting, and groping for each other's bodies as if it would be the last time they'd touch. *What happened to that intensity*, she wondered. Kate ran her hand over the engraving, feeling the passion of that night in her fingertips. Tears welled in her eyes as she whispered, "I miss you Tom."

~

After the waiter brought menus, Tom looked across the table at the executive from Halloway. "Ms. Borgman," he began.

"Please call me Arianna," she interrupted. She had a warm smile and beautiful, odd colored eyes. They were sort of lavender and blue and green all at once and Tom found it hard to not look at her eyes. He wondered if she wore colored contacts but felt it inappropriate to ask.

"Arianna," he continued, "before we get to business I have to ask you why you chose this particular restaurant?"

The shock on her face was all Tom needed to see to know that something strange was going on. She became visibly uncomfortable almost to the point that Tom felt he needed to assure her that everything was fine. "So," he said, "obviously there is a reason you wanted to meet *here.*"

She nodded. Silence fell between them and finally Arianna asked, "Are you a spiritual man?"

Tom wasn't typically asked this question during a business lunch, or anytime for that matter. He hymned and hawed and stuttered for an answer, "Um, yes, I suppose you could, uh, say I'm spiritually inclined."

Arianna leaned in closer and spoke quietly. "Do you believe in spiritual things like dreams and miracles and God's revenge and justice?"

Tom was feeling completely uncomfortable now, but Arianna continued. "Do you believe in the father's sins being passed onto the son, and the grandson, like a generational genetic encoding in the flesh?"

"I'm sorry," Tom said, the uneasiness becoming hard to hide, "what does this have to do with meeting here or with Halloway retail."

She leaned back in the booth with a look of disappointment. "It doesn't have anything to do with Halloway," she acknowledged.

"Then why are we here?" Tom asked.

Arianna shifted in her seat and ran her fingers through her shoulder length blonde hair. "If I tell you you're going to think I'm crazy," she said. "And if I don't tell you I feel like I'm not being true to something, or someone." Tom stared at her intently. Maybe she was crazy.

"Why don't we start from the beginning and you tell me why you called this meeting and why you asked for it to be at Murrays," he explained. She nodded and Tom added, "I promise to listen until you're finished and withhold my judgment on whether or not you're crazy." He smiled in an attempt to ease the tension. She smiled back and with a sigh, she slowly began to tell Tom the story she rehearsed.

~

Kimberly paid the bill and got a to-go box for Kate's salad. When Kate came back to the table, it was obvious she had been crying.

"I'm sorry Kate," Kimberly said, "maybe it was too soon to bring you here." Kimberly stood up and hugged Kate tightly. "I just felt this tugging to have lunch here and I thought it was some sort of sign."

Kate laughed. Everything was a "sign" in Kimberly's world. Kate remembered when Kimberly tried to give her highlights in her hair and forgot to set the timer. Kate's ends were so fried she had to get them cut off. Kimberly told her that was a "sign" that Kate would look better with shorter hair. Or the time Tom got hit in the mouth with a softball during a co-ed game and Kimberly said it was a "sign" that he talked too much.

As they walked toward the door Kate caught a peripheral glimpse of Tom. She saw the back of Tom's head and the face of a beautiful blonde sitting across from him. She paused and studied the woman's face. The woman spoke with feeling and emotion and looked intently in Tom's eyes and Tom reached over and touched her arm. Kate suddenly felt sick to her stomach. Her hands trembled. She grabbed Kimberly's sleeve and pointed with her head to the table where Tom sat. Kimberly saw what was going on and blurted, "That asshole!" She started to walk toward their table but Kate grabbed her arm.

"No! Let's go." Kate bellowed.

Kimberly stared at Kate, "if you're not going to give him a piece of your mind I'm going to do it for you!"

"Please," begged Kate, tears now streaming down her face, "let's just go."

Once in the parking lot Kimberly ranted in defense of Kate, spewing out every four letter, foul language adjective that entered her mind. Kate stood motionless. She felt so broken inside that it was almost numbing. Her head began to pound and her stomach ached. Half way home she moaned to Kimberly, "It's really over isn't it?"

Kimberly squeezed her hand. "It is now sweetie. It is now."

Kate closed her eyes.

When they reached Kate's house Kimberly went inside but said she couldn't stay long because she had an appointment to get her hair done. "I have to foil my roots," she explained. Kate was glad because she didn't feel like being social and just wanted to lie down and cry herself to sleep. After using the bathroom, Kimberly joined Kate in the kitchen for a quick cup of coffee.

"Men are pigs," she spewed in between sips.

Kate offered a half-smile, but it was the best she could give.

"They can't control their hormones." Kimberly said flatly. "Even when they love you."

Kate spun her wedding band around her finger. "Do you think Tom still loves me?"

Kimberly sipped up the last of her coffee and walked toward the sink to set her empty cup inside. "I think Tom loves himself first. They all do."

When Kimberly left, Kate locked the door and crawled in bed. She wrapped both arms around the pillow, buried her face inside and sobbed.

~

After his lunch with Arianna Borgman, Tom headed to the Backrow Tavern for his three o'clock with private investigator, Stephen Braznovich. When Tom entered, the bar was smoky and there were few patrons inside. It didn't look like the kind of place where business deals were made, at least not the type of deals in which Tom wanted to be involved.

As Tom approached the bar, the bartender motioned with his head and said, "He's over there."

"How do you know who I'm looking for?"

"Your type doesn't frequent this establishment unless you're meeting with him."

Tom walked to the back booth in the far right corner of the tavern. "Stephen Braznovich?"

"Thomas Anthony Miller." He looked up at Tom. "Have a seat."

Tom slid into the other side of the booth and faced Braznovich. "You know my full name already, that's impressive."

"You said you needed help finding your brother?"

"Yes. I do."

"Why?"

"Excuse me?"

"Why do you want to find your brother?"

Tom thought this was a not only an odd question but a sort-of none-of-your-business type question, and his defenses flared. "Because he's my brother."

Stephen leaned back in the booth and folded his arms across his chest, tucking his hands beneath his underarms. "If you and your brother were close you'd know where he was and wouldn't be hiring me to find him. Therefore, I have to assume there is a sour relationship between you and your brother and if so, why do you want to find him?'

Tom glared at Stephen. "You a lawyer or a PI?"

Stephen grinned. "My background is in law." He shifted in the booth and leaned forward. "I don't take cases where I don't have all the facts at my disposal."

Tom grimaced. "My brother and I were never close. He's a loose cannon. He deals drugs, last I saw him he carried a .44 in his jacket pocket, and he's done jail time."

"When's the last time you saw him?"

Tom ran his hand through his hair. "Geeze, I don't know. It had to be around the time my grandfather died. So maybe eighteen years ago."

Tom could see the astonishment in Stephen's face. "Why do you suddenly want to find someone you haven't seen or heard from in eighteen years?'

Tom explained the details of Madeline's will and he could see a light come on in Stephen's eyes. "So you want me to find your brother so you can collect the inheritance money presumably left to you in your grandmother's Will. Is that the gist of it?"

"Yes, but it's more than just inheritance money." Tom exhaled. "I believe my grandfather's company, LouLineCo, was left to me as well." Tom knew Stephen was aware of what this meant. LouLineCo was one of the largest oil companies in the country and one of the largest employers in the state of Kansas.

"How long have you been searching for your brother?"

"Since my grandmother died six months ago. I thought Martin would at least show up at her funeral, but he didn't."

Stephen nodded. "My fee is $200.00 per hour."

Tom exhaled. "That's steep."

"We can max it out at a limit you choose. For example, you tell me to put in only twenty man hours on the case and I only charge you four grand." Stephen raised his eyebrows at Tom.

"It's still steep."

"If you're due to inherit LouLineCo, then what's four grand in the grand scheme of things?" Stephen winked at him. "We got a deal?" They shook hands. "I'll have the rest of the paperwork couriered to your office later this afternoon."

"Paperwork"

"I need genealogy information, the latest contact information, and a signed financial contract to do business, that sort of thing."

When Tom got in his car he was feeling hopeful again. He didn't like Stephen Braznovich very much. Thought he was arrogant and condescending, but he was supposedly the best in the business. Maybe his arrogance is spawned from confidence in knowing he can get the job done, thought Tom.

Upon returning to the office Tom had several phone messages. Three from Kimberly. One from another woman named Alisha. He poked his head out of his office door and hollered to Cindy, "Did Kate call?"

"No, sorry," she yelled back.

He closed his office door and dialed Alisha. He got her voicemail and decided not to leave a message. Their relationship was complicated at best. He then dialed Kimberly on her cell.

"Well, well, well," she answered, "if it isn't the back-stabbing, two-timing snake!" Kimberly was seething.

"What?" exclaimed Tom, unable to imagine what he had done to piss her off now. Kimberly was always railing on Tom about something.

"You know what!" She yelled. "I saw you today. You and your blonde little whore!" Kimberly was almost screaming into the phone.

"Kimberly you don't know what you're talking about," Tom explained.

"Yes I do," she continued, "you can't control yourself and I'm glad Kate's eyes are finally open."

"What does that mean, 'Kate's eyes are finally open'?" Tom's voice rose in volume as concern crept in. What was she talking about and what did it have to do with Kate?

Kimberly yelled, "We saw you today at Murrays with your girlfriend!" Before Tom could respond she added, "I know you can't control your male, biological tendency toward cheating, but taking her to Murrays was low even for you." Kimberly slammed down the receiver.

Tom was shaking. He sat back in his office chair and felt the world crashing down on him. How could this be happening? He wasn't cheating, not with Arianna anyway. He would never take another woman to Murrays. That was his special place with Kate. Kate had to know deep down he would never do that. He sat frozen for a moment, trying to let his brain process Kimberly's words. What did she mean he couldn't control his biological tendency for cheating? He'd never cheated before their separation, and no one knew about his indiscretions after he moved out. It wasn't something he was proud of or broadcast around. In fact, he was ashamed of what he'd done. He tried to dismiss Kimberly's words as just her being overly dramatic again, but the anger lingered and tugged at his brain. This wasn't the first time Kimberly had stirred up trouble between him and Kate. She was good at planting seeds of doubt in Kate's mind and Tom could only imagine what Kate was thinking, thanks to Kimberly. He slammed his fist on the desk and grabbed the phone. He had to get a hold of Kate and explain that his lunch with Arianna Borgman was not a date. He dialed Kate but she didn't answer. He dialed again. And again. And again. Kate never picked up the phone.

~

Cindy poked her head in Tom's office and couldn't help but notice how dark it was. The seventies style wood paneling along the side was bad enough to look at, but when all the blinds were closed and the lights were off it was like being in a cave. Tom was at his desk with his chair turned backwards so she couldn't see his face, but she could feel the heaviness of despair in the room.

"Tom," she said, her voice prompting him to turn his chair to acknowledge her presence. "I've got a last minute meeting so is it okay if I jet out of here a little early today?" She hated to ask for a favor while he was obviously feeling so down and alone, but today was the only appointment time Stephen Braznovich had available and she didn't want to have to wait all weekend to schedule another one.

Tom nodded. "No problem, it's Friday, get out of here early and go have fun." He tried to give a smile but it was evident just by looking at him how broken he was.  His blue eyes looked red and glassy.  Cindy felt a twinge of guilt, but she knew she had to leave.    She knew there was nothing she could do to help Tom with his marriage. Finding her father and understanding the big picture was more important, and to piece it together meant she needed the help of Stephen Braznovich.

## CHAPTER 6

Kate agreed to go out with Kimberly, though she didn't really feel like a night on the town. She wanted to curl in a little ball and go back to sleep, but Kimberly said that was depression trying to take hold. She insisted Kate go for a while, promising they would come home whenever she wanted. Kate hymned and hawed around making up excuses, but Kimberly refused to leave until Kate got showered, dressed and put on make-up. When Kate finally emerged from the bathroom in blue jeans, black strappy sandals and a white blouse, Kimberly shook her head disapprovingly.

"What?" Kate blurted. "What's wrong with my outfit?"

Kimberly sauntered over to Kate's closet and began flipping through the clothes. "What you're wearing now sweetie, says 'I'm forty and I'm okay.'" She pulled out a black sleeveless, backless top and held it up. "What you want to say is 'I'm young, sexy and fabulous.'" Kimberly's eyes were beaming as she raised her eyebrows and nodded her head up and down, holding up the top for Kate.

Kate sighed, "Oh, all right," she conceded, "but I haven't worn this in years. It probably doesn't even fit anymore."

Kimberly waited on the bed while Kate went back into the bathroom and changed tops. She hollered through the door, "I can't wear a bra with this shirt."

"Why do you need a bra?" Kimberly yelled back. "Bras just slow things down."

Kate giggled from behind the door. "You're so bad."

"I know," Kimberly acknowledged, "but haven't you heard, bad is the new good."

~

Everyone scurried out of the office for happy hour and weekend plans, but Tom stayed until dark. There was no reason to rush home to an empty apartment. Before leaving he checked voicemail again, hoping Kate had left a message but the only call was from Alisha telling him she'd be at her sister's house for the next several hours. Once in his car, he instinctively drove to their home and sat in the driveway. He was trying to muster the strength to go inside, knowing Kate was angry and they would fight. Still, he wanted to tell her what Arianna told him. He knew then she would understand Arianna was not his girlfriend.

The house looked dark except for the small lamp in the hallway. *That's odd*, he thought. *Kate usually has every light in the house on.* He rang the doorbell and knocked several times. It was only nine o'clock so he knew Kate wouldn't be asleep yet. "Where would she be at nine o'clock," he mumbled to himself. He used his key and quickly realized the locks had been changed. He was no longer granted access to his own home. "That didn't take her long," he ranted aloud. Tom felt angry and resisted the temptation to break a window and climb in just to prove a point. It was his house too. What gives her the right to lock him out? What had he done to her that was so terrible? He wasn't a bad husband. He didn't drink too much. He wasn't abusive to her. He took care of her. Put a roof over her head, bought her clothing and food. He was a great provider and a fine spouse. She had no right to treat him this way!

He stormed back to his car and squealed out of the driveway in an angry rage. Once on the freeway he rolled down his window and let the wind of reality smack him in the face. Despite the anger he knew the truth. The truth is he wasn't the most attentive husband. He was a workaholic. Everyone knew that. He wasn't always there for Kate and he knew he let his priorities get out of whack at times. But he did love her. He always loved her. He was a better husband than most men he thought. Tom gripped the steering wheel tighter and floored the gas. Then he yelled as loud and as long as he could. He screamed until his voice went hoarse and he had no more emotion left to vent.

Grabbing his cell he dialed Kimberly's number. "Is she there?" He blurted as soon as she answered.

"Is who here?"

"Are you alone?" Tom said through clenched teeth.

There was a pause and then a simple "yes" and she hung up.

~

The door opened before Tom could knock. He started to speak but Alisha placed her fingers over his lips and led him into the kitchen. "I know what you need," she said, handing him a shot glass of tequila. She placed a sliced lime in her lips and motioned for him to drink. He gulped down the tequila and grabbed her in his arms, French kissing her and retrieving the lime from her mouth. She smiled with a glow of seduction he couldn't resist, and poured another glass.

Several shots later their bodies lie nakedly intertwined as he thrust himself deep inside her, releasing anger, stress, loneliness, and frustration in a momentary exchange for lust. It wasn't the first time he'd held her hips between his hands as she moved back and forth on top of him. It wasn't the first time he'd fondled her breasts and caressed her in places that made her shake dramatically in his arms. He'd told himself months ago he would never do it again, but he couldn't fight it. It felt as if for a brief moment their passion numbed the pain inside.

~

Kimberly and Kate pulled in front of a local martini bar, the newest hot spot in southern Johnson County. The parking lot was crowded and Kate took a deep breath and exhaled. "Don't be nervous," Kimberly said. Kate had lost all color in her face and was breathing heavy. "We're just going to have a couple drinks and chill out."

Kate nodded. She wasn't sure why she felt so knotted inside. It was probably because she hadn't gone out as a single person in twenty years, and though she wasn't technically single yet, this felt like step one. "Let me take another pain pill before we go in. My head is throbbing." Kate pulled the prescription bottle from her purse, twisted off the lid and slid one pill into her mouth, swallowing hard.

Inside, they found a spot at the bar and ordered two martinis, an espresso martini for Kimberly and a Cosmopolitan for Kate. The first Cosmo went down easy, and Kate began to relax. The second Cosmo disappeared in a few short sips, as did the third. Kimberly looked at Kate's third empty glass, "whoa there sweetie, you better slow down before you fall down."

Kimberly's warning was too late, Kate was already tipsy. She leaned over and whispered in Kimberly's ear, "I'll be right back," then she slung her leg over the stool and dismounted like she was riding a horse. Kimberly laughed, nursing her second martini and watching Kate as she sauntered over to two men sitting across the bar. Kate looped her arm around the neck of one and whispered closely in his ear. His eyes widened with surprise and he grabbed her hand and led her toward the DJ and dance floor.

Kimberly watched in amazement, never having seen this bold side of Kate. She had to admit Kate had good taste in men. This one was the definition of tall, dark and handsome, with a little ooh-la-la thrown in for good measure. His friend moved from his spot across the bar and plopped down on the stool next to Kimberly. He was handsome in a rugged, big teddy bear sort of way. He wore a pair of Levis, black Army boots, a white tee with a dark red and brown flannel hanging open over it. The color of his hair was hard to gauge, as it was cut super short, military style, but his eyebrows were dark brown. His face was tan and sturdy, like a man who works outside all day in the sun. His six four, body builder stature looked dangerous, but his soft brown eyes, cuddly.

After ordering another beer from the bartender he swiveled on his stool to face Kimberly. "So," he started in a deep, raspy tone, "you married?"

"Divorced," she answered flatly and without turning to make eye contact.

"I'm going through a divorce myself," he said. An awkward silence fell between them. "Did you know that 43% of marriages end in divorce every year?"

Kimberly thought this was an odd thing to blurt out, but it sparked interest, so she turned toward him. "Really?"

"Yep," he nodded. "Those are the latest US Census Bureau statistics. You want to know why?" He raised his eyebrows. "Communication," he continued. "Couples stop communicating and the marriage ends."

"That's not why mine ended," Kimberly protested.

"I'm sure it is," he told her, "you just don't realize it."

"Nope," insisted Kimberly, "mine ended because he started *communicating* with someone else."

"That's too bad. I can't imagine any man cheating on a beautiful lady like yourself."

Kimberly grinned. "I feel compelled to let you know, you won't be getting anywhere with me tonight."

He took a drink and smirked. "What makes you think I'm trying to get somewhere? Can't a man pay a woman a compliment without it having a deeper meaning?"

"I don't know, can they?" asked Kimberly sarcastically. "I thought all men had hidden agendas."

"See now, we're having a communication clog."

She set her martini down and looked at him. "We're having a what?"

"A communication clog," he explained. "It's where I'm saying one thing but you're hearing another. The communication lines are getting clogged."

"Are you a therapist?"

He grinned. "No, but I know the lingo."

Kimberly picked up her drink and took another sip, looking over at Kate draped around her man. "What about your friend?"

"He's single."

"Looks like quite the ladies man."

"I can tell you this," he nodded, "he's had more than most."

Kimberly grinned. "He has that look about him."

Kate and her ladies man came whirling back over to the bar. She raised her eyebrows at Kimberly as if to say, "look at me, I still got it." At least Kimberly thought that's what she was saying, though it was hard to read through Kate's drunken haze.

"Kate, sweetie, we should be getting home soon." Kimberly was trying to be nonchalant in her approach of pulling Kate from what could be a potential mistake.

Kate leaned in toward the ladies man and planted a big kiss right on his lips. "Will you take me home?" She asked him.

Kimberly almost fell off the stool. What happened to pure, perfect Kate? *Mental note*, she thought, *add alcohol and you get horny, seductive Kate.* Though she was amused by such a dramatic difference in Kate's persona, Kimberly wanted to make sure she took Kate home before anything regrettable happened.

Despite her urging otherwise, the ladies man agreed to take Kate home. Kimberly grabbed Kate's arm, but Kate snapped at her, "Stop trying to ruin my fun!" Then she threw her arms around her neck and slurred, "I love you."

"I love you too," answered Kimberly with a sigh and an eye roll. She held Kate's face between her palms and looked intently in her eyes. "Are you sure you want him to take you home? It's not just the liquor talking?"

"Of course it's the liquor," she slurred, "but the liquor is gonna get me laid." Kimberly grinned. She didn't recall Kate ever using the word "laid" and it somehow didn't fit. Kate put her hand over her mouth and giggled like a little kid about to do something naughty. Suddenly, eyes wide, she grabbed Kimberly. "Oh my gosh!" She gasped.

"What?"

Kate leaned in close and whispered, "do they still do it the same way?"

"Do what?" Kimberly asked.

Kate stared Kimberly in the eyes, nose to nose and Kimberly could feel her eyes crossing and trying to regain focus. "IT." Kate overemphasized the T and spit in Kimberly's face.

Kimberly laughed out loud and wiped off her chin. "Oh, well, I don't know. How long has it been since you've done IT?"

Kate flipped her hair over her shoulder and frowned, "don't even get me started," she said, "suffice to say it feels like FOREVER!"

Kimberly reassured her that technique hadn't changed and she would be just fine. "Like riding a bike," she teased.

"Great," Kate mumbled, "I always fell off my bike."

Kimberly hugged Kate goodbye and watched her leave with the ladies man. Then she dashed back to the bar to pay their tab. She wasn't going to hinder Kate from having fun but she was going to follow them and make sure she was safe. After all, this man could be a serial killer. He could be a rapist. He could be some weirdo who chops people up into little pieces and keeps their body parts in the fridge. Kimberly knew just because a man was good looking didn't mean he was safe, and even if he was safe, drunk as she was she might need someone to take care of her later.

Reaching for her purse she felt a strong hand grab her wrist and she turned around to see the man she had been talking to earlier. Kimberly looked down at his hand wrapped tightly around her wrist. "Can I help you with something?"

Without releasing her arm he answered, "yes doll, you can sit back down and finish our talk."

Kimberly twisted her wrist to break free but his grip tightened. "Excuse me," she demanded, "you're hurting my arm!"

"You look like a smart gal," he explained, "the sooner you sit back down the sooner I let go."

Kimberly slid one butt cheek onto the bar stool. "There," she snapped, "happy?"

"Now," he said calmly and quietly, "here's what we're going to do." As he detailed his plan for Kimberly she swallowed hard, feeling her heart start to race and her palms get sweaty. "You keep your pretty little mouth shut and a smile on that face and everything will be fine," he instructed. Within a matter of minutes they were in the back of the restaurant in a corner booth, with Kimberly pressed between him and the wall. They were virtually unseen by anyone entering or leaving. The bartender and waitress were given crisp hundred dollar bills and explicit instructions to leave them alone.

Kimberly stared at him, feeling fear and anger rise up in her. "What do you want?" she blurted.

He grinned. "I told you doll, I want to finish our talk."

"I have nothing else to say," she seethed.

"Then I guess we'll just have some quiet time together," he smirked, "and give your friend and my friend a chance to get to know each other."

Kimberly's eyes widened. "You're keeping me here so I don't follow Kate?" Kimberly tried to stand up and slide across the table, but he caught the back of her jeans and yanked her back into the booth.

He grabbed her hand and placed it against his left side, by his ribs. She felt something hard, long. A leather holster with a gun. He stared at her with a clenched jaw. "Don't make me use it," he warned. "I don't want to hurt you." Kimberly lowered her eyes to the table. "I just want to talk," he said. Her hands were trembling and her breathing shortened. Should she scream? Should she try to crawl under the table? What was happening to Kate? Her mind whirled and her pulse raced. She sat frozen.

~

As he drove, Kate leaned her head on his shoulder, kissing his ear lobe and running her tongue down his neck. Ordinarily Kate was not aggressive, but six months of separation from Tom left her longing for a man's touch. She was drunk and desperately needed to feel wanted. "Besides," she told herself in the corner of her mind, "Tom's with someone else so why should I be alone?" She ran her hand across his chest and felt his muscular form, then grabbed his arm and the protruding firmness of his bicep made her wonder if anything else was getting firm. She let her fingers dance lightly over his tightened abs, noting in her mind how powerfully built he was beneath his black sport coat. Heat rushed through her as her hand slowly slid down his stomach and over the bulge in his jeans. Her stomach twirled with nerves as she reached down to grasp his rigid form, but just before she took hold, he gently lifted her hand away.

Kate looked up at him, the shock shining in her eyes. "You don't want me to touch you?" she asked.

He gave her hand a tender squeeze and smiled in a way that told Kate he did want to be touched. She leaned forward and kissed his lips, sliding her fingers once again toward his prize.

Pulling off on a side street, he stopped the car. He took her hand and held it against the seat. "You don't even know my name," he said, turning to face her.

Kate felt a flush of shame replace desire for a moment and leaning back in the seat, she tried to think clearly. He was right. She hadn't even asked his name. "I'm sorry," she stammered, "I must seem easy to you." She let out a big sigh and stared dizzily at the floorboard. "I don't know what I'm doing." Kate buried her face in her hands, embarrassed by her actions. "I don't know anything anymore."

He tugged at her hands until she lowered them from her face, then he brushed away a piece of hair that had stuck to her lipstick. "I'm Stephen," he said, "and I think you know a lot more than you let on."

Kate looked up at him and felt the flush return. His brown eyes were warm and safe and erotic all at once. Desire flooded her body and her breathing quickened as he ran his hand around the nape of her neck toward the back and pulled her into him. His tongue caressed hers in an explosion of longing that made shivers run down her back and warm places she thought would never feel lustful urges again. His kiss told her he was no stranger to the needs of a woman and Kate blushed as she envisioned in her mind what he might do with that tongue. Laying her back in the seat, he leaned down on her just enough so she could feel his wanting. Kate's body responded in ways she hadn't felt in a long time. She gripped his arms and moved her hips in slow rhythmic circles against him, as their kiss grew deeper. His hand slid under her shirt and up from her waist to her breast in one fluid motion. Now she was thankful she wore the top that required no bra. He stroked her with fingers of experience and Kate let out a sigh of pleasure as his hands explored her, each touch making her body ache for him that much more.

"Take me," she whispered, with a boldness to which she was unaccustomed. It must have been the mixture of morphine and martinis that paved way for Kate to lay all rules and responsibility aside and lose control.

He lifted himself enough to look into her eyes. "Are you sure?" He asked, with caution in his voice. She knew what he was thinking. She was drunk and he was not and there were rules about such things.

Kate nodded, "please." A few seconds later she felt her world spinning and everything went black.

## Chapter 7

"I wish we didn't have to rush off," Alisha said, watching him pull on his pants and step into his shoes.

"I know, but neither of us can stay here," he reminded her. "You and Kimberly don't get along well enough to have prolonged visits to her house without raising suspicion."

"That's for sure," she exhaled. "I don't understand how we can be even half related. We're total opposites." Alisha grabbed her clothes and scurried into the bathroom while Tom finished getting dressed.

There was no question they were opposites. Kimberly was loud, rude and sarcastic and Alisha seemed soft spoken, caring and sweet. Kimberly had frosted blonde hair that looked too sprayed, wore too much make-up, and wore what Tom always noted as big jewelry. Alisha had soft brown hair, looked as if she hardly wore any make-up and wore a diamond stud in each ear. No one would ever guess they were related. They had the same father but different mothers and it seemed evident to Tom they each got a whole unique set of genes.

Once outside, Tom hurried to his car and sped off. He didn't know where Kimberly was but getting caught at her house with her sister would not be easy to explain. In the quiet of his car Tom felt the usual remorse rush over him. Technically he and Kate were separated so he wasn't really cheating. Though he was sure Kate wouldn't see it

that way.  Technically he had nothing to feel guilty
about.  Then why did he feel awful?  An even better
question was why did he continue to run to Alisha
when he knew he'd be riddled with regret
afterwards?  Was he driven by loneliness?   Was it
out of anger toward Kate for locking him out, first
emotionally and now physically?  The emptiness
filled him as he drove and he promised himself
he'd never touch Alisha again.

~

His cell phone buzzed on the table and
Kimberly jumped.  She studied his face as he
nodded and listened to whoever was on the other
end.  "Working on that as we speak," he said into
the phone and winked at Kimberly.  "We'll find out
if she knows her."  Shutting his phone he slid out
of the booth and into the other side, facing her.
Kimberly thought she might be able to make a run
for it now, but he swung his leg onto the seat next
to her and in a low raspy tone warned, "Don't even
think about it."
    "What do you want?" Kimberly asked, her
voice quivering.
    "I'll ask the questions doll." He reached
into her purse and pulled out her wallet.
    "What are you doing?  Are you robbing
me?"
    This made him chuckle to himself, but he
didn't answer her question.  He pulled out her
driver's license.  "Kimberly," he said.
    Kimberly snatched her purse back.  "You
could have just asked me my name."
    "Would you have told me?"  She looked
away, knowing she would have given him a fake
name or told him to go to hell.
    "Calm down.  This will be over soon."  He
reached his hand into his front jean pocket and

pulled out a pack of cigarettes and a lighter. "Mind if I smoke?" He angled the pack toward her, offering her a cigarette, but she turned her head away. "It's polite for a man to offer the woman a cigarette first, before taking his."

"It's a little late for manners don't you think?" Kimberly glared at him.

He lit the cigarette and blew smoke over his right shoulder. "I dunno. I don't think it's ever too late for manners." He shifted his weight and reached into his back pocket. "In fact, I forgot to properly introduce myself." Kimberly followed his every movement with her eyes. She half-way expected him to pull out the gun and threaten her, but instead, he retrieved a policeman badge and ID and placed it on the table. It read: Officer Ernie James.

Kimberly's eyes widened. "You're a cop!" she exclaimed.

~

Stephen pulled up in front of Kate's house and left the car running as he opened her purse and fumbled through it until he located her keys. Once the front door was opened, he lifted an unconscious Kate from the passenger side of the car and carried her in. It didn't take long to find Kate's bedroom, located down the long hall, last door on the right. He gently laid her on the bed and slid off her shoes.

He considered trying to wake her up, but Kate was passed out cold, and things had already gotten way out of control. Stephen had a personal policy never to mix business and pleasure and tonight was the first time he crossed that line. He was silently reprimanding himself, reminding himself that he was merely involved with Kate to gain information about the Miller family, nothing else. *What happened in the car should not have happened and could not occur again,* his mind scolded. Stephen pulled the bottom of the bedspread over her legs and brushed the hair off her face. He stood for a moment looking at her. "You are beautiful," he mumbled in a half-whisper. He shook his head and told himself there are a lot of beautiful women in the world, and she is nothing special, but his heart knew otherwise. There was an innocence to Kate that made Stephen want to protect her and hold her close. It was an unshakeable feeling of comfort that logic told him he shouldn't have with someone he just met.

He turned on the small lamp by her bed and placed his business card on the nightstand next to her keys. Before leaving the room, he glanced under the bed and peeked in the closet. Feelings or no feelings he was a private investigator and he needed to take advantage of her being passed out. In a quick peripheral search he found no boxes or crates of pictures or family photo albums. He made a fast search of the two guest rooms as well but nothing notable jumped out. He quickly walked through the rest of the house to get a basic layout in his head, but found nothing suspicious or relevant. Then, stopping in the hallway, he saw the pictures of Tom and Kate hanging on the wall. His gut sank. He was investigating Kate Miller to find a link to Cindy Miller and had no idea Kate was Tom's wife. "Ernie is not gonna believe this irony," he uttered to himself.

Unsure of how much time he had before Kate would wake up, he quickly went to the den and opened the desk drawers one by one. He saw the file folder marked "Journal Entries" and slid it under his arm. He then made a beeline for the door and locked it on his way out.

~

Tom sat in his car in front of his apartment for about fifteen minutes. He didn't feel like going inside and being alone for the rest of the night. It was 11:40pm and he told himself he'd drive by the house one more time and see if any lights were on. If the lights were on, he'd knock and see if Kate would talk to him.

Pulling into the driveway he found Kimberly sitting in her car. She jumped out and ran toward Tom. "Thank God!" She yelled. "I've been calling your cell for the past ten minutes!" Kimberly was out of breath and visibly upset.

"What's wrong?" Tom could see the panic in her eyes.

Kimberly ranted, "I'll tell you everything later but right now you've got to open the door and see if Kate is home."

"Where else would she be," asked Tom, "it's almost midnight."

"Tom, please just open the door!" Kimberly blurted.

"I can't," said Tom.

"Then give me your damn keys and get out of the way!" Kimberly snatched the keys from his hand and pushed by him. Tom ran to catch up to her and grabbed at the keys.

"No," he demanded, "I can't because I don't have a key." Dead silence fell between them and the humiliation of being locked out of his own home was evident on Tom's face.

Kimberly rolled her eyes and cursed. "Is there another way to get in the house?" Her voice was trembling and more high pitched and manic than Tom had ever heard from her.

"We can break a window," Tom shrugged.

Kimberly followed Tom around to the back of the house where the guest room window stretched a foot off the ground. They had the window extended several years ago because Kate complained there wasn't enough light in the room. It was going to be the baby's room and Kate said she wanted it bright and cheery.

Tom wrapped a large rock from the garden in an old t-shirt he found in his car and twisted the end so it would be easier to hurl through the window. He looked at Kimberly and asked one last time, "This is absolutely necessary?" Kimberly nodded. He swung the rock back and forth, working up a nice momentum, and then let it fly against the glass. The rock broke the glass enough that Tom was able to kick through the rest of it and reach in to unlock the window. He stared at Kimberly, who immediately started to push the window up and climb in. "Wait," Tom said, "I'll climb in and then let you in through the door."

"No!" snapped Kimberly, "you go to the door and I'll let you in. Go!" she motioned, "I'll see you at the door."

Tom was reluctant but left Kimberly hanging half in and half out of the window, and headed to the front door to wait.

Once inside, Kimberly crept through the guest room, down the hall and peaked into Kate's room. She saw Kate lying on the bed, fully clothed. Kimberly checked the bathroom and the closet, peeked under the bed and then headed down the hall to open the door for Tom.

Tom was growing impatient. What was taking her so long? When she finally opened the door, he entered quickly and breezed passed her without a word. He was in the bedroom for a moment, then came walking back and found Kimberly in the kitchen. He sat down at the table across from her and let out a long, exhausted sigh. Before Kimberly could say anything, Tom opened his hand and slid a business card across the table. It read: *Stephen Braznovich, Private Investigator.*

"You want to tell me about this?" Tom's eyes pierced into Kimberly's forehead.

She sighed. "There's nothing to tell."

Tom slammed his fist on the kitchen table. "Is this the man Kate was with tonight?"

"I don't know," Kimberly hollered back. "I just knew she left with someone and I was worried something bad had happened to her."

"If this isn't the man she was with, then how did she get this business card?"

Kimberly stared at the card and re-read it. "I don't know Tom," she sneered, "maybe she hired him to follow you and your little whore girlfriend."

Tom's mind clouded with emotion. He felt enraged that Kate was with another man, and guilty that he had no right to feel angry. Could it be possible that she hired the same private investigator to find out if he were cheating? Was that how Stephen Braznovich already knew so much about Tom when they first met?

Questions flood his brain and he glared at Kimberly. "I want to know what happened tonight. I want every detail from the minute Kate met whoever she left the bar with."

Kimberly smirked at him. "Jealous, much?"

~

When Alisha got home the house was dark and empty. She turned on the kitchen light and noticed her husband, Dale, left a note on the table. He was working late again and the note said not to wait up. Alisha and her husband had grown apart the past year. She was in nursing school and he was busy working on another case. He was always working a big case. Anytime he was obsessed about some unsolved crime, they grew apart, but this time was different. This time her career aspirations drove her to study and his pressures at work drove him to drink.

His drinking is what made her leave him six months ago and go stay with her half-sister, Kimberly.

Alisha wasn't sure who was harder to live with, Kimberly or her husband. She and Kimberly were fourteen years apart in age and had different philosophies about life. Alisha thought Kimberly was a bitter divorcee with more interest in money than people. Kimberly thought Alisha was a tree-hugging vegetarian, married to a man who cared more about his job than her. They were never close, but Alisha had nowhere else to turn. Kimberly was her only family to speak of. Alisha stayed with Kimberly ten days before she couldn't stand it anymore and moved back home. Every so often when her husband drinks too much and gets verbally abusive Alisha shows up on Kimberly's door for a night or two. This was how she met Tom.

Tom was newly separated from Kate and had dropped by Kimberly's house to beg her to talk some sense into Kate. He thought Kimberly could influence her to give their marriage another shot. Kimberly was out of town that night and Tom and Alisha ended up drinking tequila and sharing relationship sob stories. It wasn't until the wee hours of morning that the tequila paved a way through inhibition, and they found themselves entangled in naked passion. She thought their affair would only consist of this one night. Neither of them seemed like the affair type. It was something that happened out of loneliness, she told herself. It was two people in a moment of weakness fueled by alcohol. She never meant for it to continue, but every time they made contact she couldn't bring herself to tell him no. Tom looked at her in a way her husband hadn't in a long time and Alisha couldn't deny it felt good. Tom made her feel beautiful and desired, and that feeling was difficult to walk away from.

Alisha showered, slipped on her nightgown and crawled into bed with remote in hand. Flipping on the local news, she sat upright as the newscaster announced a woman had been shot in her home in Forest Lake, a sub-division located a mere four miles up the road. "A neighbor found the body," the newscaster reported. Alisha shivered. Not only did the murder creep her out but it was in her husband's jurisdiction which meant he wouldn't be home anytime soon. Alisha sat staring blankly at the TV when the phone rang. It was him.

"I know," she said, "I just saw it on the news."

"Don't wait up," he told her, "this is a biggie."

"Do you know who killed her?"

"Not yet," he said. "You know I can't give you details, but I have a strange feeling this is linked to the case I've been working on for a long time."

"The one from six months ago about the guy who died in a car accident but you think it wasn't really an accident?"

"It wasn't an accident!" He belted out louder than he meant to.

Alisha remembered this case because Dale was obsessed with it. Everything else in his life went by the wayside, including their marriage. Dale took a lot of flack for it at the station and was basically told to drop the case or suffer severe career impediment. The fact was a fifty-something year old man was killed in a hit and run accident. Dale said the angle of the hit led him to believe it was intentional, that and the fact that the car was hit twice. The real mystery lie in the fact that the man had no identification on him. No wallet. No insurance card. No credit cards and no business card. Not even a receipt from a gas station or convenience store. There was no cell phone, and no car maintenance sticker on the windshield. Nothing was in the vehicle to evidence his identity or even direct police to someone who might have known him. Even the VIN number was missing from the car. The really gross thing was that his fingerprints had been burned right off. Dale believed the killer removed everything from the vehicle and burned the victim's fingers after he was dead. Furthermore, no one ever filed a missing person's report that fit his description. It's as if he was truly a nobody from nowhere-ville.

"So, what makes you think the murders are connected?" She probed. "Are you going to get in trouble if the Captain finds out you're still working that case?"

"He won't," Dale answered matter-of-factly, "I've hired some outside help. I'm going to break this case wide open, I can feel it."

Alisha tried to sound supportive, but she had heard those words before and her faith was wearing thin.

"I can't tell you anything else, babe, don't wait up." Alisha hated that he couldn't share his work with her, but she understood when they married that confidentiality was par for the course in his line of work. Still, at times it made her feel isolated from his life.

He started to hang up but Alisha stopped him with another question. "Dale, can you tell me her name?"

"We haven't released that to the press."

"Why? Doesn't the family know yet?" Alisha knew the press could be held off if the victim was a minor or if the family had not yet been notified, otherwise the name was almost always released.

"There's some controversy over the identity of the victim," he said quietly. "I can't tell you anything else right now. Love you."

Alisha hung up the phone. Finally solving this case would mean he wouldn't be gone as often nor stressed out all the time. It might even make him a contender for a promotion. They could certainly use the extra money and less stress might mean less drinking, which could only mean less fights. Alisha daydreamed for a moment in the blissful land of 'what if.'

~

Kimberly recanted the evening for Tom, beginning with them arriving at the bar. To hear about Kate drinking and dancing and flirting with another man made him visibly uncomfortable, and it was obvious Kimberly took pleasure in telling him every little seductive detail. Tom glared at her, fighting the urge to say things he'd later regret. When Kimberly spewed more detail about Kate kissing Stephen, Tom came unglued, jumping to his feet and slamming both palms on the table.

"Knock it off Kimberly," he seethed at her, "that's my wife you're talking about."

"Not for long," Kimberly smirked. "You can't have your cake and eat it too Tom." Kimberly's tone was snide and meaner than he felt was deserved. He stood with his back to her, trying to control the anger boiling inside.

"Just get on with the story," he said through clenched teeth.

Kimberly continued telling him all about what happened after Stephen and Kate left the bar. "Wait a second," Tom blurted, "you mean this Ernie guy was a cop and held you there with a gun?"

"Yes," said Kimberly, "but I didn't know he was a cop until later," she explained.

"That's got to be illegal. You can't just hold an innocent person at gunpoint."

Kimberly squinted and wrinkled up her nose. "Well, he didn't really hold me at gunpoint exactly."

"You just said he had a gun."

"He did. I mean, I think it was a gun. It felt like a gun."

Tom shook his head and raised his eyebrows, then spoke slowly, over emphasizing his words. "Kimbeeeerlyyyyyy, did the man have a gun or not?"

"Don't talk to me like I'm an idiot!" She snapped. "I don't know. I think so. At least I thought so."

Kimberly went on to tell him that she overheard the telephone call Ernie took while at the table and that she thinks Ernie and Stephen are trying to get information from Kate about some woman.

"That's ridiculous! Kate doesn't have any information about anything." Tom emphatically spewed. "What could they possibly get from her?"

Kimberly shrugged. "I don't know and when I pried I was told it was confidential." Kimberly held up her fingers to make dramatic quotations around the word confidential.

Tom exhaled. "I don't like this a bit." His jaw tightened. "Do you even know for sure if this Ernie guy is really a cop?"

"Well, I wasn't about to stop and inspect his badge closer after he finally told me I could go." Kimberly rolled her eyes, "I thought the man had a gun, Tom. When a man with a gun tells you he's a cop you nod and say okay you're a cop!"

"There's no need to yell."

"Well, sometimes you're such a jackass."

"Nice." Tom turned and stared out the bay window, mumbling to himself, "and you're a real peach."

Silence fell between them. It was obvious they couldn't stand each other, but Tom knew they were going to have to get along long enough to figure this whole thing out.

"Okay," said Tom trying to replace the irrational emotion with logic, "first things first, I'm going to call the police and see if an Officer Ernie James exists." He reached in his pocket for his phone but it wasn't there. Feeling both pockets and coming up empty, he excused himself to his car to see if he'd left it in there.

"I don't think it's in there," said Kimberly, as he walked toward the door. "I tried to call you a bunch of times earlier, and surely you would have heard it ringing if it was in your car."

Tom searched his car to no avail. Then it hit him. His phone must have fallen out of his pocket when he was with Alisha at Kimberly's house. Tom's heart stalled and he felt a nauseating knot inside. How would he explain his phone being in Kimberly's house?

~

Alisha must have dozed off because the phone jolted her up in bed. She leaned toward the nightstand and grabbed it just before the third ring. "Hello?" She could hear the caller breathing, but they never spoke. After offering a polite "hello"

three times she hung up. The second ring sent
chills through her. This time the caller spoke. His
voice was low and garbled, like he was trying to
disguise it. He said, "Tell your husband to look up
the Kansas hit and run murder of Lou Miller."
Then he hung up.

Alisha immediately called Dale's cell but it
went straight to voicemail. "Call me right away,"
she said, trying to hide the uneasiness she felt
inside. She scurried out of bed, retrieved a shoe
box from underneath and pulled out a Smith &
Wesson semiautomatic. She checked the clip, fully
loaded, pushed it back in until it clicked in place
and crawled back in bed with the gun next to her.

~

Tom convinced Kimberly to stay the night
so they could both talk with Kate first thing in the
morning. This bought him some time to figure out
a way to get his phone back. He told her to take
the spare room closest to the master bedroom.

"You go on to bed," he said, "I'm going to
stay up and make some phone calls."

Once the spare bedroom door closed, Tom
dove for the home phone and dialed Alisha's cell.
No answer. He dialed again and again. Voicemail.
He was sweating. He knew he had to get his phone
out of Kimberly's house before she found it. He
paced around the den and then caught a glimpse
of hope as he entered the kitchen. There, on the
counter, next to the wine rack sat Kimberly's
purse. Feeling like a naughty kid snooping on
Christmas morning, he crept over to the purse and
peeked inside. There in her purse, shining like a
beacon of salvation, were her keys. Tom grabbed
them and sneaked quietly out the front door to his
car. His heart raced as he started the engine and
backed quickly out of the driveway, keeping the

lights off until he was well up the street. As he
drove to Kimberly's house, he mentally considered
all the places his phone might be. It could have
fallen out by the couch, in the kitchen or by the
bed. He'd have to be quick, get in, get out and
hopefully get back before Kimberly noticed he was
gone.

## Chapter 8

Stephen sauntered past the bartender of the Backrow Tavern, to the back booth carrying several file folders. He slid in across from Ernie. "She passed out before I could talk to her. I managed to pull a file but I don't think it'll have what we're looking for. Near as I can tell it's just a bunch of personal thoughts and feelings. Reads like a diary." Stephen dropped the folder on the table and rubbed his eyes.

"So there's no mention of Cindy Miller?" Ernie asked.

Stephen shook his head, "not that I saw in a quick skim through."

"Damn," cursed Ernie, slamming his fist on the table. He lit a cigarette and inhaled deeply. "You think we got the right Miller family?"

"Ironically, I think we have the right Miller family for both cases." Stephen went on to explain the pictures in the hallway and how Kate is Tom Miller's soon-to-be-ex-wife.

"I'll be damned," Ernie snorted. "Well, that makes things easier."

"Maybe." Stephen rubbed his eyes. He was still uncomfortable with what happened between him and Kate and worried this would complicate the investigation.

"Let's review what we know so far," Ernie lit a cigarette.

"We know Cindy Miller is the daughter of the big oil tycoon, Lou Miller right?"

95

"Sort of," snorted Ernie. "We know that Cindy Miller's mother told her that her father was in the oil business, but that don't mean he was an oil tycoon."

"But we have a birth certificate that proves Lou Miller is her father."

"Correct, but there are a lot of Lou Millers."

Stephen tilted his head back and forth. "How many Lou Millers are somehow linked to the oil industry in Kansas?"

Ernie exhaled smoke over his right shoulder. "I'm guessing not many."

Stephen continued. "We know Cindy was born in Kansas. We know her biological last name is Miller and we know her father was in the oil business." Stephen motioned with his fingers. "There were twenty-seven male Millers that fit the age, date and location parameters and of the twenty-seven only four are linked to the oil business."

Ernie squint his left eye as he blew out smoke and stared at Stephen. "Let me guess, those four are all related."

Stephen grinned. "Lou, his son Louis Jr. and the two grandsons, Martin and Tom."

"And as fate would have it," Ernie exhaled a giant smoke ring right over the center of the table, "Tom Miller just happened to hire you this afternoon to locate his brother Martin."

Stephen smiled, "yep."

"And you just happened to be at the same bar as Tom Miller's wife, Kate, who just happened to fall all over you and you happened to drive her home and just happened to snoop around her house."

"What's your point?' Stephen raised his eyebrows at Ernie who bellowed a raspy smoker's laugh.

"There's just a lot happening, that's all."
Ernie cleared his throat. "That and you're the
luckiest bastard I've ever seen."

"It's not luck. It's skill." Stephen grinned.
"It's a well known fact that women will expose
family secrets a lot easier than men, so getting an
inside track with Kate is, well, dare I say it, a
stroke of genius."

"Okay, genius, when do we tell Cindy we
found her long lost fraternal family?"

"Soon," Stephen answered, "but first we
need to find out if Cindy is the daughter of the
grandfather or his son. They both have identical
names."

"You said the son's name was Louis Jr."

"That's a legal name, but he could have
gone by Lou, just like his dad, so he could have
put Lou on the birth certificate." Ernie lit up
another cigarette while Stephen talked. "We also
need to find out what happened between Lou and
Cindy's mother. She's going to have questions."

"She'll have questions all right," Ernie
gleaned, "and the first one will be where's my share
of daddy's oil money?"

"Anyway," Stephen continued, "Lou's son,
Louis Jr. died in Florida a little over five months
ago."

"Guess we can't question him then."
Stephen shot Ernie a look. "I'm just saying."

Stephen added. "Looks like he wasn't
much of a father because he left his kids with Lou
and Madeline to raise and he never came back for
them."

"Sounds like a nice guy. How'd he die?"
Ernie asked.

Stephen flipped through a couple pages in
one of the folders. "Says here he was hit while
crossing 39th street in Tampa." Stephen continued

to skim read aloud.   "Looks like it was a hit and run case."

"Police ever find the schmuck who hit him?" Ernie asked.

"Doesn't look like it," said Stephen. "Still filed as unsolved."   Stephen continued, "So, we need to focus on the only living possibilities we have."

"The grandsons," Ernie interrupted.

Stephen nodded.  "Martin and Tom Miller. You begin an extensive search for Martin, which shouldn't be hard because he has a rap sheet two hundred yards long." Stephen slid Martin's file to Ernie. "I'll concentrate on finding which Lou is Cindy's father by investigating the Miller family history further."

"Got it."

Stephen smiled.  "So I'll investigate Kate and you find Martin."

"You mean Tom," Ernie corrected.

"No, you find Martin."

Ernie shook his head and blew smoke right in Stephen's face. "You investigate Tom not Kate."

Stephen grinned. "Oh, right, right, right. I'll investigate Tom. Did I say Kate? I meant to say Tom."

Ernie rolled his eyes. "You get to do all the fun stuff."

"Let's hope." Stephen grinned.

~

A couple gin and tonics later and Stephen and Ernie had mapped out a game plan.  Ernie told Kimberly he was cop and needed information from Kate. Now it was time to go one step further and find out if or what Kimberly knew.

"Girlfriends talk," Ernie said, "so if Kate knows any family gossip the probability is high that she would have shared it with Kimberly."

"Right," Stephen nodded, "but Kimberly wouldn't share it with us."

Ernie shook his head. "You surprise me friend." He took a deep drag and let the smoke pour out his nostrils. "We throw Lou or Cindy's name out and see how she reacts. Her reaction alone will tell us if she knows anything."

Stephen shoved in the last bite of his club sandwich and checked his watch. Time to make the call. He pulled out his cell and dialed Kate's number.

"What makes you think Kimberly will be at Kate's house?"

Stephen shook his head, "now you surprise me friend," he imitated Ernie's inflection. "After what happened tonight, I guarantee you Kimberly made a beeline to check on Kate and she's probably still there."

"How can be so sure?"

"I know women."

"I bet you do." Ernie spouted causing Stephen to chuckle.

Kimberly had just climbed into bed when the phone jolted her up. She dashed into the hall expecting to find Tom on the couch. She looked in the bathroom, the kitchen, the den. He was nowhere to be found. Surprised the phone hadn't awakened Kate, she grabbed it just before the fourth ring. "Hello?" She answered.

"This is Kimberly, correct?" Stephen spoke in his usual smooth, deep tone.

"You must have the wrong number," Kimberly stammered, her heart beating rapidly.

Stephen spoke calmly. "No, I don't have the wrong number. I know Kate is still sleeping and I know you have questions about tonight.    I want to answer your questions." Stephen paused and Kimberly wasn't sure whether he was waiting for her to speak.

"Okay," she uttered almost breathless, all the while looking for Tom and wondering where he went.

"My partner Ernie and I are working on a case and I need you to tell me everything you know about Lou Miller."

Kimberly's mouth went dry and she slammed down the phone.

"Well?" Ernie asked when Stephen disconnected.

"She hung up."

Ernie smiled, "that's the reaction I was hoping for."

~

The house was pitch black and Tom felt his way into the foyer and straight back to the kitchen. The moon shone through the window above the sink, giving him enough light to see that his phone was not anywhere on the floor. He went over to the couch in the family room and began moving cushions. Then it hit him, duh, just call yourself and follow the ring. He wondered why he hadn't thought of that sooner. He made his way back to the kitchen and dialed his cell from Kimberly's home phone. Sure enough he heard it ringing from the bedroom. "Thank God!" he sighed, keeping the receiver in his hand and heading down the hall. Nothing could have prepared him for what he would see when he turned the corner.

There she stood, in her nightgown, holding his phone in one hand and a gun in the other.

"I knew you'd come back for this," she said, holding up the phone. Tom stood speechless, intensely aware that the gun in her hand was pointed at him.

Alisha lowered her aim to the floor. "Sorry," she sighed, "a girl can never be too careful."

Tom felt a little more at ease, but still on edge. He studied her face. It was obvious she was tense.

"I got your message about your phone, so I ran over to see if I could find it for you." She held out the phone for Tom to take.

Tom stared at her, letting his eyes go from the gun, up her arm and to her face. She followed his gaze and rolled her eyes. "You're probably wondering why I have a gun."

"It crossed my mind," he answered, reaching out slowly and taking his phone.

Alisha sat down on the bed and took a deep breath. "Aside from being a verbally abusive drinker, my husband is a policeman," she explained. Tom was shocked. In all the times they'd talked about him she never let on that he was a cop. Tom pictured him as some low life, jobless scum who sat on the couch all day with one hand tucked in his waistband and the other on the remote. "He's rarely home at night and I get afraid so I keep a gun handy." Tom sat down next to Alisha and quietly listened. "Don't worry," she continued, "I'm totally trained on how to use it. I got the best score in the gun training class when I got licensed."

Tom nodded. "Good to know." But it didn't really make him feel any better. He couldn't help but wonder why she brought the gun with her to Kimberly's.

Before he could ask, Alisha continued, "I've had a weird feeling all evening, probably just from the news about that woman getting murdered. That and how it somehow ties into a case my husband's been working on. It just makes me jumpy."

"Who was murdered?" Tom asked.

"Some woman in Forest Lake was shot," she answered.

"Who was she?" Tom probed.

Alisha explained that the identity hadn't been released to the press yet and that her husband said there was some controversy over it. Tom sat silent. Hearing about murder on the news was one thing, but when it happens so close to home it causes an uneasy feeling inside and Tom wasn't sure how to respond. After an awkward moment of silence Alisha rose from the bed and stammered, "Well, you have your phone so we should probably go. I don't know when Kimberly will be home."

Tom stood up. "Kimberly is at my house so we don't have to rush off. We can talk some more if you want." Even as the words left his mouth he couldn't believe he was saying it. He knew damn good and well he didn't want to talk, he wanted to touch.

Alisha turned and met his stare. She swallowed hard. The temptation to fall into his arms felt overwhelming. "How do you know she won't come home?"

Holding up Kimberly's keys, he grinned, "Because I took these from her purse."

Alisha felt a smile cross her lips. "This is wrong," she uttered as she felt his arms grab her close and his lips enclose on hers in a kiss that spoke only of wanting. Despite the red flags going off in her head she surrendered to him.

~

Kimberly's pulse increased as she paced in the living room. Who were these men, how did they know she was at Kate's house? Why were they asking her questions? She felt this pressing need to get out of there so she grabbed her purse from the kitchen and headed to her car. She dug her hand into her purse but couldn't find her car keys. "Damn," she mumbled, searching harder. She finally emptied her purse onto the hood of the car and realized her keys were nowhere to be found. She dashed back inside Kate's house and retraced her steps, no keys. Her heart beat so violently she could feel it pounding in her temples. She searched everywhere. No keys. Frustrated, Kimberly plopped down on the couch, replaying the night in her mind. All of sudden it hit her. Tom must have taken her keys. "That jackass!" She muttered out loud. "He wanted to make sure I couldn't follow him!" She grabbed her phone and dialed his cell. No answer.

~

Tom and Alisha heard his cell ringing but ignored it. The passion they shared left no room for interruption. The only sound they could hear were the moans of unspoken approval. As they lay sweaty in each other's arms and the euphoric arousal of the moment subsided, Tom reached his hand to the floor and picked up his phone. He looked at the call log. "It was Kimberly," he said.

Alisha bolted up. "We should go. We should go now!" There was fear in her voice.

Tom grabbed her around her waist and pulled her back down. "It's okay," he assured her. "Remember, I have her keys." He tried to comfort her with gentle kisses on her lips and her neck, but Alisha was visibly upset and her once relaxed body was now rigid with fear. She pushed Tom to the side and leapt from the bed, searching the floor for her panties and nightgown. One of her sneakers managed to work its way under the bed and Alisha bent down on all fours to retrieve it.

Tom sat up and grinned at her position. "Better watch it," he warned, "you make this dog want more."

Alisha couldn't stop the smile from filling her face. "I'm trying to get my shoe," she explained, rolling her eyes "not trying to turn you on."

Tom slid off the bed and position himself behind her, pulling her hips back firmly against him. "You don't have to try."

She pulled away from him, turned around and gave him a token peck on the lips. "We have to go," she said, standing up and sliding into her shoes.

"What's bothering you?" Tom asked.

Alisha glared at him. "Oh, I don't know," she groaned, half sarcastic, half sincere, "maybe it's that I'm in my half-sister's house committing adultery with a married man. What could possibly be wrong?"

"I'm separated," defended Tom.

"I'm not." She retorted. For the first time Tom realized he had never thought about how Alisha might be feeling. He had selfishly only looked at their relationship from his perspective. It never dawned on him that she, too, might be struggling with feelings of guilt and remorse.

Tom sat down on the bed next to her. "Geeze Alisha, I'm sorry," he whispered.

"Me too."

## Chapter 9

Tom pulled into the driveway and found Kimberly sitting on the hood of her car. As he approached her it was evident she knew about her keys and was pissed off. "You son of a bitch!" She screamed, jumping off of the car and getting right in his face. "Where the hell were you?" She cursed at him. "How dare you leave us here after what happened tonight!" Kimberly's arms were flailing and Tom grabbed her simply to protect himself. She struggled and kicked at him, but she was no match for his strength. He pulled her back against his front and held her arms crossed in front of her body so she couldn't move.

He put his lips directly to her ear and told her to calm down. When she continued to struggle he squeezed around her ribs until she winced from the pain. "Calm down," he yelled.

"Where were you?" She demanded.

"I had something to take care of." Tom didn't anticipate Kimberly finding out about her keys, so he hadn't come up with a story for his whereabouts. He naively thought he could sneak out and sneak back in with no one knowing.

"Why did you take my keys?" Kimberly struggled against Tom and he noted in his mind that she was a helluva lot stronger than she looked. "Let me go!" She screamed loud enough that Mrs. Netbaum's front porch light switched on. Tom released his grip and Kimberly whirled around and smacked him across the face. Kimberly swung at him again, but Tom grabbed her wrist before she made contact. She kicked at him with her spiked heel and Tom pushed her against the side of the car.

"Stop it," he scolded, leaning down inches from Kimberly's face.

"What are you doing?" The voice came from the front porch and Tom whirled around to see Kate standing there with a look of concern and awe. "Are you fighting?" Neither Tom nor Kimberly spoke to answer that question. "For Heaven's sake, get inside before the neighbors see you." Kate held open the door and shook her head at both of them as they entered the house like two scolded children. "What will the neighbors think?" Kate slammed and locked the door then breezed by them and led the way to the kitchen.

~

Tom sat at the kitchen table while Kimberly paced back and forth and Kate made coffee. There was a thick, silence in the room and no one wanted to be the first to break it. Finally Kate spoke. "My head is throbbing," she moaned, grabbing her forehead with one hand and balancing against the countertop with the other.

"That's because you inhaled three martinis in thirty minutes," blurted Kimberly, whose tone implied she was blaming Kate's irresponsible actions for everything that occurred tonight.

"I'm sorry," retorted Kate, "but obviously I'm not the only one in the room with some explaining to do." Her eyes darted to both Tom and Kimberly with a steely glare.

Tom lowered his eyes to the floor and exhaled, "I'll go first," he said. Kate stared at him with her jaw set tight and her nostrils flared. She was ready to shoot him down at the first sign of indiscretion. Tom folded his hands on the table and took in a deep breath. Kate's stare made it clear he had one shot at this and he'd better phrase his words perfectly. "You saw me at Murrays with another woman and you were right to think I was involved with her." Kate studied his face and Tom slumped in his chair. "I would have thought the same thing if I had seen you there with another man." Tom raised his eyes to meet Kate's and continued, "it was stupid of me to meet her at Murrays and for that I'm sorry."

Kimberly threw her hands up in the air, "what the hell does this have to do with everything that happened tonight?" She crossed her arms angrily and scowled at Tom. "This isn't exactly the right time for you to clear your conscience," she seethed. "This isn't all about you Tom!" Kimberly's voice was downright hateful and even Tom was shocked by the bitterness in her tone.

"You're right Kimberly," he hollered, jumping to his feet with such force he knocked over the chair, "this is about Kate and Kate deserves the truth!"

Kimberly laughed with disdain. "What do YOU know about truth?"

Tom didn't know how to answer. He didn't know what her statement meant or on what facts she was basing her words. What element of truth was he lacking? Was there something about Kate he didn't know? Was she implying that he was hiding something? Before he could come up with a rebuttal, a teary eyed Kate lashed out.

"Look at you two," she yelled, "look how selfish you are!" Kate stormed out of the kitchen, down the hall and slammed the bedroom door. She was awestruck by the intensity of anger between Kimberly and Tom. It was no secret they didn't like each other, but she had no idea the depth of their mutual hatred.

Kimberly glared at Tom, "way to go jackass."

## Chapter 10

Kimberly glanced at the clock. 2:00 am. "I'm going home," she announced to Tom, grabbing her keys from the table and making a beeline for the door.

Tom quickly followed her outside, "wait," he pleaded. Kimberly whirled around and stared at him. Tom felt short of breath as he asked, "Where were you headed when you realized I had your keys?"

She smirked at him and retorted, "Where were you headed that you felt the need to take my keys so I couldn't follow you?" Tom realized there would be no reckoning this without revealing his relationship with Alisha, and that was not an option.

He shuffled his weight from foot to foot and ran his hand through his hair. "C'mon Kimberly," he said, "I'm just trying to figure out what's going on."

"Me too!" She blurted.

Tom stepped closer to her which made Kimberly stiffened in her stance. "Can't we work together on this?"

"I tried to work with you Tom," she said, opening her car door. "I told you all about my evening but you haven't told me anything about yours." She glared at him as if she were looking right through him. "So," she demanded, "where were you?"

Tom knew telling her about Alisha would be the final nail in the coffin of his marriage. He couldn't let that happen. "Goodnight Kimberly," he said and walked back to the front door.

"You were probably with your girlfriend," Kimberly yelled, "infidelity runs strong in your veins doesn't it Tom!" He turned to comment but she had already slammed her door and started the car. He was still standing on the porch when she angrily sped off.

Once inside Tom debated whether to knock on the bedroom door or leave Kate alone. He chose the latter, fixed himself a bourbon and water and settled into the comfort of his old chair. With everything that happened tonight, Tom wasn't about to leave Kate by herself. The night's events replayed in his mind as he tried to understand. He planned to call Stephen Braznovich in the morning and find out how his business card ended up on Kate's nightstand. With that thought, he suddenly remembered he wanted to call the police and see if Officer Ernie James existed. He leapt from his chair and hurried to the desk in the den to get a phone book. If Ernie James was an officer, Tom wanted to give him a piece of his mind. He wanted to let him know legal action would ensure for the manner in which he handled things with Kimberly and Kate. If Officer James didn't exist, well, that was a whole different set of concerns.

Tom found the number to several local precincts and began calling. The first two claimed there was no Officer by that name. Tom's pulse began to quicken. The third call proved a bit more helpful as the operator put his call through to another Officer, a policeman named Dale Gordon. Tom's palms got sweaty as he listened to the voicemail message, knowing it was nearing the beep and his time to speak. At the tone he stammered nervously, trying to convey who he was and why he was inquiring about Officer Ernie

James. He ended the message by leaving his cell phone number.

Sitting back down in his chair, Tom tried to calm his mind. He flipped on the television and began scrolling through channels. Red lettering across the bottom of the screen that read "Breaking News" caught his attention, particularly since it was a local news station. He listened intently to the newscaster as she read from the prompt, "A woman was found tonight murdered in her Forest Lake home. The victim's name was Jeanette Carlen. Police are searching for leads as to the motive and assailant. If you have any information about this crime please contact the police at the number listed on your screen."

Tom shook his head and took a swig of his drink. Forest Lake wasn't far from here. That must be the murder Alisha was talking about. He closed his eyes momentarily and tried to let the stress melt from his body. It had been a long night and he knew he needed sleep, but he couldn't shut his mind off. When he opened his eyes to reach for his bourbon, his world suddenly went into slow motion. He stared at the face on the TV, the blonde hair, the beautiful, oddly colored, alluring eyes. He could hear his heart pounding in his ears as he jumped to his feet to move closer to the set.

The newscaster repeated the name of the victim, "Jeanette Carlen." Her voice echoed in his brain as Tom blinked and stared at the screen, shaking his head. Chills bolted up his arms and neck as a clammy disbelief encompassed him. He backed up and caught his foot on the edge of the ottoman, hurling himself into the end table and knocking his drink to the floor.

The crash made Kate open her door and dash down the hall, gun in hand. "What happened," she yelled, seeing Tom on the floor amid broken glass and ice. "Are you alright?" She reached for his hands but Tom already sat up, put his elbows on his knees and held his forehead in his palms. He was trembling and for a moment Kate's anger was replaced by concern. "Tom," she bent down next to him, "what's happening?" She placed her hands on his knees. "Please talk to me." Her voice cracked with emotion. "Are you having a heart attack," she grabbed his wrists to pull his hands away so she could see his face. His eyes were glassy and Kate knew there was something terribly wrong. Tom was a man who never cried. She couldn't remember the last time she'd actually seen tears in his eyes. It was probably at grandmother's funeral six months ago. She searched his face for answers. "Do I need to call 9-1-1?" she uttered with panic.

He shook his head no. Then pointing to the TV he said, "That woman is not Jeanette Carlen." Kate was confused. She turned around, glanced at the screen and back at Tom. Clearly the name below the picture read Jeanette Carlen. Tom's voice cracked with every word as he tried to swallow the emotion. "That is the woman I met with at Murrays. Her name is Arianna Borgman and she's an executive with Halloway retail."

Kate looked at the television again and back at Tom. "You must be mistaken Tom, maybe she just resembles the lady you met with."

Tom shook his head and uttered, "No, no, no, no, it's her Kate. It's her. I know it's her. "

Kate didn't know what to believe. She knew Tom was under a great deal of stress, that the separation had been hard on him. She thought perhaps sheer exhaustion was distorting his memory. Tom grabbed Kate's hands in his, "you saw her at Murrays," he pleaded, "You saw her right?"

Kate's mind took her back to that horrible afternoon. Standing in the middle of Murrays, watching this blonde woman talk intimately with Tom. Seeing him touch her arm tenderly. Kate pulled her hands away, "yes, I saw you with her."

"Then you know that's her!" Tom demanded, sitting up straighter now.

Kate jumped to her feet and ruptured into a tirade of emotion. "So what!" she screamed. "So what if it IS your girlfriend? Am I supposed to feel sorry for you and get all sympathetic because the woman you've been screwing behind my back is dead?" Kate's eyes swelled with tears. She knew how awful that sounded but she didn't care. She was angry and hurt and she had a right to be.

Tom leveraged himself slowly off the floor, realizing the gun was still clenched in Kate's angry hand. This was the second gun pointed at him tonight and he was starting to feel a bit jumpy. He moved slowly toward Kate, reaching her shoulders and running his hand down her arm until his hand covered hers and the gun. She released her hold immediately, surrendering the gun to him. Tom breathed easier. He set the gun on the coffee table and pulled Kate close him.

"She's not the woman I'm screwing." He said, stroking her hair. He knew that didn't come out right. Kate sobbed. "Please," begged Tom, "please let me tell you what Arianna Borgman told me because then you'll know she was never my girlfriend."

Kate wanted to stop crying but the tears flowed beyond her control. She felt so many emotions, anger, rage, fear, heartache, loss, confusion. The past three days had been more than she could handle. She hadn't told anyone what the police had told her at the hospital, how the accident wasn't an accident at all. She could scarcely believe it herself. Instead, she'd held it in, pretending everything was okay. Now the flood gates were open and she couldn't stop the tidal wave of emotion.

Tom wiped the tears from each of her cheeks. Holding her face in his hands, he looked directly into her eyes and begged, "can we please sit down and talk?"

Kate blinked slowly and nodded.

~

Kate fell asleep on his shoulder and it took Tom a couple minutes to slide his arm from behind her without waking her. Finally free, he stood up and stretched his back, wincing from the stiffness. The sun was beginning to turn the sky from deep black to smoky gray as morning approached. His head felt like tongs were clamping down on each temple and his heart ached from the sheer stress of the past twelve hours. Kate told him the policeman's theory on her car accident which left him feeling more than unsettled. He never got around to telling her what Arianna told him at Murrays. Kate was too emotional and after telling him about her meeting with the police she couldn't keep her eyes open. It could wait another day. He stood for a moment and stared at Kate as she slept. If the past six months apart had made him realize anything it was that his love for her had only grown deeper and he missed her with an agony powerful enough to break him. In the silence of that moment he vowed, "Somehow we will get through this together."

With Kate asleep, Tom crept to the den and opened the desk drawer. He wanted to look at the folder of Journal Entries he read the day of Kate's accident. Something in the letter grandmother wrote Kate was bothering him. He couldn't put his finger on it. He flipped through every file but couldn't find the journal entries. "Damn," he said aloud, "she probably hid them because I snooped around last time I was here." He didn't blame Kate for hiding her personal stuff; after all, he hadn't proven himself trustworthy. Still, it bothered him to think she would harbor the secrets of her soul from him. He tiptoed quietly down the hall to the bedroom and began a casual search for the journal entries. He looked under the bed. Pulled open each dresser drawer and ran his hand inside. Nothing. On the top of the dresser he noticed a business card. It read, Officer Dale Gordon. Tom felt a nauseating sensation in his stomach as he realized this was the name of the officer he left a message for in regards to the supposed policeman, Ernie James. Could Officer Gordon and Ernie James be working together on solving Kate's car accident? How did Stephen Braznovich fit in?

Kate's voice startled him and he whirled around to face her. "What?" he gasped.

"I said, what are you doing in here?" Kate was irritated and her face shown with both disgust and exhaustion. "What are you looking for?" She held both hands up in the air and Tom could tell she was upset. This was strike two in the snooping department. Like a dog with his tail between his legs, he followed Kate to the kitchen, trying to explain. Every once in a while she'd sigh or roll her eyes at him or shake her head and he could tell he was making no lead way.

All excuses aside Tom looked at her and spoke his heart, "Kate, I know I've screwed everything up, just like grandmother said in her letter that we Miller boys do." Hearing Tom quote grandmother made her stop fiddling with the dishes in the sink and turn to face him. "The thing is," he continued, "I know I've been insensitive at

115

times and I know I've put my work first and I know I've left you lonely…" His voice faded and cracked as he fought back the lump rising in his throat. "I've done things," he paused and swallowed hard, "things I never thought I'd do. Things I'm ashamed of." Kate studied his face, letting each word lower her defenses. "But the truth is," he took a deep breath, "I don't want to live my life without you and I'm scared to death of losing you for good." Tom's eyes were glassed over and his struggle to contain the tears was evident.

Kate's breathing quickened as she walked closer to Tom. There were so many things they needed to work out, but for a brief moment the problems felt trivial. She wrapped her arms around his neck and when he returned her embrace a well of emotion was unleashed. For the first time in years, they wept in each other's arms.

It must have been the release of emotion that gave way to a different sensation long since unprovoked by Tom. Or maybe Kate was still reeling from the events of the night before. Whatever the reason, she was suddenly aware of the strength of Tom's arms around her back, and the feel of his chest against hers. He held her firmly and her body grew more aware of his closeness, nursing to life a longing inside her. Kate's breathing deepened as a warm rush filled her. She wondered if Tom felt it too. A wanting so powerful she couldn't imagine ever letting go. She slowly raised her head from his right shoulder, turning and hesitating with her lips only centimeters from his. Neither one spoke words but their bodies communicated, as they carried on a conversation only lovers understand. His lips met hers first tenderly, then longingly, as desire erupted within. He pressed her against the countertop as their kisses grew deeper and hungrier. He couldn't stop and she didn't want him to. They fumbled with buttons and zippers and left pieces of clothing in the kitchen and down the hall. It had been six months since they'd touched at all, and over a year since they'd passionately pleasured one another.

Their tongues danced wildly across the other's body, bringing chills of delight, as they reveled in a sensual affection they both missed. Groping like teenagers, they caressed and explored every inch of each other with an intense erotic need, refusing to be stifled. Though their minds knew of all the problems between them, their bodies knew only of a deep, carnal need to re-connect. Sounds of satisfied moans and salacious sighs filled the room as Tom and Kate trembled in each other's arms and fulfilled their longing.

Wrapped in the scent of passion's aroma, Tom held Kate close. As the intensity subsided, reality began to seep in and the rush of heartache returned. They were separated. They were divorcing. It would be naïve to think this changed anything. They were always good in bed and everyone knew good sex wasn't enough to hold a marriage together.

Tom kissed Kate on the forehead. "I've missed you," he whispered.

"I've missed you too."

Tom could hear the anguish in her voice and he knew she was thinking the same thing he was. This didn't change anything between them. A couple orgasms weren't enough to save their marriage, no matter how incredible they were.

After they showered, Kate made coffee and they sat at the kitchen table. An awkward silence fell between them. There were things they needed to discuss, but neither knew how or where to start.

Kate exhaled deeply. "Tom, I still love you but I can't escape this feeling of distance between us."

Tom's defenses leapt alive. "Distance?" He exclaimed. "You weren't feeling distant about thirty minutes ago."

Kate's face worked into a scowl. "I knew you'd do this."

"What am I doing?"

"I knew you'd think this changed everything, but it doesn't."

Tom leaned back in the chair and crossed his arms. Her words felt like an ice pick in his flesh. He knew she was right, what just happened didn't change everything, but it changed something.

Kate continued. "I feel like there's this huge gorge between us and there's no way to cross."

Tom listened but every word felt like a bullet to his already worn thin armor. He wasn't sure how much more he could take. "Explain to me how two people can be on the opposite side of a gorge and make-love the way we just made-love?"

Kate shrugged. "We were just lonely, that's all it was."

Tom shook his head and stood up. She was wrong. He pointed to the bedroom, "that was more than just loneliness. That was passion and connection and belonging."

Tom could see confusion encompass her and he knew that she knew he was right.

"I just can't rush back into our marriage and wake up five years from now as miserable and stagnant and alone as I've been the past few years."

"I understand you're afraid. I'm afraid too, but when we connect like we just did the fear goes away." Tom's heart was pleading.

"But how long will that connection last?"

Tom sat down and grabbed Kate's hands in his. "I know I've made mistakes, but I also know what I felt and what I feel now and I know what I see in your eyes. We can make this work Kate."

Kate shook her head no. "It's like there's this river between us and it's raging and I can see you on the other side, but I can't get to you."

Tom squeezed her hands and joined her in the metaphor, "there's a log we can use to cross."

Kate lowered her eyes to the floor, remembering the poem in Madeline's journal. "The log it already broken," she whispered.

Tom tightened his jaw. "Then I'll chop it up and build a damn bridge if that's what it takes."

Kate could see the determination in his eyes and for a brief moment hope leapt alive in her. Maybe, she thought, just maybe this isn't the end.

## Chapter 11

Despite the chaos of all that was happening, Tom felt better. Hopeful. He and Kate had connected and regardless of what made it happen, he was grateful. He knew he should head to his apartment and get some sleep, but he hated that apartment. He hated the rental furniture in it. He hated the musty smell of the building. He hated how his mailbox key always stuck in the hole and he had to jiggle it back and forth to get it open. He hated that his neighbor smelled like cat pee. The thought of going to his apartment made his stomach knot and burn. After a moment of pondering his options, he decided on a drive-thru cheeseburger and headed to his office. Since it was Saturday he would have it all to himself and could review the last twelve hours of events without interruption. Maybe he could make some sense of all this.

Woofing down the last bite and following it with a gulp of coffee, Tom began to pace around his office and recant aloud each occurrence beginning with Kate's car accident. A new determination had been birthed in him and he was not going to give up.

~

Mrs. Netbaum arrived shortly after Tom left. She brought Kate a cheese filled strudel and asked how she was feeling. "I'm feeling much better," Kate assured her.

"Well, I'm happy to hear that," Mrs. Netbaum said, making the sign of the cross over her body and breathing out a huge sigh of relief. "When I saw that man carry you inside last night I thought you were dead."

Kate felt her face flush. She had forgotten all about how flirty she was and how she left the bar with a complete stranger. When Mrs. Netbaum mentioned last night, a flash of images filled Kate's head and redness flood her cheeks. What had she done?

"That man who brought you home sure was a looker though." Mrs. Netbaum fanned herself and blushed. "He got me flustered all the way from next door."

Great, thought Kate, now the whole neighborhood probably knows some strange man brought me home and thinks I'm a slut.

"Then there was all that commotion. Kimberly was in your driveway and your husband showed up again."

"Again?" Kate asked.

"Yes," she shook her head with her eyebrows raised high into her forehead. "He came over earlier then sped out of here like he was a NASCAR driver. Then he came back later when Kimberly was here and then they went inside."

"Where was I?"

"You were already inside dear."

"Where was the man who took me inside? Was Tom here when the other man was here?" Kate started to panic, trying to piece it all together.

"Oh, no, dear, the good-looking man was gone long before Kimberly or Tom showed up. He was only in your house for a few minutes." Mrs. Netbaum narrowed her eyes, "you have a snout full did ya?"

Wonderful, thought Kate. Now I'm not only the neighborhood ho, I'm a lush too.

When Mrs. Netbaum left, Kate made a dash to her closet to see if the manila envelope was still there. All of a sudden she felt paranoid, like all these people were traipsing around her house doing God knows what while she was unconscious. She knew she was being irrational, but ever since the accident she felt this pressing need to keep her eyes on that envelope.

Relieved to see it still on the shelf, she snatched it down and opened it. She pulled out the contents, revealing a photograph of a little girl with blonde hair and a birth certificate. Kate guessed the little girl to be about a year old in the picture. She was holding a daisy shaped barrette in her hands and smiling. The barrette looked enormous in her tiny fingers. Kate remembered looking at this picture six months ago, the day Martin stopped by and gave her the envelope, but she never noticed the picture had been cut. Now, looking closely, she could see someone's hand on the little girl's shoulder. It was a man's hand. It looked like a man had been purposefully cut out of the picture.

Kate thought back to the day Martin brought the envelope to the house. He was out of breath, almost frantic, as he emphatically told her that no one was to see the envelope, not even Tom. He made Kate promise she would hide it away and told her he would return to get it as soon as he could. She didn't like hiding things from Tom, but they had just separated and it never felt like the right time to bring it up. Before Martin left, Kate told him about grandmother's Will and how both he and Tom had to be present for the Will to be read and released. Martin looked stunned then mumbled something about Grandma Madeline being a smart old brood. Kate didn't understand the context and before she could ask him what it meant, he was gone. She hadn't heard from him since.

Kate dropped the picture back into the envelope and picked up the birth certificate. Her mouth fell open and her heart stalled when she read the name of the birth mother: Arianna Borgman. Her brain rushed with awareness that this was the same name as the woman Tom met for lunch at Murrays, the one he swore was killed last night. The birth fathers name had been blacked out as well as the date of birth, and though she held the certificate up to the light, Kate couldn't make out even one number or letter.

Questions flew in and out of her head faster than she could develop feasible conclusions. Who is Arianna Borgman? Why did Martin give Kate a file with Arianna Borgman's daughter's birth certificate? Why was the birth father's name blacked out? What did Arianna have to do with Tom? Then it hit her and a nauseating anger welled inside. Tom must have had an affair with Arianna Borgman and they had a child together. Logic fought emotion in a losing battle as Kate's mind filled in all the blanks. Tom wanted children and since she couldn't get pregnant he had a baby with someone else. He's probably been paying her child support for years, she surmised. "I bet Martin found out and is probably blackmailing Tom for money," she mumbled to herself. Kate's mind ran full speed away from any sense of rational thought and the anger raged inside her. She got up to get the phone and call Kimberly, but the doorbell interrupted her.

Kate quickly stuffed the birth certificate back in the envelope, shoved it under her bed and rushed to the door. Peering through the window she was shocked to see Stephen Braznovich, holding a bouquet of wild flowers and a bottle of white wine. Her heart thumped wildly in her chest and she felt a warmness fill her cheeks, replacing the angry thoughts about Tom with a buzzing excitement. She ran her fingers quickly through her hair, fluffed it then hesitantly opened the door. Before Kate could say a word, Stephen breezed past her and walked straight to the kitchen. Kate sarcastically mouthed, "Won't you come in" as she closed the door and followed him.

"You didn't call me," he said, "so I thought I'd drop by."

"You didn't leave me your number," she answered flatly.

"Oh contrar," he explained, "I left my business card on your nightstand right after I tucked you in." He winked at her and Kate could feel the blood rush to her cheeks. There was very little she remembered about their encounter, but what she did know was she boldly made herself sexually available to him. Stephen saw her flush, "Don't worry," he said. "You have nothing to be ashamed of."

Kate looked up with narrowed brows. Is that a good thing or a bad thing, she wondered, knowing she was overanalyzing the statement, but unaware of whether he was saying the sex was great or telling her nothing happened.

He came closer. "Let's start over," he proposed, "this time we'll have less liquor and more getting to know each other." He extended his hand. "I'm Stephen Braznovich. Nice to meet you."

"Kate Miller." She said, shaking his hand. "Likewise."

Kate couldn't stop the smile from flooding her face. There was no refuting the fact he was charming. Not to mention hot. Kate silently commended herself, even drunk she had good taste in men. She accepted the flowers with a thank you and pulled a vase from the top shelf of the pantry. "So," in an attempt at small talk, "how much of each other did we get to know last night?"

He laughed out loud, which made Kate feel more at ease. His smile was gentle and something in his dark brown eyes made her feel warm and secure. "I was a perfect gentleman," he said with a slight nod of his head, "well, maybe not perfect."

Kate smiled, "And I was..." Her voice faded slowly, signaling him to fill in the blank.

He caught her gaze and raised one eyebrow, "you were...," he drew out the word for the mere pleasure of watching Kate on the verge of wincing, "passed out," he concluded. "Nothing happened."

Kate exhaled loudly, which made Stephen laugh a deep belly laugh. "My," he said, "I've never seen a woman so happy to have NOT slept with me."

"It isn't you," Kate explained, "it's, well, I'm married sort of."

"Hon, you're either married or you aren't. There's no married sort of category."

"I'm separated."

"I know. And you haven't had sex in what seems like FOREVER." He slurred his words to mimic her from last night.

Kate gasped. "Did I tell you that?" She cupped her hands around her mouth.

"I think you told the whole bar," he teased.

Kate buried her face in her hands. She couldn't believe it. Stephen laughed harder. "It's okay," he consoled, "I get the feeling you don't frequent that place so you probably won't see any of those people again."

The phone was a welcome interruption from the humiliation she felt, and Kate jumped to answer. It was Kimberly. "I'm coming over with wine and chick flicks and we're going to have a late afternoon slumber party." She sounded giddy or drunk. Kate wasn't sure which.

Hating to squash Kimberly's plans, as it sounded fun. "I can't," she said delicately.

"Why not?" Blurted Kimberly. "I'm not going to let you sit around and sulk."

"I'm not sulking," Kate walked further away from Stephen and spoke softly. "I'm not alone." There was silence. "Are you there?   Kimberly, did you hear me?"

"Is it Stephen?"

Kate giggled like a teenager.

"It IS, isn't it?" Kate laughed at Kimberly's dramatic tone.   "How long is he going to be there?"

"I don't know," Kate shrugged, "I didn't even know he was coming over."

"Kate," Kimberly warned, "you don't even know this guy and you don't know what happened last night."

Kate whispered into the phone, "he already told me nothing happened.  He was a perfect gentleman."

"That's not what I'm talking about."

Stephen found Kate in the den and handed her a glass of white wine.  Kate nodded a thank you then spoke into the phone.  "I'll call you in a little bit.  Bye."  She set down the receiver and joined Stephen on the couch.

"Hope you don't mind," he said, holding up his wine glass, "but I found the glasses and took the liberty of filling them."

"It's fine. Thank you."

"I don't typically drink wine in the middle of the day," Stephen said.

"I do," Kate answered sarcastically, "middle of the day, middle of the night, all the time really."

Stephen chuckled, "yes, I guessed from last night that you have a very high tolerance for liquor." Kate laughed out loud. It was no secret she was a light weight.

Kate was beginning to relax and turned her body to face him. She bent one leg up under the other, and rested her arm on the back of the sofa. As they talked Kate noted in her mind how easy their conversation flowed. Stephen made her feel comfortable. The way he looked at her made her feel interesting and pretty, even though she'd hardly gotten any sleep the night before and knew she looked like a train wreck. He kept his eyes on hers while she spoke. He'd smile at her and she couldn't help but blush, feeling the giddiness of flirtation rush over her. The attention from someone new, a man other than Tom, felt refreshing. Not to mention the fact that he had olive skin, brown hair that was so dark it was almost black, a kid-like playful grin with dimples and deep brown eyes that oozed sensual sweetness. He was a tasty morsel.

"So," she said, "have you ever been married?"

"Ah, the age old question," he grinned. "No, I haven't."

"Why not"

"Because I'm the smartest man on earth."

Kate shot him a look that said, "C'mon!"

"Okay." Stephen took a deep breath. "I grew up with divorced parents. They did the best they could but their relationship was volatile and hostile. They loved me but hated each other. I decided I was never going to live that way and never going to put a kid through that life. So, I haven't married."

Kate studied his face. "Have you ever been in love?"

"Nah, love's not for me." He leaned forward and poured more wine in both glasses. "Besides," he added, "love has nothing to do with whether a marriage is successful or not."

Kate was floored by his statement, as she knew she and Tom were living proof.

Stephen cleared his throat. "It's like this," he began, "marriage is a foundation of love expressed in legal form. It's an agreement, a commitment to stay together regardless of whether you feel in love or not."

"Go on," said Kate.

"Well," he continued, "when I was a boy I spent a lot of time at my grandparents' house because my parents were always fighting. My grandpa was a Preacher. He taught me about the Bible and when I got older he taught me about girls." Stephen grinned, which made Kate smile. "He taught me about marriage and how it is a covenant designed by God to be shared between a man and a woman. It's an unbreakable bond."

The phrase "unbreakable bond" took Kate back to her conversation with Madeline the day she gave her the wedding ring.

"Am I getting too deep," asked Stephen.

"What?" Kate realized she had zoned out while thinking about Tom's grandmother.

"You had a spaced out look on your face and you started spinning your wedding band. I'm probably boring you with this stuff." He apologized.

"I want to hear more," said Kate, "please."

Stephen took a sip from his glass and continued. "Grandpa used to tell me that God made the marriage covenant as a vow of

permanence. A promise that cannot be broken."
He looked at Kate. "That's a lot of pressure."

"Do you believe it's even possible to have a successful marriage?" She asked.

"I think it's a balancing act. I think every marriage teeters on the edge of failure at any given moment. I think spouses give up at separate intervals in the relationship and if they both happen to quit at the same interval than the marriage is over." Stephen took a breath. "I have a handful of close friends. Out of all of them, one couple is still married." He shook his head. "That tells me something about marriage."

"It's hard sometimes," Kate said softly.

Stephen put his hand on her knee. "They call it the institution of marriage. How many institutions do you find it easy to live in?" They both smiled.

"Now, it's my turn to ask questions." Stephen leaned back on the couch and crossed one leg over the other. "When did you and Tom, is it?" Kate nodded. "When did you and Tom get married?"

Kate inhaled deeply. "Right out of college, so, eighteen years ago."

"Do you get along with his family?"

"Tom doesn't actually have much family," she said matter-of-factly. "I never met his parents. He was raised by his grandparents. I think his grandpa liked me but he died the same year we were married so I didn't have the chance to really get to know him. Tom's grandmother, Madeline, loved me the most." Kate smiled thinking about grandmother.

"What was she like?"

Kate sighed and laughed simultaneously. "Wow." She took a deep breath and exhaled. "She's a tough one to describe. She was quite a spunky lady," she explained, "and wise in a different sort of way." Kate's eyes narrowed as she searched for the right words to describe Madeline. "She was open and free-spirited and yet there was this depth to her that I've only recently begun to understand through reading her journal"

"She left a journal?" Kate nodded. "Have you read the whole thing?" Stephen probed. Kate shook her head to indicate she hadn't. "How many pages is it?" Kate could see that Stephen was trying to mask an interest in the journal. What she didn't know was he was searching for a connection between his client, Cindy and one of the Miller men, and hoping the journal might give some indication as to Martin's whereabouts.

"The pages aren't numbered," Kate explained, "but it's about an inch thick."

"Is it like a family genealogy?"

"No, it reads more like a diary."

"Does it list family members at all, like a family tree?" Stephen probed and Kate narrowed her eyes at him, thinking his interest in Madeline's journal was over-the-top.

"No. It's more like a culmination of her thoughts and life experiences." There was an awkward pause and silence filled the room. Kate shifted on the couch and stared out the window.

"I'm bombarding you with questions aren't I?" Stephen reached out and touched her knee. "I'm sorry, it's the private investigator in me that gets carried away and fires questions at people like they're in a damn interrogation."

Kate smiled and Stephen set both their glasses on the table and took her hands in his. He inched closer to her and she felt a nervous twinge in her stomach.

"You know this isn't going to be our first kiss." He said, moving slowly closer.

130

"It's the first one I'll remember."

A genuine smile filled his face and he belly laughed. "That's right; I forgot you were blatto last night." She rolled her eyes. "It doesn't say much for my kissing when it's that easily forgettable." Stephen's dimpled grin made him almost irresistible. "What do you say you give my kissing another chance to make a lasting impression?"

Kate's heart raced in her chest as he drew closer and placed his hand on her cheek, gently guiding her lips to his. His kiss felt tender, and soft, but passionate too, sending warm chills through her. As he pulled back she opened her eyes and met his gaze.

"How was that?" He asked.

She grinned. "Um, I don't know. Already I can't remember it," she teased.

"That's it," he smirked, "I'm going to make sure you remember this one." He pulled Kate into his arms and kissed her with an intensity that made her whole body come alive. She wrapped her hand around the back of his neck and pulled him closer, deepening their kiss, and pressing their bodies together. There was no mistaking his physical expression of desire pressing firmly against her, and no denying her body's warm response of readiness.

The doorbell jolted them both from the couch, and they quickly adjusted their clothing. Kate ran her fingers through her mussed hair as she hurried to the door and peaked through the peep hole. No one was there but a floral delivery truck was pulling out of the driveway. She opened the door to find a bouquet of white daisies sitting on the porch with a card that read: "Thank you for an incredible morning. ILYWAMH."

Guilt put an instant damper on the passion she felt for Stephen, and now she felt like a coke addict crashing down from a once great high. Anger followed the guilt, as the temptation to sleep with Stephen merely to get back at Tom rushed through her mind. "He was with that woman at Murrays and probably fathered a child behind my back," her defenses boldly proclaimed. "Why should I feel guilty for desiring another man?" Her psyche spewed, pointing out that she deserved to feel pretty and she needed to feel wanted. "This is good for me," she tried to tell herself. Somehow, though, the guilt was winning.

Kate carried the daisies into the kitchen and set them on the counter. Her stomach was tied up and she was sure Stephen would sense the sudden change in her mood. She stood for a moment staring out the bay window, trying to separate her emotions. She liked Stephen. Not only was he hot but he made her feel young and interesting, which was something she hadn't felt in a long time. She loved Tom, but the passion was gone, or had been until this morning. "This morning was a fluke," she told herself. It was stress-induced sex and it would probably never be that good again.

"You're separated," her mind screamed, "go for it, have fun, you need this." Her heart just couldn't get on board no matter how badly her body wanted it. And it wanted it.

Kate was too deep in her own thoughts to realize Stephen entered the kitchen and was standing behind her, peering out the window. "What was that?" His voice jolted Kate back to reality and she jumped.

"What?"

"I thought I saw someone running across the back yard."

Kate joined him in staring out the window, but didn't see anything. "Are you sure?" The back yard was a heavily wooded area that backed up to a small pond. It wasn't odd to see a deer or a wild fox run through every now and again.

"Well, I'm sure I saw something," he explained, "but I'm not sure if it was a person or maybe a big dog." He shrugged his shoulders. "Do you have a big, light haired dog?"

Kate shook her head.

"Do your neighbors have a big, light haired dog?" He probed, still staring out the window. Kate shook her head.

She studied him for a moment. "You really saw something?"

"Yes, I did." He turned to face her. "You think I just stare out windows, making proclamations of sightings simply to amuse myself?" His sarcastic wit made Kate grin.

"It was probably a deer." Kate seemed calm on the outside, but inwardly she was feeling jittery. Ever since the car accident and the talk with Officer Gordon, Kate felt jumpy, like she was being watched or targeted. She thought about telling Stephen but decided it was too heavy a topic. She didn't want to appear as some weak, scared little girl who couldn't take care of herself. The past six months she had learned how much she could take care of herself. She loved her new found independence. She loved cooking what she felt like cooking and not what Tom wanted to eat. She loved doing whatever she wanted when she wanted and not being tied down by Tom's schedule. She loved her new freedom. The only part missing was someone to hold her at night, someone to sit and watch television with, someone to make her laugh. It seemed the price for freedom was loneliness and Kate hadn't yet decided if it was a price she could pay long term.

They just returned to the couch when Stephen's cell phone buzzed. He checked the caller ID and excused himself to the other room. Stephen spoke in a low voice and though Kate strained she was unable to overhear. When he came back, Kate knew by his expression their evening had come to an abrupt end.

"Forgive me," he said, "but this is a meeting I can't miss."

"You have meetings on a Saturday?"

"Unfortunately, the investigating business doesn't get weekends off." He moved quickly toward the front door.

Kate forced a half-smile. "I understand."

Stephen leaned in and gave her a quick kiss on the lips. "I would love to hear more about your grandmother's journal," he said, "can I call you later?"

"Sure," she answered lightly. She closed the door, feeling a mixture of disappointment and relief. The twinge of let down from being ditched for work was all too familiar a feeling. Still, she knew the relief she felt stemmed from the fact that regardless of how good Stephen's attention made her feel, he just wasn't Tom. Kate walked back to the den, grabbed her glass of wine and took a big gulp, letting it warm her as it went down. Then sauntering over to the phone she dialed Kimberly to tell her she was free for a slumber party after all. No answer.

## Chapter 12

Alisha was at the kitchen table studying when Dale shuffled in exhausted. He plopped down next to her and rubbed both eyes. They were bloodshot and outlined in dark circles. "You look awful," Alisha noted, "do you feel as bad as you look."

Dale exhaled, "It was a long night and a longer morning," he said. "So, yes, I probably do."

"You need to take a nap. You can't keep going like this." Alisha wanted to encourage him to sleep instead of drink.

"I'm so close on this case," he told her, "I can feel it."

Alisha touched his arm. "If anyone can solve it, you can babe, but you have to sleep for your brain to function."

He nodded. "Is that what all these nursing books say?"

"Yes," she grinned, "as a matter of fact it is."

Alisha got up to make him some coffee and a sandwich. She got out bread, bologna, and chips and went back to the fridge to retrieve the mayo. Dale rubbed his eyes and let out a loud yawn. "I got a big break last night," he said matter-of-factly. "You remember the mystery caller that gave you the name Lou Miller?"

"Yes. He scared the crap out of me. I slept with a loaded gun."

"That's my girl," Dale grinned.

135

Alisha smirked and shook her head. She didn't know why the thought of her with a gun turned him on. "Go on with your story."

"I pulled the file on Lou Miller. He was the big oil tycoon down in Stillwell. You know, the one that started LouLineCo?"

"Okaaaaay," Alisha said, wondering how this fit with the John Doe hit and run and the woman who was shot.

"Turns out Lou was killed in a hit and run and I'm thinking the two are related." He dropped his head and leaned on the table, resting his chin on his arms.

"Sounds like a long shot."

"That's because I haven't told you everything yet. A couple hours after your message, I got a call from a man who wanted to know why Officer Ernie James was harassing his wife and girlfriend."

Alisha interrupted, "Ernie James? Is he still an officer? I thought he was demoted or decommissioned or whatever after that big coke bust a year ago."

"He was, sort of, it's a long story. He was acquitted. Now we use him un-officially for undercover type work."

"So, what, he's like a freelance cop?" She mused.

"Yeah, sort of." Dale unlaced his boots and slid them off. "I hired a private investigator to help me get to the bottom of the John Doe case and my PI works closely with Ernie. Ernie was the mystery caller who gave me Lou Miller's name."

"Dale, you didn't really hire a PI did you?" Alisha stared at him. "What will the Captain say if he finds out you're still on this case and now you're using funds for outside investigators?"

"I'm not using police funds." The second the words left his lips Dale knew it was a mistake.

"How are you paying for a private investigator?" Alisha looked at Dale and felt the anger rising in her throat. "We don't have the money for this!" She yelled, slamming a plate onto the counter. "We're barely scraping by as it is!"

Dale jumped up and grabbed Alisha's arms. "Babe, listen, I know this is a strain but when I crack this case wide open I'll get the promotion I deserve, and we'll have more money. A lot more money. I promise." He tried to make eye contact with Alisha but she kept darting from his glare. "I'm close here. I know it. I can feel it." Alisha let out a big sigh. "Bear with me on this a little while longer okay? Please?"

Alisha conceded. "Okay, but I'm going to have to quit nursing school and get a full time job if you don't solve this soon."

"You won't have to do that," Dale said confidently, sitting back down at the table. "I have a feeling the man who called last night is the missing link."

"How so?"

"I dunno yet. I have to meet with Ernie first. But I can feel it."

"What's the guy's name?" Alisha spread mayo on the sandwich, twisted the lid back on the jar and headed to the fridge.

"Tom Miller." Alisha froze. Her stomach crashed inside just about as fast and hard as the mayonnaise jar when it hit the floor. Dale jumped up. Alisha's hands were shaking. "What's the matter babe?"

Her heart raced as she tried to form words. Dale stared at her and she knew she needed to regain composure fast. "I haven't been feeling well," she blurted, "I think I'm getting sick.

"All of sudden?"

"Yes, it comes and goes."

Dale helped her pick up the broken glass from the mayonnaise jar. "Maybe you should go lay down," he said. She nodded, but her mind raced with questions as to why Tom would call her husband and how Tom would even know Dale was her husband. In all the times they'd talked she had never even told Tom her last name.

Alisha set Dale's sandwich and chips on the table, then retrieved a glass from the cabinet and filled it with ice and water. She set the water in front of Dale and returned back to the mayonnaise mess on the floor. "So, what makes you think this Tom Miller guy is related to the oil tycoon guy?" Alisha tried to fane nonchalant interest.

"A hunch," he said, taking a big bite of the sandwich, "but that will be easy to confirm. Simple genealogy search."

Alisha shook her head, "I don't get it," she said, "even if this oil tycoon guy and Tom are related, how are they connected to the John Doe case?"

Dale shook his head, "I don't know yet, but the fact that the private investigator connected Lou with my John Doe on the same night that Tom called, tells me somehow they're all interconnected." Dale took another bite and washed it down with a long drink of water. "Anyway, I'll have the proof I need soon enough."

"What kind of proof?" Alisha unwound more paper towels from the roll and mopped up the mayonnaise.

"Phone records for starters." Dale shoved some chips in his mouth. "If Tom and John Doe are connected then maybe they've been in contact within the last year. Maybe they were in constant contact up until the last six months because John

Doe was killed. Maybe Tom even killed him." Dale shrugged and threw three more chips in his mouth. "It's a process of elimination babe."

A chill ran up Alisha's back and she wanted to throw up. Tom's phone records would have her cell number on them. Dale would recognize her cell and question how she knew Tom, how long she'd known him, and the nature of their relationship. Alisha could feel the blood drain from her face as the inevitability of getting caught sank in.

"How long does it take to get copies of phone records," she asked, trying not to seem overly interested in his answer.

"For civilians, several weeks," he explained, "but for me, I'll have them first thing Monday morning, maybe sooner."

Alisha stood frozen. She needed to warn Tom. They needed to get their story straight before everything unraveled.

~

Tom had been pacing around his office all day. He made a timeline of sticky notes beginning with Kate's car accident and they were spread out across the desk. His mind kept drifting back to Arianna Borgman and the meeting at Murrays. Why Murrays he wondered. If her name really was Jeanette Carlen, why did she pretend to be Arianna Borgman, as if that name was supposed to mean something to Tom, but it didn't? Was it a coincidence she was killed right after she met with Tom? Was that somehow connected to the reason someone tried to run down Kate? Why would anyone try to kill Kate? None of it made sense. He sat at his desk and rubbed his eyes, fighting the exhaustion in hopes of coming up with a plan of action that would render him answers.

Feeling his cell phone buzz in his pocket, he pulled it out and saw a text message from Alisha. "We need to meet now. Urgent. Tell me where."

Tom stared at the screen with a pit in his stomach. Alisha had never texted him before and never was there an urgency in meeting. He sat for a moment then texted back. "Come to my office. 2889 Centre Creek Blvd." He then scurried around picking up the timeline of sticky notes he had so carefully constructed. He stacked them neatly in reverse-sequential order so he could easily lay them back out once Alisha left.

Alisha texted, "Ok. Ten minutes."

Tom had no sooner read Alisha's text when he heard the jingling of keys in the hall outside his office door. He listened quietly, knowing the janitorial staff wasn't due to come until tomorrow and few employees held keys to the building. He quickly turned off his office light and stood behind the door, listening to the sound of footsteps approaching. When he heard the key enter his lock, Tom slid into the corner behind the door, next to a coat rack that held an umbrella and a black wind breaker he wore only on golf outings. He held his breath as the key turned in the lock and the door pushed open. Tom crouched into the shadows behind the door and watched as Rita entered his office, leaving the door standing open.

She approached his desk and looked inside each drawer, scanning carefully. Tom couldn't imagine what she was searching for and he fought the urge to jump out and catch her, but he knew he'd gain more information by secretly watching. She obviously parked her car in the front and didn't see Tom's car parked in the back lot.

Rita picked up the pile of sticky notes and flipped through them. "Hmmm," she hummed to herself, "I didn't know Kate was in an accident."

She set the sticky notes back where she found them and moved to the bookcase. She ran her fingers across the bindings of several books in a row, and then reached behind them. Tom could see she was disappointed to find nothing.

Rita let out a loud sigh and spoke to herself, "I know Martin gave him an envelope, now where did he hide it?"

Tom couldn't believe Rita would stoop this low, invading his private office to search for something she believed came from Martin. Other than his casual taunting her by insinuating he had found Martin a couple days ago, what would make her think he possessed something worth hiding? Furthermore, what would Rita want with it? Knowing Rita it had to have something to do with money, specifically relating to LouLineCo. The more Tom tried to figure it out the angrier he became, on top of it, he was nervous that Alisha would show up any minute.

When Rita finally left, closing and locking the door behind her, Tom put his ear to the door and listened. He wanted to make sure he heard the whoosh of the front office door open and close before he came out of his office. When he was certain Rita was gone, he turned on his office light, grabbed his cell phone and text Alisha, "park in back."

~

Ernie looked up when he heard Stephen stumble inside the front door of the Backrow Tavern and hit his knees on the hard wood floor. A trickle of blood ran from his forehead, down his left temple and under his jaw line. He was panting as Ernie helped him off the floor, shuffled him to the back and dropped him into their usual booth. He grabbed a napkin off the table, dipped it in his water glass and handed it to Stephen to wipe the blood.  Stephen dabbed at the cut with the napkin. "How bad is it?"  He asked Ernie, wincing from the pain.

"You could probably use a stitch or two." Ernie grabbed the cigarette he left burning in the ashtray and inhaled deeply. "What the hell happen?" He asked, blowing out a big ring of smoke.

"Somebody tried to run me off the road," Stephen said, anger building in his voice. "You should see my car."

Ernie squinted at Stephen and cleared his throat, which sounded like a pool of phlegm was grumbling around in his esophagus. "You get a look at the driver?"  Stephen shook his head no. "Type of car?"  Stephen shook again. "Damn," Ernie blurted, digging his cigarette butt into the tray.

"It happened so fast," Stephen explained, still blotting the blood from his forehead.  "I left Kate's and as soon as I hit Metcalf this car came out of nowhere and tried to run me off the road." Stephen explained how the other car came at him head on.  He swerved to avoid a collision, sending his vehicle into a spin which resulted in a light show of sparks as his passenger side scraped the metal guard rail for a good twenty feet.   "The darn thing of it is," Stephen spattered, "they didn't even stop.  They just sped off."

Ernie held up his hand.   "Wait a minute, did you say you left Kate's house?"

Stephen nodded.  "That's where I was when you called me."

"Who knew you were there?"

"No one. Just Kate."   Ernie lit another cigarette and let out a loud exhale.  Stephen knew what he was thinking, but there was no way Kate could have tried to run him down. "She didn't do it," he said, gripping Ernie's vodka tonic and taking a gulp.

"I didn't say she did," Ernie blurted.

"You were thinking it." Stephen took another gulp before Ernie grabbed the glass from him.

"Order your own," he barked.

"Touchy. Touchy." Stephen grinned.

"You don't like my theory, you don't get my liquor." Ernie tucked the glass under his arm and took a drag from his cigarette.

Stephen conceded, "Okay, tell me your theory on my random car accident."

Ernie narrowed his brows and glared at Stephen. He didn't say it but Stephen knew he was thinking "you moron." They both knew the almost collision was no random accident, but either an attempt on his life or a warning to back off. Either way it meant they were getting closer to the truth.

Changing the subject, Stephen asked, "Any luck on finding Cindy's real father?"

"I'm focusing on finding her mother now, as she's the only one who can verify whether the biological father is Lou Sr. or Lou Jr."

"Okay, so any luck with that?" Stephen re-wet the napkin with water and pressed it against his bloody head.

"Here's where we're at: I found an apartment registered under Arianna Borgman, but not one neighbor could give me any type of description." Ernie shrugged his shoulders. "A couple neighbors commented they'd never even seen her before." Ernie ruffled through some papers. "I asked what kind of car she drove and everybody said something different. One said a white suburban. Another said a silver Cadillac."

Ernie dug his cigarette butt into the ashtray. "You sure we can't just ask Cindy to get us an appointment with her mom?"

Stephen pursed his lips and scowled at Ernie. "You know we can't do that. Cindy specifically asked that her mother not know about our investigation. We can't break our code of confidentiality."

Ernie lit another cigarette. "So," he said, "I started asking myself why so many different cars?"

"What are you thinking, she drives rentals?"

"Bingo," smiled Ernie, "so I made a few calls to some local rental places and looky here." Ernie flipped open a folder that was on the table. Inside were several rental agreements all signed by Arianna Borgman.

"Maybe she rents every time her car is being worked on," Stephen suggested.

"Maybe," breathed Ernie, exhaling a line of smoke across the booth. "But I went ahead and got the make, model, color and date of each car she rented."

"Okay," muttered Stephen, wondering where this was going.

Ernie grinned, "I have a hunch if we cross reference these cars and date of rental with the collision date of the John Doe car, we'll find a suspicious match in paint color." Stephen looked at Ernie who was beaming.

"You mean the John Doe case Officer Gordon gave us?"

Ernie nodded and slid the file over to Stephen. "Now all you have to do is have the lab make paint color comparisons on the two cars and if there's a match, we have solved the John Doe case."

Stephen laughed, "So you're saying there's a possibility that Cindy Miller's mother killed John Doe." Ernie nodded. "You realize that's speculation?" Ernie nodded again. Stephen stared at him, "you realize how ludicrous that sounds?" Ernie nodded a third time, and coupled it with a big grin and a raised eyebrow. Stephen shook his head. If Ernie didn't have a knack for this, Stephen wouldn't even entertain the idea. But Ernie had a gift for solving the unsolved. "Okay," he said, "I'll check out your paint colors and see what pans out, but it still doesn't tell us the identity of John Doe."

Ernie pulled the cigarette from between his lips, "I'm working on that," he said. "One more thing," he added. "I looked up what I could find on this Lou Miller guy and he's been dead a long time, like almost eighteen years."

"Yeah, so?" Stephen said, casually paging through the file of rental agreements.

"Well," Ernie took a swig of his drink, "what stands out is he was hit by a car."

Stephen abruptly stopped paging through the file and met eyes with Ernie. "Who hit him?" he asked.

"Hit and run," said Ernie. "Unsolved hit and run."

"Seems to be a trend."

"Seems to be."

Stephen sat back in the booth and exhaled. "You're thinking we're dealing with the same killer aren't you?" Stephen studied Ernie's face. "You're saying the killer in both hit and run accidents is Arianna Borgman?"

"Maybe even three." Ernie raised his brows and blew a big smoke ring above his head. He shrugged. "The method seems to be working for 'em so I'm just saying it's possible." Ernie had an uncanny way of cutting right to the chase. He had good instincts and Stephen learned years ago to trust Ernie's odd way of doing things. He hadn't been wrong yet, knock on wood.

Dale walked up quickly. He was off duty, out of uniform and wore dark sunglasses even inside the bar. Ernie slid out the side of the booth and to the other side next to Stephen and Dale sat down across from them. It wasn't until he was hidden in the booth that he took off his glasses.

"Don't call my house with tips again," Dale scolded, "only call my cell. You had my wife so freaked out she slept with a gun."

Ernie belted a gruff laugh. "Talk about adding some bang in bed." Dale wasn't amused. "Sorry man, it was the only number I had for you."

Dale darted his eyes to Stephen who quickly admitted, "My bad, I gave him that number. It won't happen again."

Dale, now noticing the gash in Stephen's head, asked, "What the hell happened to you?"

Stephen and Ernie exchanged glances then Stephen said, "I had some car trouble." Ernie chuckled through a mouthful of smoke.

Dale eyed them both. "Something I need to know about?"

"Not yet," Stephen said, "we'll keep you posted."

Dale motioned the waitress over and ordered a gin and tonic. "Where'd you say you got the name Lou Miller from?"

"From another case." Stephen's answer was curt and Dale knew that meant he couldn't give details.

Dale raised an eyebrow. "If you're working two cases that overlap I need to know about it."

Stephen took another swig of Ernie's drink and Ernie snatched the glass away from him. "Our agreement is I tell you whatever information is pertinent to your case, period." Stephen's face was stern and pressing. "How or where I obtain my information is none of your business."

Dale swallowed hard. He didn't like these rules but he knew that was their agreement. Moreover, he knew he couldn't solve this case without Stephen and Ernie's help. "Agreed," Dale said. He continued to tell them about the phone call he received from Tom Miller regarding, and he emphasized the quote, "the treatment his wife and a girlfriend received by Officer James."

Ernie shook his head. "I had to keep her there so Stephen could question her friend. What were my options?" Ernie picked up his glass and slurped the rest from the bottom. "Not all of us get to play kissy face ya know." Stephen smirked.

Dale glared at Ernie. "Look," he said, "I know how and where you get your information is your business, but when I start getting complaints you're going to catch some flack for it." Dale was pissed and Ernie huffed off to the bar for another round. He returned shortly with two gin and tonics and set one down in front of Stephen.

"There," Ernie said to Stephen, "drink your own."

Stephen lifted his glass and lowered his head, gesturing gratitude, then turned his attention back to Dale. "Have you run a check on this Tom guy who called to complain about Ernie?"

Dale shook his head. "I was working on finding the identity of a new stiff all night. Haven't even had a chance to call the guy back. I'm going to have Emily run a background check tomorrow."

"It wasn't a hit and run stiff was it?" Ernie blurted and Stephen shot him a shut-up glance.

"No," answered Dale, "but we did have a hit and run attempt on a woman's life just this past Tuesday." Dale took a drink.

"She survived?" Asked Stephen.

"Yep," answered Dale, "but it totaled her car and put her in the hospital for a night."

"Any leads from it?" Ernie probed.

"Nah," Dale shook his head, "she didn't see the car or the driver."

"What about last night's victim?" Asked Stephen.

"It was a female, shot in her apartment in Forest Lake. A neighbor found her late Friday evening. We're still waiting on exact time of death. She was in her late-thirties, a dancer, and wannabe actress by trade, named Jeanette Carlen."

"You think these two have any connection to each other or any link to John Doe," asked Stephen.

"Nothing concrete." Dale sighed, ran his fingers through his hair and took a drink of his gin and tonic. It went down smooth. "Just my hunch," he said, letting frustration and exhaustion seep through his words.

"What was the problem with the new stiff's identity?" Stephen squint his eyes as Ernie exhaled smoke.

"She had two ID's so it took us a while to ascertain which one was the real one."

"You have to fingerprint?" Stephen asked.

"Couldn't," said Dale, crunching a piece of ice in his teeth. "Fingerprints were burned off."

They all knew what this meant. John Doe's fingerprints had been burned off too. The person who killed Jeanette Carlen was the same person who killed John Doe. All they needed to figure out now was how the two were connected.

Stephen looked at Ernie. "What's your gut on this one? Same killer or a copy cat?"

"Same," muttered Ernie without missing a beat.

Stephen turned his attention back to Dale. "You said she had two ID's. What name was on the fake ID?"

Dale looked up with narrowed brows. "Arianna Borgman, why?"

~

Tom unlocked the back door to the office and let Alisha in. He could tell right away something was wrong. She had tears in her eyes and her lip quivered each time she started to speak. He walked her back to his office, closed and locked the office door. He sat down across from her and studied her face.

"What's going on?"

Big tears filled her eyes and flooded onto her cheeks. He couldn't help notice her hands were trembling so he got up and moved to the chair next to her, placing her hands in his.

"Please," he prodded, "I can't help if I don't know what's going on." Tom stared at her. "Is it your husband?"

Alisha burst into sobs nodding her head up and down. "Was he drunk again? Did he hit you? Did he hurt you?"

She shook her head no, and then she whispered, "He knows."

Tom's breathing stopped. "About us?"

"Uh-huh," she sobbed.

"How?" He demanded. "Did you tell him?" Tom was out of his chair pacing. "Why would you tell him?" Before Alisha could answer Tom fired off question after question. "Damn it, Alisha!" He yelled, "How could you do this?"

"I didn't tell him!" She screamed at the top of her lungs and it startled Tom.

"Then how in the world does he know?"

They stared angrily at each other. Tom was panting from the blinding emotion of the situation. Alisha sank back into the chair and put her face in her hands. "Phone records," she sighed. "He'll have your phone records first thing Monday morning and my number will be on them."

Tom stood motionless while his mind processed what the hell she was talking about. Why would her husband need his phone records? He started to formulate questions in his mind, but Alisha interrupted his thoughts with the answers. "My husband," she said while wiping tears from her face, "is Officer Dale Gordon, the man you called last night."

Tom sank back down into the chair next to Alisha. She looked up at him. "He's been working on a case for a long time and was given an anonymous tip last night about a man named Lou Miller."

Tom gasped, "That's my grandfather's name."

Alisha looked up at Tom and goose bumps shimmered up her arms. "A couple hours after he was given this name, you called and since your last names are the same, and since you were asking questions about an officer working on the case, he had a hunch you might be somehow connected so he's having a back history of phone records drawn up on you." Alisha exhaled.

Tom put his hand on her knee and squeezed tenderly. His mind was soaking it in and trying to come up with a believable scenario for why he and Alisha would be in contact. Anything he came up with would seem far fetched, with the exception of the truth and that was no option.

"Tom," Alisha cried, tears welling up again in her eyes, "he's going to know we were lovers and he'll leave me." She burst into sobs and Tom knew that fear all too well. He pulled her close to him and draped his arms around her.

"He won't find out," Tom promised, "we'll think of something and we'll stick to our story." Tom's stomach knotted and he felt sick.

## Chapter 13

Ernie and Stephen locked eyes. The cases were spilling over into each other more than they imagined. Stephen knew it was time to tell Officer Gordon what he knew about Arianna Borgman. He flipped Ernie his car keys and asked him to go retrieve his briefcase from the trunk.

They all ordered another round and some sandwiches and Stephen outlined first what he knew of Lou Miller, the man killed years ago in an unsolved hit and run. Then he shared that he was hired by Cindy to obtain an original birth certificate with her father's name on it. Her biological father being either the Lou Miller killed in the unsolved hit and run eighteen years ago or his son, Lou Miller Jr., who died in Florida six months ago. Her biological mother is Arianna Borgman. "Cindy hired me to track down her father so she could take part in the inheritance she believed her mother deserved."

"If her father is dead," interjected Dale, "wasn't the inheritance already paid out?"

Ernie and Stephen shot each other a glance. "Not totally," said Stephen.

"It gets even better," Ernie added, "just wait."

Stephen continued. "Genealogy research shows that Lou Miller had two grandsons, Tom Miller and Martin Miller. Tom is presumably the man who called you last night. Martin we haven't been able to track down yet.

"But we think we're getting closer," interjected Ernie.

Stephen went on. "Tom is married to Kate Miller. Kate and her friend Kimberly are the two ladies we met at a martini bar last night. The one Ernie, here, harassed." Ernie rolled his eyes.

Dale nodded. It was a lot of pieces to put together but Stephen could tell Dale was keeping up. Dale lifted his glass but paused before it got to his mouth, as if relevance overtook him and left him unable to move.

"You gonna drink that or sniff it?" Ernie chuckled.

Dale stared motionless, finally uttering, "Kate Miller. You said Tom is married to Kate Miller?"

"Yes," answered Stephen, "Kate is the one I was trying to get information out of last night and again today."

"Kate Miller is the name of the woman I spoke with at the hospital earlier this week. She was the hit and run attempt I told you about."

"No." Stephen shook his head. "It couldn't be the same one. She never mentioned an accident."

Ernie listened intently. He inhaled long and hard, leaning his head back against the booth. Then he blew out smoke in one fluid motion. "I think we got the right Miller family and so does the killer."

Dale dialed Emily on his cell. When she answered he instructed her to pull the Kate Miller file and send the relevant stats to his PDA. Within a couple minutes Dale read Kate's stats out loud, confirming her home address as 3755 Hyacinth Court in Stanley, Kansas.

Fear nested in Stephen's stomach and his heart sank in his chest. "Does she know the accident was a possible attempt on her life?"

Dale nodded. "Without going into too much detail I told her I believed someone intentionally tried to harm her."

Stephen felt awful. He had no idea Kate was in an accident, nor that she was a potential target. He was merely using her to try and find out more about the Miller ancestry and how Cindy Miller tied in. He couldn't imagine the kind of stress she must be under.

The concern shown on his face and Dale leaned in closer. "Are you emotionally involved with this woman?" Stephen adjusted in the booth and shook his head no. "I need clear heads on this case you got it?" Dale studied Stephen's eyes. "I can't have you clouded by emotions here."

"I'm not clouded."

Dale leaned back. "Did you get any information from her?"

Reaching in his briefcase Stephen pulled out the file folder marked Journal Entries. He felt a twinge of guilt as he pulled grandmother's letter from the file. "Most of these are personal writings about her marriage and her feelings, but there is a letter from the grandmother," he explained, handing a copy of the letter to Dale. "I've highlighted the one sentence I think is relevant."

Dale skimmed the letter until he got to the highlighted area. He licked his lips and nodded. "So," he said, "whatever this family sin is, grandmother knew and covered it."

Stephen nodded in agreement. Ernie added, "We figure someone dug it up and somebody else didn't like that."

Dale sat back, took a deep breath and exhaled long and slow. "Let's suppose these murders are all connected and we're dealing with the same killer from the hit and run of Lou Miller, to the dead John Doe six months ago which was another hit and run, to the attempt on Kate Miller to the dead actress who's fake ID just happened to be the name of the birth mother of your client."

"You're missing one." Ernie lit a cigarette and squinted at Dale.

"Who?"

"The hit and run of Lou Jr. in Tampa." Ernie blew out a smoke ring.

Dale blurted, "Son of a..."

"Oh yeah, she's a bitch alright," Ernie interrupted Dale mid-sentence.

"Assuming we're dealing with one killer, what's the motive?" Dale stared at Stephen.

Ernie held up his fingers and rubbed his thumbs over his fingertips to indicate money.

"What money?" Dale asked.

Stephen explained how Tom Miller hired him to find his brother Martin so they could open their grandmother's will and distribute the inheritance. Ernie chuckled at the disbelief on Dale's face.

"I know," Ernie said, "it's all freaky at first, but give it a second and it'll settle in your brain and start making sense."

Dale crunched an ice cube in his teeth. "So you're telling me that someone is slowly wiping out members of the Miller family?"

"Looks that way," Ernie answered gruffly.

Stephen shook the ice in his glass and slurped down the last gulp. "Okay, assuming we are dealing with one killer and one motive, which may or may not be accurate, this at least gives us an age range."

"How do you mean?" asked Dale.

155

"I mean a person who ran someone down eighteen years ago would have had to be at least sixteen to drive then, which would make them a minimum of thirty-four now."

Ernie added, "That eliminates our client Cindy from the suspect list."

"Acting alone, yes, but she could be an accomplice, or she could know about mommy's past sins and decide to re-invent them in the present." Dale never missed an opportunity to apply guilt to anyone. In his mind there was always a way for someone to commit a crime if they wanted it bad enough.

Ernie chimed in, "the problem is just because Cindy's full name is Cindy Miller Borgman doesn't mean the woman she knows as mom is the real Arianna Borgman. Cindy could have been adopted by a third party."

Stephen glared at Ernie, "are you trying to make things more complicated?"

Ernie grinned, "It's what I do."

"We could set up a meeting with Cindy and her mother and that would answer that question?" Stephen suggested and Ernie threw his hands up in the air. "What?" Stephen turned to Ernie, acknowledging that the frustrated arm throw was meant for him.

"I suggested setting up a meeting earlier and you said we were bound by client confidentiality." Stephen could see Ernie was peeved and that he didn't like Stephen presenting his good idea to Dale as if it were his own.

Stephen grinned. "I stand corrected." He looked at Dale with a snide smirk. "Ernie, here, thinks we should set up a meeting with Cindy and her mother." Ernie scowled at Stephen's sarcasm.

"See if you can set it up and I want to be there." Dale looked as antsy as a little kid being told he had to wait to open his birthday presents. Stephen knew he wanted to solve this case right now, and regain some of the respect he had lost at the station. "Prime suspects are also Tom Miller and Kate Miller."

"Kate's not a suspect," Stephen blurted without thinking.

Dale shook his head at Stephen. "You better keep your heart and your dick out of your head or people might end up dead."

It was a harsh warning, but Stephen knew Dale's advice was right. He needed to stay emotionally unattached and level headed to solve this case.

"I want to know where Tom Miller was the day of his wife's accident." Dale shrugged. "And for God's sake, somebody find this Arianna Borgman."

Ernie stuck his finger in the air. "On it."

"Good." Dale rubbed his eyes. He was wiped out and in desperate need of sleep. Before heading out he reviewed their new assignments. Stephen was to find out from Kate anything he could about the Miller family history and see if he could set up a meeting with Cindy and her mother. Ernie was to find the missing Martin Miller. Dale would review the paint colors with those taken from the accidents and find out what evidence the phone records showed. They'd all meet again on Monday at noon. Dale got up to leave. He arched his back to stretch and put on his dark glasses. "Remember," he said, "we never met here today and we aren't working on this case together. Everybody got that?"

"Got what?" Ernie mused.

"Good," Dale said and he left.

~

The banging sound was driving Kate crazy. She followed the noise down the hall and into the guest room. Opening the door she froze when she saw shards of glass all over the floor and realized the window was broken. A slight breeze blew through the opening, causing a wooden picture frame, hanging to the left of the window, to lift slightly and bang methodically against the wall. Someone had broken in. Kate's heart beat uncontrollably in her chest and she couldn't breathe. She backed out of the room and ran to her bedroom, locking the door behind her. She pulled the gun from the nightstand drawer, checked the clip and took the safety off. Her hands trembled as she grabbed the phone and dialed 9-1-1.

"9-1-1 Operator," a voice came through the phone.

"Help me," Kate whispered. "Someone's broken into my house."

"Did you see the perpetrator?"

"No," she whispered.

"Do you know if they're still in the house?"

"I don't know," she said, her voice cracking.

"Can you get out of the house?"

"No," Kate said quietly, "I'm locked in my room with a gun, please send help."

"Stay on the line with me ma'am, we're sending units to your location now."

"Hurry," said Kate, "please hurry."

~

Officer Dale Gordon had just turned onto the freeway when the 9-1-1 call came through. He was off duty, but closest to the location, and when he heard the address his gut sank. He radioed in and placed the emergency light on top his vehicle. Then he turned on the siren and sped up, unsure if he would find Kate Miller dead or alive, with fingerprints or without.

Stephen hung around with Ernie and finished another drink, talking over more details before heading their separate ways. When Stephen left the bar he headed straight to Kate's house. He was bothered by the fact that she was the woman in the accident, and knowing that if this person tried to kill her once, they would most likely try again. He was also kicking himself for leaving abruptly after thinking he saw someone or something behind her house. It was probably nothing he told himself, but something inside feared otherwise. He should have checked it out before he left. As he drove he dialed her number but it rang endlessly, no voicemail, no machine. It could mean she's on the other line and not clicking over. It could also mean something was wrong. He instinctively pressed harder on the gas.

By the time Stephen reached Kate's street it was lit up with police cars, the flashing lights of an ambulance and fire truck. Stephen's mouth went dry as he realized they were in front of Kate's house. He threw his car in park, one house up and made a dash toward Kate's front door. Two men in uniform blocked him. "I'm sorry sir, this is a crime scene. No one is allowed to enter," said the officer to his right.

"What happened?" Stephen blurted.

The officer on his left let go of his arm and asked, "Are you family?"

"No," said Stephen, "I'm, I'm a friend of Kate."

The officer to his right kept a tight grip on Stephen's arm. "Officer Gordon has given strict instructions that no one is to be let in."

"Dale Gordon?" Stephen interrupted. "Tell him Stephen Braznovich is here. He'll let me in."

One officer stayed with Stephen while the other went inside. He emerged with Dale right behind him, motioning Stephen inside.

"She's pretty shaken up," Dale said, "but otherwise okay."

Stephen breathed a sigh of relief. He hadn't realized how much he cared until he thought something terrible had happened to her. "Where is she?"

Dale stopped walking and turned to face Stephen. "Not emotionally involved my ass," he said.

Stephen lowered his eyes. "I care about her okay. She's a good person and I don't want to see her hurt."

Dale nodded. "She's in the back bedroom."

"Is anyone with her? I mean, any family or friends?"

"No. We tried to call her husband but he's not answering his cell." Stephen started down the hall when he heard Dale holler, "don't touch anything. We're still bagging up evidence." Stephen lifted both hands up as if it to say he wouldn't touch a thing.

Peeking in the bedroom he saw Kate sitting on the end of the bed. Her eyes were puffy and red from crying and she looked fragile. When she glanced over and saw him she burst into tears and dove into him. He couldn't remember being hugged so tightly and he felt awkward. He could feel her body trembling in his arms as he stroked her hair and tried to quiet her.

Two hours later, the police cleared the house and Stephen sat on the couch in the den with Kate. He knew this was the time to ask specific questions. His private investigating experience taught him that the most information spills out during the height of emotional trauma.

He felt guilty and didn't want to manipulate Kate, but he also knew the sooner he helped Officer Gordon solve this case the safer Kate would be. Stephen moved closer to her on the couch and held her hand in his. "Earlier today," he began, "you were telling me about your grandmother's journal."

"It's Tom's grandmother's journal," Kate corrected.

"Can you tell me more about it?" Kate wiped her nose in a tissue and exhaled. "I don't know what to say about it really," she uttered. "It's an amazing book about her life, her dreams, her struggles and her incredible faith." Kate's eyes danced when she spoke of Tom's grandmother. "She had a wisdom I hope I will have one day," Kate explained, "such a depth of understanding and forgiveness that I think most people never reach."

Stephen's mind leapt alive. The word "forgiveness" was his segway into questioning her. "What do mean by forgiveness," he asked, "forgiveness for what?"

Kate stared off in the distance for a moment. Her eyes were glassy from the tears and it looked to Stephen as if she were contemplating whether to tell him something. He squeezed her hand. "Kate," he said, "you can tell me anything."

"You're a private investigator right?" She asked rhetorically. He nodded. "Are you here because you're investigating me?" Stephen licked his lips, pursed them together and released her hand. She gazed up at him with eyes that sought only the truth and he knew she deserved it. He let go of her hand, stood up and walked across the room.

"I'm going to get a glass of water if that's okay. Would you like one?" Kate nodded and Stephen disappeared into the kitchen. Within

161

moments he handed her a glass and leaned against the front of the desk, watching while she took a drink, and choosing his words carefully.

"Yes." He exhaled. "I intentionally followed you to the martini lounge last night to talk to you for the purpose of gaining information about a case I'm investigating."

"What case?"

"I can't tell you that. It's against client confidentiality."

Kate nodded her head and bit her bottom lip. "So last night was just your typical way of investigating?"

"No."

Kate continued despite his answer. "But I passed out last night and you couldn't get whatever information you were after so you came back today."

"No. Not exactly."

"The flowers and wine were a nice touch. I guess you've learned that from past investigations, huh."

Kate's sarcasm was apparent and Stephen dropped his chin to his chest. It sounded very cold the way she said it. "Kate, I came back today because I wanted to come back and talk with you."

"No, you had to come back to get information from me."

He began to pace again as he emphatically tried to explain his intentions. "When I found out it was you that was almost the next hit and run victim, I could barely breathe." Kate stared blankly at the floor while he spoke. "I drove here tonight because I was worried about you."

"You don't have to worry about me. I'm fine. I can take care of myself." Hostility oozed from her tone. "I don't need you or anyone else toying with my emotions." Kate put her hands up to hide her face.  She didn't want to cry and she didn't want him to see her hands shaking.

He sat down next to her on the couch and took her hand in his.  "I'm not toying with you.  I am worried about you and the only way I can help you is to solve this case quickly."

Kate's defiance and independence leapt alive in her.  "I don't need your help."

"Yes, Kate.  Yes you do need my help." Stephen got off the couch, walked across the room and leaned back against the desk to face her.

"I don't want your help," she spewed and glared up at him.

Stephen hollered back at her.  "Someone tried to kill you and they tried to run me off the road earlier this evening.  They've already killed several people.  You need my help Kate.  This isn't a game."  Silence fell between them.  "Being brave is one thing.  Being stupid is another."

Kate exhaled loudly, "now you think I'm stupid."

"No.  I think I hurt you and I was wrong." Kate stared up at him.  "I'm ashamed of last night. Not because I didn't feel something, but because I allowed myself to cross a line I've never crossed.  I let desire cloud my judgment."  Kate lowered her chin and stared at the floor in front of her.  "You're a beautiful woman Kate, and I'd be lying if I told you I didn't want to make-love to you.  I do."  Kate smiled and felt her cheeks flush with color.  "But in this situation it was wrong of me to let things go as far as they did."

"Because of your case or because of Tom?" Kate made eye contact for the firs time since he began his heartfelt explanation.

"Both."  Stephen walked back over and sat down next to her.  "It's unethical because of the case I'm working on and it's immoral because you are another man's wife."

Kate nodded.

"I know you've felt it too. I've seen the guilt in your eyes."

Kate leaned her head on his shoulder. "Yes and I hate it. Why does he get to be with another woman but I can't be with you?"

"Wait, how do you know he's been with another woman?"

Kate's eyes teared up. "I think he may have had an affair years ago and even fathered a child."

Kate could feel Stephen's body tense up and his breathing quicken. "Why would you think that?"

"I can't tell you why, I just know."

"That's not good enough Kate. I need you to tell me what you're talking about." Stephen stared deep in her eyes. "I need you to trust me."

Kate led Stephen down the hall and into her bedroom.   She pulled the manila envelope from under the bed where she had stashed it earlier and handed it to him.

"What's this?" He asked.

"It's the envelope Tom's brother, Martin dropped off six months ago and told me to hide. It has a birth certificate and a picture that I think Martin was probably trying to use to blackmail Tom."

"Does Tom know you have this?"

"No. I never told him because it was right after we separated and he moved out."

"Have you seen Martin since?"

"No.  He promised he would come back when it was safe."

Stephen pulled out the contents. "Does anyone else know Martin gave this folder to you?"

Kate shook her head. "No, I forgot about it until the other day when I climbed up in my closet to get the gun down."

"You have a gun?"

"Does that surprise you?"

His lips curled into a half-smile. "Well, you don't seem like the gun toting type."

"It isn't mine, its Tom's. Actually it used to be his grandpa's and Tom kept it in the closet in case we ever needed it. I put it in my nightstand after the car accident and grabbed it tonight when I saw that the window was broken. The police took it away from me when they got here."

"What did they do with it?"

"They put it in a bag and took it I guess." Kate's voice was uneasy.

Turning his attention back to the manila folder, Stephen looked at the picture and said, "I don't think Tom is the father of this little girl."

Kate didn't answer him; she just stared and blinked slowly.

"I don't think Martin was trying to blackmail Tom." He added, but Kate stood motionless. All of a sudden Kate felt sick. Her head started getting light and the sound of his voice grew hollow and more distant. "Kate?" Stephen dropped the envelope and grabbed her right as she lost consciousness. She fell on him like a rock and it took him a few moments to drag her to the bed and lay her down. She would be out for the next hour or so thanks to a substantial dose of Lorazepam. He didn't like taking these measures, especially now that she was giving him the information he needed, but he had no way of knowing she would be willing to talk when he placed the drug in her drink. He needed answers and there was no time to be her emotional support.

With Kate out of the way he began searching for grandmother's journal. He started in the closet and it didn't take long to find it tucked neatly inside the hat box. Stephen phoned Ernie who was there in a matter of minutes to pick up the journal and take it to be copied. "Hurry," said Stephen, handing the journal and the manila envelope to Ernie, "these have to be back here when she wakes up."

## Chapter 14

Dale called Alisha's cell again. He'd tried four times already and figured she was mad that he was working late on his day off, so she wasn't answering. He didn't know she was at Tom's office, ignoring his calls because she and Tom were racking their brains, trying to come up with an explanation for how they knew each other.

Dale filled his coffee mug for the third time and stared out the station window. He was waiting for the finger print and hair analysis results on the specimens they pulled from Kate Miller's broken window. So far there were no matches, but Dale wasn't giving up hope.

"Good news," Emily said, as she bounced down the hall with her red pony tail flopping wildly behind her.

Dale whirled around with anticipation. "We have a match?"

"No," she said flatly, "but your phone records are already in."

"I didn't expect them 'til Monday morning."

"I know," smiled Emily, "but I have a friend who has a friend who called in a favor." Emily winked and handed him a stack of papers. "One full year's worth."

Dale started going thru the print out number by number until he felt like his eyes were crossing. He then flipped to the day of Kate Miller's accident. Nothing unusual stood out. Refilling his coffee he decided to start backwards, and work from the most recent to the past. The most recent activity was yesterday. He quickly realized the phone company had issued records for Tom Miller's home phone and cell phone. Dale divided these into two separate piles. It took only a second for Alisha's cell phone number to leap off the page and smack him in the face. He sat stunned and counted six phone calls last night from Tom Miller's home phone to Alisha's cell. He grabbed Tom's cell phone records and found Alisha's number on there multiple times the past six months. Dale pounded his fist on the desk and kicked a chair on wheels across the room.

Emily quickly approached his desk and leaned down in his face. "What is it?" They had been partners for a couple years and Dale knew Emily could read him pretty well. "C'mon Dale, you know you gotta let me in on this so I can help." He knew she was right but he didn't like it.

He jotted down Alisha's cell phone number on a piece of paper and handed it to Emily. "I need phone records for the past six months on this number and I need them now." Dale's jaw was set.

A few minutes later Emily returned and slid into the chair next to Dale. "That number belongs to your wife," she whispered, as if she expected him not to know. "You still want me to run the records?" Dale gritted his teeth at her.

"I don't want anyone to know about this, you understand?"

"Got it," she nodded.

"One more thing," he said, "I need to know who this number belongs to." He handed her another phone number.

"Okey dokey," she said and scooted quickly down the hall.

~

Kate began to stir and Stephen sat down on the bed next to her and placed her hand in his. They had timed it perfectly, as Ernie returned the journal and manila envelope three minutes before Kate started waking up.  She blinked several times before she was able to keep her eyes from rolling back in her head again.  She focused in on Stephen's face and her mouth formed a half smile. "I'm sorry," she said, "I don't know what happened. I got dizzy."

"It's okay," he answered, "you're under a great deal of stress and you're exhausted." He brushed the hair off her face.  "I should go and let you rest," he said.

Kate sat upright in bed, "no, please don't go," she begged.  "I don't want to be here alone." Her breathing quickened and Stephen could hear the panic in her tone.  "The police took my gun and I don't feel safe here."

"Okay, why don't I sleep on the couch tonight so you're not alone?"

Stephen started to stand up but Kate grabbed his hand.  "Stephen," she blurted, sounding more desperate than she intended, "will you sleep in here with me?"

Something inside him winced.  Under any other circumstances he'd have jumped at the invitation, but he knew he was in too deep with Kate.  He'd known her less than thirty-six hours and already he genuinely cared for her.  Despite his reservations, Stephen turned off the overhead light and laid down on top the covers, wrapping his right arm around Kate.  She nestled back against him and intertwined her fingers with his.  Holding Kate felt comfortable and Stephen closed his eyes, mentally reminding himself this was business. Within a few moments he felt Kate's body go limp and her breathing deepen.  She drifted to sleep in his arms.

~

Kate jolted up in bed.  She dreamt about the accident again.  It was becoming a nightly ritual.  The room was filled with sunlight and the clock indicated it was 7:00am.  Stephen was already at the door talking to Officer Gordon when Kate crept down the hall.  "Good morning," she said sheepishly.

Stephen had a serious look in his eyes as he turned to face her.  "Officer Gordon needs to ask you some questions."

"Okay," Kate said, "can I make coffee while we talk?"

They sat around the kitchen table and Dale laid out copies of phone records from Tom's cell phone and their home phone.  "Now," he said pointing to the various colors of highlighted lines, "can you tell me the name of the person whose number is in yellow"

Kate glanced, "that's Kimberly's number," she said matter-of-factly.

"And who is Kimberly?" Dale asked.

"She's a close friend.  She's actually been my closest friend for the past couple years."

"Kimberly is the friend Kate was out with Friday night when Ernie and I met them at the martini lounge," Stephen added, helping jog Dale's memory.  "She's the one Ernie kept occupied."

Dale nodded then diverted his attention back to Kate.  "Can you tell me the name of the person whose number is in green highlighter?"

Kate looked but she didn't recognize the number.  "I don't know that number off the top of my head.  I could check my address book if you want."

Dale smirked, "Mrs. Miller," he mused, "you called this number six times in a row, late Friday night."

Kate looked back at the record. "No I didn't," she retorted.

"Mrs. Miller, you can't deny physical evidence. The record shows you called this number six times on Friday night from your home phone." Dale's voice raised and Stephen narrowed his brow and shot him a glance to calm down.

Kate raised her voice. "I didn't call anyone Friday night because I was passed out." She looked at Stephen. "Just ask him."

Stephen nodded, "that's the truth Dale, I carried her in and put her to bed and she was out cold."

Dale exhaled. "How do you know Alisha Gordon?"

"I don't know anyone by that name," answered Kate.

"Was anyone else in the house with you on Friday night?" Dale asked, exasperated by Kate's denial.

"No," Kate said, "actually yes, but not until much later than when these calls were made."

Kate explained how she woke up and found Tom and Kimberly screaming at each other in the drive way and how she let them inside and then she ended up getting angry and storming off to her room because they were fighting.

"Why were they screaming at each other?" Dale questioned.

"I don't know," Kate said, "it was a strange evening." Kate thought for a second, "I think it was something about Kimberly's keys."

"Dale," Stephen interjected, "Kimberly was in the house with Kate before that time."

"How do you know that?" Dale asked.

"Because I called and Kimberly answered," he explained, leaning closer to get a better look at the phone record. "Look on the incoming calls, there should be one from my cell," Stephen ran his finger down the page, "there, right there."

"How did she get in?" Dale asked.

Stephen shrugged, "I don't know. I locked the door behind me."

Dale diverted his eyes to Kate. "Does Kimberly have a key?" Kate shook her head no. "Is there a hide-a-key somewhere she could have used?" Kate shook again.

"Was anyone with her?" Dale asked.

"I don't know," Stephen emphasized again. "I wasn't here."

Dale looked at Kate. "I was drunk and passed out, but I know who might know." It was against Kate's better judgment and she didn't want to say it. "Mrs. Netbaum."

A few minutes later Mrs. Netbaum sat at Kate's kitchen table with a cup of coffee in hand. She told Dale everything she knew about that night, including how Kimberly and Tom broke into the house through the guest window. "If it had been anyone else I would have called the police," she explained, "but with the troubles Kate and Tom have been having I just assumed it was best for me to let them work this out. Besides, Kimberly was there and I sure do like that Kimberly. She's a sweetheart she is."

Kate snorted, "How do you know Kimberly?"

"She stops by and says hello from time to time, whenever she comes to visit you." Mrs. Netbaum took a dainty sip of her coffee and smiled. She reached across the table and patted Kate's hand. "You have some real sweet girlfriends," she said, "you should be thankful they care so much about you."

Kate looked dazed. She had no idea what or who Mrs. Netbaum was talking about. "What girlfriends?"

"I'm sure I don't have to tell you who your true friends are dear. Take Rita for instance."

Kate almost fell out of her chair. "Rita? Rita hates me!"

"Who's Rita?" Dale and Stephen asked in unison.

"Oh, don't be silly dear." Mrs. Netbaum shook her head. "Rita cares so much about you she asked me to keep an eye out and to let her know if Tom's violent brother ever came around to bother you."

Kate and Stephen locked eyes.

"What the hell is going on?" Dale clenched at Stephen.

Stephen held up his finger to Dale. "Give me a second and I'll fill you in." Then he looked to Mrs. Netbaum. "Mrs. Netbaum, did you ever see Tom's brother here?"

"Just once about six months ago."

"Did you tell anyone you saw him?" Stephen asked.

"Oh my yes, I called Rita right away. Told her he carried an envelope into the house and I was keeping a close watch." Mrs. Netbaum patted Kate's arm, "that's what good neighbors do."

Stephen glared at Kate. "Who is Rita and what interest would she have in Martin?" Kate gave a summarized version on the history of LouLineCo, grandfather's inheritance tied up in grandmother's will and Rita's desire to get her hands on both Tom and the money. Dale leaned his head back and exhaled. He then thanked Mrs. Netbaum for her time, told her she may be needed for more questioning later, and escorted her home.

Dale placed a call to Emily ordering a full background check on Rita, including family history, phone records, you name it. Dale hung up and returned his attention to the phone records. He pointed to a highlighted number. "You said this was your friend Kimberly's number?"

"Yes," Kate answered, "that's her cell." Kate peeked down the rest of the list. "This is her home number."

"Something's not right here," Dale studied the records. "If this is her home number then she called Tom's cell phone from her home phone around the same time Stephen called your home phone and talked with Kimberly." Kate was befuddled in the numbers and times.

Stephen grabbed the records, processing it in his mind. "I know I spoke to Kimberly so she couldn't have been the one who called Tom from her home phone. Someone else had to have used her home phone to call Tom's cell."

Dale looked at Kate, who shrugged her shoulders. "I know you were drunk."

Dale grabbed his cell and dialed. "Emily, the phone number I gave you last night... you got the name it's registered under yet?"

Emily answered and Dale hollered in the phone, "what?"

He looked at Kate, and cupped his hand over the speaker of his phone, "is your friend Kimberly's last name Sutton?"

"Yes," nodded Kate.

Dale knew Alisha had been spending time at Kimberly's house and now he wondered if it was time spent with Tom. The thought made him flush with anger. He un-cupped the phone. "Emily, get me the phone records on Kimberly Sutton for the past six months." Then he hung up.

Dale took a deep breath and tried to figure out how his wife and her half-sister were somehow connected to Kate and Tom Miller. He ran his fingers through his hair. "Mrs. Miller," he said, "after you found your husband and Kimberly screaming in your driveway, then what happened?"

"I let them in. They fought. I got mad and went to my room and closed the door." She looked at him as if to say I already told you that.

Dale threw up his hands, "then what? They left?"

All of a sudden Kate remembered about Tom breaking his glass of bourbon and telling her the woman on the television wasn't Jeanette Carlen but was named Arianna Borgman. When Dale heard this he shot up in his chair. Stephen gripped Kate by her arm and said, "Are you sure?"

Dale blurted, "How did he know her name was Arianna Borgman?"

"He met with her at Murrays." Kate dropped her chin. "He said it wasn't a date but it looked like an intimate conversation from what Kimberly and I could tell."

"You and Kimberly were on your husband's date?" Dale looked skeptical.

Stephen stepped out of the room, dialing Ernie and leaving a voicemail about this new connection to Arianna Borgman.

"We weren't ON the date," Kate stammered, "we just happened to be there having lunch."

Dale studied her face. "You happened to be at the same restaurant at the same time?" His tone told Kate he wasn't buying her story.

"Yes," she said emphatically. "It was a coincidence."

Dale raised his eyebrows at Kate and quickly redirected his attention to his cell phone now buzzing on the table. He answered and after muttering several uh-huh's he hung up. He abruptly walked over to Kate and began issuing her Miranda rights, "Kate Miller," he stated, "I am placing you under arrest for the murder of Jeanette Carlen. You have the right to remain silent. You have the right to an attorney. Anything you say or do can and will be held against you in a court of law."

Stephen came back into the kitchen, "are you out of your freaking mind Dale?"

Dale stared at him, "we've got a match on the gun."

"What gun?" Stephen stammered.

"The gun used to kill Jeanette Carlen is the same weapon we physically removed from Kate Miller's hands last night."

"That can't be," cried Kate. Her eyes darted to Stephen. "It's not true," she said, "I didn't kill anyone." Her voice cracked with fear.

"Dale," Stephen begged, "you know you've got the wrong person here."

Dale's expression turned stone cold. "I have to take her in."

Stephen helplessly watched as Dale cuffed Kate, escorted her from her home and placed her in the back of his car. He stood on the front porch, his mind reeling, knowing he had to figure this case out quickly before Kate was charged with a murder his gut said she didn't commit.

~

Stephen left Kate's house and called Ernie. They arranged to meet at the Backrow Tavern right away. Then he dialed Officer Gordon. When Dale answered, Stephen laid into him. Cop or no cop Stephen was going to give Dale a piece of his mind.

"Take a breath," Dale said mid-way through Stephen's ranting. "I know she didn't do it."

Stephen was momentarily stunned silent. Then he shook his head and blurted, "Then why did you arrest her?"

"Two reasons. First, she's a target which means she has something or knows something that somebody wants. I need that information first." Stephen exhaled loudly. "Second, she's safer at the station and whoever the real perpetrator is will get sloppy if they think we've stopped looking."

"So you're using her to flush out the killer."

"Yes," Dale answered, "just like you've been using her to get information."

Stephen didn't appreciate the implication he had used Kate. He didn't like Dale's tactic of using her as bait either, but it made sense. Kate would be safer at the station and past experience told him odds are the killer will get sloppy. Stephen sighed.

"You find out everything you can," Dale concluded, "I'll take care of your girlfriend."

"She's not my girlfriend."

"Right. Clearly there's no emotional attachment." Dale hung up.

~

Kate called Tom from the police station but he didn't answer. She left a very long winded voicemail, spewing out details of phone records and the gun and Arianna Borgman. She rambled until the message cut her off.

After listening to Kate's voicemail, Tom flew out of his office and made a beeline for the police station. He and Alisha stayed at his office late last night trying to come up with a believable story. She left around ten and he slept on the small, uncomfortable, brown tweed couch. He dug in his console for a piece of gum since he didn't keep a toothbrush at the office and didn't want to arrive at the station with morning breath. He hated morning breath. That taste, coupled with the hollow despair in his stomach made him feel like he could vomit. The whole thing felt surreal. How could anyone think Kate could be a killer? It didn't make sense. Tom's eyes watered as he weaved in and out of traffic on the freeway, pressing the gas to the floor. "I'm coming Kate," he mumbled to himself, "I'm coming."

~

Stephen and Ernie settled into the back booth and spread out the copies of grandmother's journal and the contents of the manila envelope. Ernie lit up cigarette and Stephen scowled and waved the smoke away from his face. "Sorry man," said Ernie, "chain smoking helps me think." Stephen nodded. He hated the smell of smoke and particularly disliked it in his face, but right now he'd take anything that would help him solve this case.

"Hell," he said, "I'll buy you another pack if it'll help us figure this out faster." Ernie grinned and they both went back to reading.

Ernie pulled out the birth certificate they retrieved for Cindy Miller. He noted the birth father's name was Lou Miller. He then pulled out the birth certificate that had been hidden in the manila envelope. They were exactly the same except the father's name was blacked out. He then looked at the picture of the little blonde girl holding the barrette. She was standing with her palms up, holding a silver and pearl barrette. He squint his eyes and stared at it for a long time. "Let me see the picture in the front of grandmother's journal."

Stephen flipped to the front. "What picture?"

"A few more pages in," he instructed, "keep going, you should come across a picture of grandmother and Lou."

"Here it is."

Stephen handed the picture to Ernie. Ernie's eyes darted from one photograph to the next, squinting and studying every detail. He laid the pictures face up on the table and turned them toward Stephen. He grinned with satisfaction and Stephen knew by his expression he was onto something. He'd seen that smirk on Ernie's face before and it always turned out good. "What do you got?" Stephen asked.

"Our little girl here," Ernie explained, "is our client, Cindy Miller."

Stephen's eyes widened and he pulled the picture closer to his face. There was a resemblance but that was hardly concrete. "Could be," acknowledged Stephen, "but it's far fetched."

"Look at her right wrist." Ernie confidently spewed.

Stephen squinted, "you mean the little blotch on the picture?"

"That's no blotch, that's a birthmark." Ernie grinned. "Know how I know?" Stephen shrugged. "Remember the first meeting you had with Cindy?" Stephen nodded. "I was walking out as she was coming in. I shook her hand and saw the birthmark on her right wrist. I remembered it because it's an unusual place for a birthmark."

"Okay," said Stephen, processing what this meant. "Say you're right and Cindy Miller is the little girl in the picture, what does that mean exactly?"

"It confirms the link between the two cases."

Stephen blinked slowly and grimaced.

"We already have a link and this doesn't prove anything."

"It proves there's a cover up in the Miller family and someone wants to keep it that way." Ernie argued.

Stephen shrugged, "I'm not impressed yet. Wow me." Ernie slammed his fist down on the table which made Stephen jump. "I'm sorry man, but its all speculation."

"But you know I'm right," Ernie blurted.

Stephen looked at Ernie, "keep smoking."

Ernie scowled and leaned forward, holding up both pictures in front of Stephen's face. "See what the little girl is holding? Now look what is in the old lady's hair."

Stephen took the pictures from Ernie and looked closer. It was the same ornate daisy barrette. It was a barrette unlike any you would find in stores today. Maybe in an antique shop. Looked to be made of silver or possibly white gold and strewn with pearls. "Now," grinned Ernie, "we have something more tangible to go on." Ernie leaned back in the booth and lit up another cigarette, grinning.

"But it still doesn't prove anything," Stephen added, glancing at the caller ID on his buzzing phone.

"It proves grandmother knew little Cindy existed." Ernie bulged his eyes at Stephen.

Stephen held up a finger signaling Ernie to be quiet. "Great," he said to the person on the phone, "we'll be there, thank you." Hanging up, he turned to Ernie, "that was Officer Gordon. They're going to interrogate Kate and he wants us there to listen."

Ernie pursed his cigarette between his lips and gave Stephen two thumbs up.

~

Tom couldn't believe how awful Kate looked. Her eyes were fear stricken, glassy and red. She could barely speak to him without breaking into sobs and trembling. She kept repeating, "I didn't do it" over and over.

Tom grabbed her face, "I know you didn't do it Kate. I'm going to clear this up. Trust me."

An officer came into the room and escorted Kate out. It broke Tom to see her this way. A moment later Officer Gordon entered and introduced himself. Tom had little room for niceties left. "My wife didn't kill anybody," he blurted.

Officer Gordon stretched out his arm, motioning for Tom to take a seat. "I promise you," he said, "we're going to get to the bottom of this and if your wife is innocent she will be free to go."

"Not if," Tom seethed, "she IS innocent."

Dale stared at Tom, and it was evident he was letting his mind do an official overhaul. "Mr. Miller," he began, "we'd like to ask you a few questions."

"Am I under arrest?"

"No," Dale answered, "but any information you can give us may prove helpful in clearing your wife."

Tom stood up and moved to the door. "I'll answer your questions, but not without my attorney present."

Tom stepped into the hall and dialed Jace. When he answered Tom stammered, "I need an attorney."

The emotion was loud in Tom's voice. "I'm sorry you couldn't talk her out of it, but don't worry I've got a great divorce lawyer."

"No," Tom interrupted, "I need a criminal lawyer right now."

There was a gasp and then silence on the other end of the phone. "Holy shit Tom," Jace uttered, "what did you do?"

~

Kate's fingers were ice cold when they led her down the hall and into the interrogation room. She sat for a few moments by herself, praying, before the door opened and Officer Gordon entered and sat down across from her. Stephen and Ernie stood quietly behind the two-way glass and watched. "Kate," Officer Gordon began, "all we need you to do is tell us the truth." Tears ran from Kate's eyes, down her cheeks and around her chin. She didn't know what truth he was talking about. She wasn't even sure what happened that made her a suspect in a murder. Officer Gordon continued, "Did you kill Jeanette Carlen?"

Kate cried harder, "no," she sobbed, "I don't even know who she is."

Dale leaned forward and looked Kate directly in her eyes and asked, "Did you kill a woman named Arianna Borgman?"

"No, I've never met either of these women." Kate wiped her eyes. "I told you, my husband had lunch with Arianna at Murrays the other day."

"And you were there?" Dale asked.

"Not at lunch with them, no," Kate tried to clarify. "I was at Murrays with a girlfriend and we saw Tom and Arianna."

"What did you think when you saw your husband with Arianna?" Dale prodded.

Stephen slammed his fist against the wall. "He's baiting her!" He yelled. "He told me he knew she was innocent." Stephen paced back and forth while Ernie stood staunch, arms crossed, staring through the glass.

"I was upset because I thought he was on a date," Kate admitted.

"Was this the first date he'd been on with Arianna?"

Kate's theory about Arianna and Tom swarmed her brain. "He said it was."

"Do you believe it was?" Dale's eyes stared right through her.

"I don't know." Kate wilted.

"Did you follow Arianna home?"

"What?" Kate looked at him with wide eyes. As his implication sank into her mind, she sat up straight and wiped her tears. "I want legal representation before I answer anymore of your questions."

"Thata girl!" hollered Stephen from behind the glass. He was growing ever more pissed at Dale. Dale came back behind the glass and Stephen laid into him. He grabbed Dale by the shirt and slammed him against the back wall.

Ernie pried Stephen off, yelling "think it through man, you gonna assault a cop?" Stephen was panting. "Where will that get you?" Stephen knew Ernie was right but he could scarcely control his anger.

Stephen yelled at Dale, "What the hell are you doing? You know she's not guilty!"

## Chapter 15

Tom paced in the front area of the station, periodically peering out the glass doors, looking for Jace, who promised to be there soon. When he finally arrived with Donald Bracker in tow, Tom hurried through the double doors and met them on the sidewalk. Donald Bracker stood five foot eight inches tall, had coal black hair and wore an Armani pent striped suit that Tom assessed cost at least fifteen hundred dollars. He wore a large gaudy ring on each hand and a gold bracelet on his left wrist. He appeared a bit flashy for Tom's taste, but the way he saw it beggars couldn't be choosers. A quick exchange of formalities and a brief introduction let Tom know Donald Bracker was a criminal defense attorney, with a reputation for details.

"If they forgot to dot an I or cross a T, and they always do," he smirked, "you and your wife will be out of here in no time."

Tom, Jace and Donald talked strategy for a few moments and Tom summed up what he knew about the case against Kate. Then they walked back inside. Taking a seat, Tom felt jittery as he was certain his nerves were fried end to end. He put his palms on his knees and tried to wipe the clamminess away, but it didn't work. He couldn't believe this was happening. Jace studied his face. "Relax man," he said, "Donald's one of the best."

Tom nodded but it didn't make him feel better.

It wasn't long before Officer Gordon emerged from the hallway and escorted them to an interrogation room in the back. Tom felt a sick pit in his stomach and noticed his legs felt weak and wobbly as he walked down the hall. Taking a deep breath seemed virtually impossible and made the nausea worsen. Officer Gordon, Emily, Tom and Jace took a seat at the rectangular shaped table. Donald remained standing. "Is my client under arrest?"

Dale looked at him with a glare that acknowledged Donald's bold stature and understood he would be taking the law to the letter. "At this point, no," Dale answered.

"Then he doesn't have to agree to answer any of your questions," Donald retorted.

Dale's jaw tightened. "No," he said, "this is a voluntary interview."

"Then we request it is stated in your report that my client voluntarily offered information to assist the police in their criminal investigations." Donald's tone was no-nonsense, direct and matter-of-fact. Tom was impressed. Before Dale could respond, Donald continued, "We would also like the recording device for this voluntary meeting to be turned off." Dale locked eyes with Donald and scowled, but Donald continued despite Dale's irritation. "You are well aware that it is illegal to record a conversation without the consent of all those being recorded." Dale nodded. "This voluntary interview will not take place while being recorded by any device."

Dale exhaled, then turned to face the two-way glass panel and motioned with his arm across his neck to cut the tape. He then glared at Donald, "satisfied?"

Donald nodded and took a seat, turning to Tom. "You may answer any question and you may also choose, under the Fifth Amendment, not to answer any question." Tom looked at him, unsure if this was his way of instructing Tom to hide information he thought might incriminate himself or Kate. He shook his head to indicate he understood, but he really didn't feel like he understood anything. The only thing he knew for sure was there was an underlying uneasiness swelling in his gut.

~

Stephen and Ernie returned to their favorite brainstorming spot in the back booth of the Backrow Tavern, and began pouring over Madeline's journal. Stephen knew the answer was somewhere in this book, he could feel it.

Ernie squinted as he exhaled smoke into the air above his head. "We know Cindy Miller is the daughter of Arianna Borgman and Lou Miller, right?" Stephen nodded and Ernie continued. "We know Lou Miller was killed in a hit and run accident, right?" Stephen nodded again. "We know Cindy has the same hair barrette that Madeline had right?"

Stephen jumped in, "that's an assumption," he said, "but we can go with it for now."

"Maybe Lou Miller gave little Cindy the hair barrette as a goodbye gift." Ernie held up the picture of the little blonde girl with the barrette in her hands.

Stephen looked up from the journal and repeated, "A goodbye gift." They stared at each other, letting that idea flow through their heads and trickle down to the effect a goodbye would have on each person. Stephen talked it through, "Lou Miller wouldn't leave his wife, who was Tom's grandmother, even though he had an affair with Arianna Borgman which resulted in the birth of

186

Cindy Miller Borgman." Ernie nodded. "He gave her the expensive barrette as a parting gift and mom, a.k.a. Arianna, didn't think that was enough so she ran him down."

Ernie grinned, "That's all speculation," he said, mimicking Stephen.

Stephen pursed his lips and narrowed his eyes at Ernie. "So what does this mean?" He asked rhetorically, but Ernie had an answer ready.

"It means..." Ernie paused, lighting up another cigarette. "Cindy's mom is our killer. The question is, does Cindy know?"

"Wait," said Stephen, holding his finger up, "what if the barrette belonged to grandmother and she got pissed that her husband gave it to his mistress so SHE ran him down?"

Ernie inhaled until his face narrowed and his cheekbones protruded, then he let the smoke pour out his nose. Stephen thought he looked like a bull every time he did this, but he didn't tell him. Ernie shook his head. "Nope," he retorted, "not grandmother."

"Why not her?" Argued Stephen.

"Because for now we have to assume all the murders are related and grandmother has been dead for six months." Ernie smashed his cigarette butt into the ashtray, "our killer is still alive. Besides," he added, "she just tried to get rid of Kate and probably you."

Stephen pondered, "Do we have any concrete evidence to support the notion that the hit and run of John Doe six months ago, and the hit and run attempt on Kate Miller's life are connected?"

Ernie reached into his brown leather briefcase and pulled out the file of rental car agreements. "Bear with me," Ernie said. Stephen leaned back in the booth and closed his eyes. He wanted to focus on every word. Ernie began, "each rental contract was signed by Arianna Borgman and she purchased insurance on each vehicle."

Stephen opened his eyes. "That would indicate that she either doesn't have auto insurance of her own, or she was anticipating damage to the car." Ernie nodded in agreement.

Ernie lit up another cigarette and continued. "Six months ago she rented a silver sedan from Budget, returning it after a collision with damage to the front quarter panel and the rear panel, both on the driver's side."

Stephen opened his eyes again. "Both on the driver's side?"

"That's what the report says."

Stephen tried to paint the picture in his mind. "So she could have hit the car head on, damaging the front quarter panel, then backed up and hit the car again, damaging the back panel?"

Ernie shrugged. "It's possible." Stephen closed his eyes and Ernie continued. "The paint found on the silver rental sedan was black, and according to the police report, the paint found on the black car our John Doe drove, was silver."

Ernie shifted in the booth and flipped to another page and continued his out loud analysis. "Last Tuesday she rented a white suburban from Avis, with insurance, returning the vehicle with damage to the driver's side front panel and remnants of tan paint."

The hair on Stephen's neck stood up and he felt the anxiety building in his chest. "What color was the paint on Kate Miller's car?"

Ernie flipped to the police report. "Kate Miller drove a tan Acura, damage to the front quarter panel, with remnants of white paint."

Stephen sat up straight, it was sketchy, but conceivable that Arianna Borgman was the driver in both accidents.

Stephen's heart beat faster. He pulled out his cell phone to dial Officer Gordon, but Ernie held his hand up. "Wait a minute," Ernie said, "you haven't heard the rest of my theory."

~

Officer Gordon jotted a telephone number down on a piece of paper and spun it around to face Tom. Staring directly in his eyes he asked, "Mr. Miller, can you tell me whose telephone number this is?"

Tom glanced at the paper. "Yes sir," he said, "that is my cell phone number."

"Thank you." Officer Gordon's tone was curt as he pulled the paper away, jotted down another number and turned it back to face Tom. "And this one?" He asked, locking eyes with Tom.

"Yes sir," Tom said, "that is the cell number of my wife's best friend's sister."

Officer Gordon thought it odd Tom didn't use Alisha's name. "Can you tell me why, two nights ago, you called this number six times from your phone?"

"I didn't call from my phone," answered Tom calmly. "I called from my wife's home phone because I couldn't find my cell phone."

Dale was losing patience. His jaw tightened and he spewed, "why would you call Alisha in the middle of the night?"

Donald butted in, "who's Alisha?"

Tom answered smoothly, "Officer Gordon's wife." Dale and Tom's eyes locked in a stare Tom knew Donald was concerned might result in one of their heads being vaporized.

Donald turned to Tom, "you called his wife six times in the middle of the night?"

Tom shook his head and folded his hands on the table. "Officer Gordon's wife, Alisha, is the sister of my wife's best friend, Kimberly. She happens to have a key to Kimberly's house which is where I accidentally left my cell phone." Tom exhaled, repeating the story exactly as he and Alisha rehearsed. "I couldn't get a hold of Kimberly so I called Alisha."

Dale studied Tom's face. Donald shook his head. "In lieu of this little tidbit of information," Donald said, "I'd like to request another officer head up this case as personal interest may cloud professional judgment."

Dale stood up abruptly and left the room with Emily trailing behind him. Donald turned to Tom with a flash of anger in his eyes. He slammed his hand on the table and through gritted teeth spewed, "you better tell me right now if you're screwing around with Officer Gordon's wife." Tom shook his head in denial.

When Officer Gordon walked back into the room it was with a stride of confidence and a smirk of condescension. He sat back down and handed Donald a piece of paper. Donald perused it quickly, then shaking his head he handed it to Tom. "What is it?" Tom asked.

Dale grinned, "A statement from your wife."

Tom read the page and sighed with despair. Dale snatched the statement off the table. "See Mr. Miller," he examined, "according to your home phone records you were in the house calling my wife six times between 12:25 and 12:40am." He stood up and paced around the table. "Then according to your wife she found you and Kimberly arguing in your driveway somewhere around 1:40am." He stopped and faced Tom, "so my question is where were you from the last time you called my wife to the time your wife found you in the driveway arguing with Kimberly about her keys?"

Tom felt like there was no saliva left in his mouth. His heart was beating so fast he thought it was echoing in the room. His hands were clammy and he could feel his face beginning to flush.

Dale slammed another paper on the table and bent over toward Tom, sliding it closer. "This is a record of your cell phone calls," he said, through clenched teeth. "Do you see this call right here?" Officer Gordon pointed to an incoming call from Kimberly at 1:10am. Another at 1:20am. "And how about this call here," he said, pointing to an outgoing call at 2:40am. "That was the call you made to me," Dale explained, "asking me about Ernie James." Tom didn't utter a word. "So," Dale summed up, "you found your cell phone sometime between 12:45 and 2:40am, is that correct?"

Tom sat motionless and mumbled almost incoherently, "I don't really know what time it was when I found it."

Dale shrugged, "of course you don't," he mused, "I'm sure you don't want me to ask where you were when you found it."

Tom was silent.

"Or maybe I should ask if you were alone when you found it?" Dale stared right through Tom.

Silence.

"Let me help you out." Pulling another paper from his file he showed Tom the phone record for the call from Stephen Braznovich's cell phone to Tom's home phone at 12:45am, explaining that Kimberly answered Tom's home phone. "You and Kimberly were at your home within a few minutes of each other."

Tom swallowed hard. "We must have just missed each other."

"Not according to a witness." Dale leaned back and folded his arms across his chest. "A Mrs. Netbaum claims she saw you and Kimberly entering the house through the bedroom window at just before midnight."

Tom froze. He hadn't thought about Nosey Netbaum.

"I'm puzzled," said Dale sarcastically, "why didn't you just talk to Kimberly then about your phone?" Dale smirked at Tom. "I'm certain she would have checked her home to see if it was there."

Tom's heart was pounding so hard in his chest he could swear it was visible through his shirt. "I don't know," he stammered, "I guess I didn't think of it at the time."

"I see," nodded Dale. "So, how did you come to leave your phone at Kimberly's house in the first place?"

Tom couldn't move. Sweat pooled at his temples and his tongue felt like sand paper. He ran his fingers through his hair and turned to Donald. "I don't want to answer anymore questions."

Dale raised his voice. "You are aware Mr. Miller that lying to an Officer to impede an investigation is a criminal offense?"

Donald stood up and addressed Officer Gordon. "My client has answered enough. If you have further questions you may contact me." He handed Dale a business card and escorted Tom to the door with Jace trailing behind.

Before Donald could open the door, Dale turned and said, "I don't suppose you want to tell me about your meeting at Murrays with Arianna Borgman." Tom knew this was a last ditch effort to keep talking, to pry out any information he could. Tom stopped and turned around to face Officer Gordon. He wanted to find out what was happening as much as anyone. He wanted to help clear Kate and himself of any assumption of wrongdoing. More than anything, he wanted all of this to go away. As a gesture of goodwill, Tom walked back to the table and sat down.

Donald joined him but not before he warned, "I am against further dialogue and think both of you need to cool off."

Dale never took his eyes from Tom as he nodded, "agreed."

Emily took detailed notation on everything Tom said about the meeting at Murrays. Tom's voice cracked with emotion as he replayed the sequence of events for Officer Gordon.

Dale interrupted, "wait a minute," he said, "your assistant booked the appointment with Arianna Borgman?" Tom nodded. Dale looked at Emily, "get me the phone records for every line coming into Tom's office. I want to know when the appointment was made and where the call came from." Emily left the room. He then turned his gaze back to Tom, "continue please."

Tom inhaled deeply and began to lay out the details of the story Arianna told him. As he began he shook his head and said, "This will sound far fetched and a little out there, it did to me too."

Dale nodded. "Go on."

## Chapter 16

Stephen leaned forward with both elbows on the table, giving Ernie his full attention. "What's the rest of your theory?"

Ernie shifted in the booth and rubbed his lips together. He pulled out Kate's file marked "Journal Entries" and retrieved from it grandmother's last letter to Kate. "See here," he said pointing to the highlighted line and read, "it says 'Forgiveness is KEY' but I think grandmother is making reference beyond the need to be a forgiving person."

Stephen squinted, "what do you mean?"

"Because of the barrette, we can assume that grandma knew little Cindy existed right?"

"Speculation," Stephen said, cocking his head to one side, "but alright."

Looking back at the letter Ernie explained, "See how the word key is in all caps?" Stephen nodded. "I think it's in all caps to indicate there is a key."

"Like a key to a map, like a code?" asked Stephen.

"Nah," Ernie shook his head, exhaling smoke through his nose, "like an actual key to a locker or a safe deposit box or an in home safe of some sort."

Stephen leaned back against the booth and thought deeply. Even if there is a key, he thought, what would she have placed in hiding that would help them solve the case? Unless she knew who killed Lou. Stephen stared at Ernie. His eyes widened. "You think grandmother knew who killed her husband?"

Ernie squinted from the smoke he exhaled and slowly nodded his head.

Stephen leaned forward again and waved smoke from his side of the table. "You think grandmother forgave the killer?"

Ernie grinned, "welcome aboard the thought train," he mused.

Stephen stared at him. "You think grandmother hid proof of the killer's identity in case it was ever needed?"

Ernie grabbed grandmother's letter to Kate and spun it around to face Stephen. He pointed to a line they hadn't paid attention to before. In fact, Stephen hadn't even remembered reading it because it was in the very beginning of the letter and seemed irrelevant. The line read: *'I see the strength in you that is needed to carry this burden of forgiveness, to protect our legacy and to hold our family together.'* Ernie grinned. "Grandmother was one smart broad," he said. "Forgiveness is key, but protection is wise."

Stephen tried to sort the information in his mind. "So, grandmother forgave the killer but passed the information down to Kate for the future protection of her family if or when it was needed."

"Bingo," said Ernie, snapping his fingers. "Now you're tracking with me."

Stephen reached for his cell phone again to call Officer Gordon, but Ernie held up his index finger to wait. Ernie leaned on his elbows and squished his cigarette butt into the ash tray. "There's more," he said. Stephen set his phone down and leaned in closer.

~

Officer Gordon sat back in his chair and exhaled. It was far fetched. It was a lot to take in, but something in the story rang true. "Let me sum this up," he said to Tom and Donald.

"Arianna Borgman set up a meeting with you at Murrays to tell you that your dead grandmother visited her in a dream and told her it was time to meet with you about her Will."

Tom nodded, knowing it sounded insane.

Dale continued. "She then told you that she was your grandfather's lover and your grandmother killed him because he was going to leave her."

Tom nodded again and Officer Gordon continued. "Arianna promised not to tell anyone that your grandmother murdered her husband provided that grandmother promise her the inheritance money she deserved." Officer Gordon leaned forward and adjusted in his chair. "Am I getting all this straight?"

"I know it sounds nuts," Tom muttered, "but that's what she told me." Tom shook his head. "The thing is there's no way she could have known anything about my grandparents unless, well, unless she really had a dream."

Dale looked intensely at Tom and stated bluntly, "and then Arianna wound up dead."

Tom jolted from his chair, "now wait a minute, I didn't kill her!"

Dale held up his hand, as a signal for Tom to calm down. "Let's change the subject," he suggested.

"Good idea," interjected Donald, with an inflection that let Dale know that another accusatory tone would end the voluntary questioning.

"Tell me about your family," Dale licked his lip and spun a pen on the table. "Your parents alive? You have any siblings?"

Donald blurted, "Relevancy?"

"Assuming Arianna's story to be true, we have a motive to keep a family secret hidden," Dale stated matter-of-factly. "I need to know who the family members are."

Donald looked back at Tom and nodded to answer Dale's question. Tom sat back in his chair and crossed his arms. "My parents are deceased. I have an older brother named Martin. He's always been a loose cannon. I don't really know where he's living now and I haven't heard from him in years."

Dale jotted down notes as Tom spoke. "Why do you think your brother is a loose cannon?"

"I don't know," sighed Tom. "He went off the deep end after mom died and our dad left."

"Did you two get along?"

"Martin is four years older so we didn't play together much as kids. We had a falling out years ago." Tom ran his hand through his hair. "Geez, it's been almost twenty years now. We just never got through it I guess. He left and we haven't talked since."

"What was the fight over?" Dale questioned.

Tom stared at the floor and it became obvious he was connecting dots in his mind. His mouth felt pasty and he licked his lips and swallowed hard. "My brother and I had a fight over Grandpa Lou." Tom stood up and walked across the room, trying to remember the details of their argument. "Martin accused grandpa of having an affair with a young woman from a neighboring town. He said he got her pregnant."

"Was there any truth to the accusation?"

"I don't know," Tom sat back down. "There were a lot of rumors back then."

"So what happened between you and Martin?"

"We had a big blow up one night." Tom recalled, "I sided with Grandpa Lou. Martin left and a couple months later grandfather died in the accident."

"Did your grandfather impregnate someone?"

"Geez, I dunno." Tom shrugged. "There were rumors but nothing I ever believed."

"Do you think your brother could have killed Lou?"

Tom shook his head. "Martin was a hot head but I don't think he was capable of murder."

Dale excused himself and stepped into the hall, closing the door behind him. He quickly found Emily and gave her instructions. "I want you to find out everything you can about a Martin Miller, the brother of Tom Miller."

Emily nodded, "got it."

"Thank you," hollered Dale, grabbing his cell and heading the opposite direction. He dialed Stephen's number.

~

Kate told Officer Emily all about Martin showing up at the house six months ago and dropping off the manila folder. She described the picture inside the folder in as much detail as she could remember. As Emily stood up to leave the room, Kate concluded, "Tom could tell you more about Martin," she added, "I never really got to know him."

Emily stood up from the table and pushed her chair against it. "Mrs. Miller," she asked, "where is that manila folder now?"

Kate thought back for a moment. It was under the bed and then she got it out to show Stephen. "I gave it to Stephen," she answered.

"Who is Stephen?"

"He's a private investigator whose been working on this case." Kate's eyes were wide with innocence and Emily could tell Kate had no idea how deep this whole thing went.

"Sit tight," said Emily, excusing herself and closing the door behind her.

Kate was tired of sitting tight in this windowless, pale yellow room. Or maybe it was light tan, Kate couldn't tell in the dim lighting. She was mentally drained from recanting details of phone calls and names of people she didn't even know. Her eyes burned from too much crying and she just wanted to go home.

~

Stephen hung up his cell and filled Ernie in on the details Tom had given Dale concerning his missing brother, Martin. Ernie lit another cigarette and hung on every word. They had work to do. First assignment was to find out everything they could about Martin Miller. Though Ernie had a strong sensation he knew his whereabouts and it wasn't anywhere he could be found. Second assignment was to pull Stillwell police records on Lou Miller's accident. Last, but not least, find Arianna Borgman.

The question was how did Lou's murder tie into the John Doe hit and run, the shooting of Jeanette Carlen, and the attempt on Kate's life?

Out of the blue Stephen blurted, "You know what's been eating at me?"

Ernie looked up, "not solving this case."

Stephen rolled his eyes. "Obviously." He shifted in the booth. "It's too coincidental that Kate and Kimberly were at Murrays at the exact same time as Tom and Arianna's meeting at Murrays."

"Stranger things have happened," shrugged Ernie.

Stephen couldn't shake the feeling of relevance there. "It's too much of a coincidence. It's like someone wanted Kate to see Tom with another woman."

"That should be easy to figure out," Ernie packed down his box of cigarettes against the table, "all we need to know is who scheduled the meeting at Murrays." Ernie looked at Stephen with raised eyebrows, to indicate his impatience. "Now, can I tell you the rest of my theory or what?"

Stephen had gotten sidetracked by Officer Gordon's call and forgot Ernie was about to tell him the rest. "Sure, go ahead. Wow me." Ernie chuckled a raspy, smoker's laugh.

"Grandmother knows who the killer is and forgives her, hiding her identity." Ernie began.

"Yes, you said that already," interrupted Stephen.

"I was backtracking to make sure you remembered where we left off." Ernie opened the carton and lit another cigarette.

"But why would she do that? Why would she forgive the other woman?" Stephen questioned.

Ernie leaned closer, "because she knows it's the only full-proof way to protect herself and her family."

"How?"

Ernie took a long drag on his cigarette and blew the smoke right over the top of Stephen's head. "Speculating that the motive for Lou's murder was money, Grandmother cuts a deal with Arianna, agreeing to put her in the Will if she disappears and leaves her alone to live and die in peace."

"That's nothing but speculation," Stephen said.

"Hear mê out before you discount my theory," Ernie rebutted. "Arianna goes away, disappears for years, waiting for grandmother to die." Ernie took a drag on his cigarette. "When she dies Arianna re-emerges under her new identity to wait for the family to search for her and give her the money she has been promised."

"Wait," Stephen interrupted, "what do you mean she re-emerges with a new identity?"

"She has to be close enough to keep tabs on the family, to know when the Will is paid out and who gets what," explained Ernie. Stephen nodded, though it sounded far fetched. Ernie continued, "shortly after grandma dies, Martin, the only living family member who knows about grandpa's indiscretions, digs around and finds out who Arianna is pretending to be. He gathers proof of who she really is and threatens to compromise her identity."

"So he takes whatever proof he has and gives it to Kate for safe keeping," Stephen interjected.

"Arianna couldn't have anyone knowing who she really is, so she killed him by the same method she killed his grandfather." Ernie exhaled smoke and cleared his throat. "What she didn't count on was the contingency grandmother put on the Will, stating that both Tom and Martin had to be present."

Stephen's mind was tracking now. "And when she learns of this contingency she's left with no other choice but to kill all remaining heirs."

Ernie interrupted, "leaving her daughter the only biological heir to Lou's oil empire."

"This is all speculation, guesswork," said Stephen.

Ernie raised his left eyebrow and grinned. "You're not wowed yet?"

"I'm wowed by your imagination for sure," Stephen said, "but we don't have a lot of facts here."

"Like what?"

"Like, how does the murder of Jeanette Carlen tie in?" Stephen couldn't wait to hear this answer.

Ernie just shook his head as if disappointed. "Are you new here?" He teased Stephen. "We know Jeanette Carlen was an actress, so we can assume she was hired to star in the lunch role of Arianna Borgman." Stephen sat up a bit straighter and narrowed his brows. It never dawned on him that someone hired Jeanette. "I see I have your attention," Ernie commented.

Stephen felt a tingle in his stomach, that feeling they were on target. "So why did Arianna kill Jeanette?"

Ernie leaned in close, "because she saw who the real Arianna was. She was a loose end."

Stephen leaned back, "wow." He sat still, deep in thought for a few moments. "How did Martin know who Arianna was?"

Ernie reached across the table and picked up the picture of the little girl holding the barrette. "First, Martin may have seen her years prior during the affair. But more importantly, Arianna has the barrette." Ernie exhaled smoke. "Grandmother gave Arianna the barrette not only as a symbol of their agreement, but as a marker of her real identity."

"So you think Lou's wife and mistress cut a deal. Arianna's silence and money in exchange for the safety of Madeline's family." Stephen leaned back and folded his arms.

Taking the cigarette from his lips, Ernie grinned. "I wowed you didn't I?" It was obvious he was quite pleased with himself.

Stephen nodded. "This is all speculation," he said, "but yes, you wowed me."

## Chapter 17

The phone rang and woke Tom. He opened his eyes and remembered he had slept at the house last night. Jace stayed over too, for moral support. Kate gave him the keys so he could let himself in. Poor Kate, he thought. She had spent the night in jail. He rolled over and grabbed the phone from the night stand. "Hello," he uttered, not caring if he sounded half asleep.

"Mr. Miller?" Came the voice of Stephen Braznovich. "We need to talk right away." Tom sat up in bed and let his feet feel the coolness of the hardwood floor. He rubbed one hand through his hair and tried to focus on the clock. "It's only 7:00am and it's been one hell of a night," he mumbled into the phone. "Can we do this later?" Tom's head was still pounding from last night's interrogation, and he didn't feel up to another round.

"Mr. Miller," Stephen continued, "I'm in your driveway right now, and I think we need to talk immediately."

Tom hung up the phone and went to the door, letting Stephen inside and following him back to the den.

Stephen began to lay out the details of what they knew, what they guessed and what information they still needed. When the doorbell rang, Stephen immediately jumped up, "I'll get that," he said. "It'll be my partner Ernie James." Tom instantly recognized the name as the officer that held Kimberly at gunpoint and he felt anger flush up around his neck.

Ernie followed Stephen to the den, nodding a hello to Tom and taking a seat on the couch. He kept quiet while Stephen told the story. Stephen pulled the copies of grandmother's journal from his briefcase and flipped open to the page marked "forgiveness." He handed the page to Tom, who studied it momentarily and realizing it was grandmother's handwriting, he leaned forward toward Stephen and clenched his teeth. "How do you have a copy of my grandmother's journal?"

"Kate allowed me to copy it," he lied. He could tell Tom didn't believe him but he wasn't here to win a popularity contest. He needed information and he needed it quickly. "See the picture of a key in the upper right corner," he said, pointing to it on the page Tom still held tightly in his grip. Tom nodded. "You see the darkening around the edges of the key," asked Stephen. Again, Tom nodded. "Well, I believe in the journal there is an actual key glued to the page," Stephen paused, studying Tom's face.

Tom chimed in, "and you want the key because you think it opens a buried treasure chest?" He oozed sarcasm and anger.

Ernie stood up, towering over Tom to such a degree that Tom stood up right afterwards. Still, Ernie's physique was intimidating. He glared at Tom and warned, "Unless we get the key whoever tried to kill your wife will try again and maybe this time she'll succeed." Ernie shuffled by Tom and mumbled to Stephen that he was stepping outside for a smoke. Tom sank back in the arm chair and stared into space.

Stephen sat quiet for a moment, and then begged, "Please Tom, I can't find the killer until I know the identity she's living under."

Tom sighed, "I'd help you but I don't even know where Kate hides that journal."

"In her closet, top shelf, in the floral designed hat box to the right."

Tom glared at him. "What were you doing in my wife's closet?"

~

Dale rolled over in bed and wrapped his arms around Alisha. He hadn't confronted her about the phone calls to and from Tom Miller yet. He wasn't sure he wanted to hear her answer. Exhaling, he rolled onto his back and stared at the ceiling. His mind told him Kate was innocent and Tom was possibly guilty of sleeping with his wife but not of murder. He fought the urge to be emotional and forced only the facts to replay in his mind. Professionalism was overrun by personal feelings and the thoughts of Alisha in another man's arms. He couldn't stand not knowing the truth. Rolling back onto his side, he let his head rest right behind Alisha's ear and whispered, "Are you awake?"

She stirred, "yes."

His heart was pounding as he tried to think how to ask about Tom Miller, but before he could say anything she rolled over and said, "Can you tell me more about the case you've been working so hard on?"

It was the segway he needed to broach a difficult subject. He rolled back on his back and she snuggled up against his chest. He began to tell her about Lou Miller's murder. Alisha lay still in his arms and listened to every word. She was young at the time but vaguely remembered the murder of the big oil tycoon. It hit the small town of Stillwell hard and the news spread fast to all the connecting towns.    Dale spilled out details about the case he had never shared with her in the past. He was always secretive about his work, but now she felt like he was no longer shutting her out. Dale talked for twenty minutes straight, pouring over every detail and processing the information as he heard his own voice speak it.   He rubbed his eyes with his right hand, keeping his left arm draped around Alisha.

She leaned up and kissed his neck.  "I wish I could help you figure it out," she said.

"Me too," he exhaled.

Alisha leaned up on her elbows and faced him.  "So, you think the killer is the same in all of the murders and it's someone named Arianna Borgman?"  Dale nodded.  "Who are your suspects?"

Dale sat upright.  "Kate Miller.  Tom Miller. Rita.  Hell, it could be just about anyone."

"But I thought you said it had to be a woman?"  Alisha felt her nerves stand on end at the mention of Tom's name.

"No," Dale explained, "I said the killer is using a woman's name.  It doesn't mean it has to be a woman."

Alisha was relieved when Dale's cell brought an abrupt end to their conversation. Closing his phone, he jumped out of bed and was in the shower in a matter of seconds.  Once the front door closed she grabbed her cell and called Tom.

When his voicemail came on, Alisha waited for the beep and then blurted, "You're a suspect!"

~

Tom, Stephen and Ernie made their way to the bedroom and retrieved the journal from the hat box in the closet.  Tom pulled it out and handed it to Stephen, who flipped immediately to the tab

207

marked "forgiveness". There in the corner of the top of the page was a small brass key.

Stephen shot Ernie a glance. "You didn't notice this when you were making copies?"

"I was moving quickly. Remember?"

Stephen looked at Tom, "may I remove this key?"

Tom nodded. "How do you know what it unlocks?"

"We don't," said Ernie, "but I bet grandmother will tell us." He winked at Tom and took the key, holding it up to the light. He flipped it over and on the side there was an engraving that read: Bank of Stillwell sdb

"My grandparents lived in Stillwell," Tom exclaimed.

Stephen looked at Ernie, "What is sdb?"

Ernie stared at the key and squinted harder. Stephen thought he could actually see the wheels spinning in Ernie's head. With a satisfied grin Ernie nodded, "Safe Deposit Box."

Stephen slapped his hands together and let out a congratulatory yelp. "Thank you grandma!" He hollered.

Ernie grimaced. "Don't celebrate yet, only grandmother or whoever she has given authority to at the bank or in her Will can access the safe deposit box."

Stephen looked at Tom. "Who was the executor of grandmother's Will?"

Tom stuttered around. "I don't know. I can't see the will until we find my brother, which I hired you to do." Stephen and Ernie shot each other a glance that was obvious to Tom. "What?" He looked from one to the other. "What did that look mean?"

What that look meant was that he and Ernie had a suspicion that Martin Miller was the

John Doe killed in the hit and run six months ago, but Stephen didn't feel it was the proper time to tell Tom.   If they were right about Arianna killing Lou, and Lou Jr. and attempting to kill Kate, it only stood to reason that she had already killed Martin and Tom was next on the list.

Ernie grabbed Tom's shoulder, "we'll tell you on the way to the station."

"Why are we going to the station?" Tom howled, "Unless it's to pick up Kate, that is the last place I want to go. Besides, we can't help Kate by sitting at the station."

"No," said Stephen, "but Kate can help us."

~

Stephen drove with Ernie in front and Tom in the back seat.  Just as he got in the car, Tom's cell buzzed a text from Rita that read, "Where are you?"

"Ah, hell," Tom uttered aloud.

"What's up?"  Stephen asked, peering at Tom through the rearview mirror.

"I had an 8:00am meeting I forgot about." Tom rubbed his eyes with his hand.

"You're late."  The next text read.

Stephen asked.  "Do you want us to drop you at work?  Ernie and I can take it from here."

Tom stared at him, thinking that's exactly what Stephen probably wants, so he can swoop in as Kate's hero. "I don't think so."  Tom forced a grin.  "I want to see my wife."  He emphasized the words my wife and was certain Stephen got the message.

This time his cell phone rang and Tom cursed aloud as he answered.  "This is Tom."

Rita's tone was perturbed.  "Why aren't you at the office?"

"I've got some things to take care of this morning and then I'll be in."

"We had an 8:00am meeting."

"I'm aware and I apologize for my tardiness."

"That's not good enough," Rita spewed. "I'm going to have the Board review your performance the past six months and inform them that I believe you are nothing more than a financial liability to this company."

Something in Tom snapped and he hollered at the top of his lungs. "You do that, you self-righteous, snotty, lying, bird-beaked bitch of a goddamned whore!" Silence filled the phone. "And while you're at it you better start updating your resume because in less than five fucking days I'm going to take over LouLineCo and you are the first rotten thing to go!" He disconnected the call.

Silence filled the car and then Ernie chuckled. "Bird-beaked bitch, that's a new one."

They all laughed. "Hope that wasn't your boss," Ernie said.

Stephen added, "I think you used every curse word known to man in one sentence."

Tom shook his head. He'd lost it and there was no sugar-coating what happened. "Sorry guys, I just had to get that off my chest."

"Who was that?" Ernie asked.

"The company Controller, Rita. She's been a puss-oozing sore in my ass for the past, well, since I was eight years old."

"Sounds like a nice girl," Ernie teased.

"I'm telling you, she's a real bitch, to the core."

Stephen and Ernie shot each other a glance. Then Stephen asked, "What's the relationship between your brother and Rita?"

"There is no relationship. They know each other because we all grew up together, but no one has seen Martin in years, not even Rita."

"Were they ever romantically involved?"
Stephen asked.

"Not that I ever knew about." Tom looked
at Stephen. "Why?"

"Just curious," Stephen answered, but Tom
felt there was more to the story.

"We better hurry and get to the station,"
Ernie interjected, then quoted Tom, "because we
only have five fucking days to solve this case."
They all chuckled again.

~

Kate sat clutching her purse against her
chest and listened intently as Officer Emily
explained they were releasing her because she had
an alibi for the time of Jeanette Carlen's murder.

"The charges against you are dropped,"
Emily explained, "you're free to go now."

"Will someone take me home?" Kate asked.
"Officer Gordon brought me here yesterday in his
car."

Emily pointed to the lobby area. "Someone
is already here."

Relief flooded Kate's whole body and she
suddenly felt exhausted. She walked into the
bathroom, washed her face with some crumpled up
paper towels, and applied lip gloss. Her lips were
so dry it was as if she could feel them soak up the
gloss the moment she put it on. She looked at her
reflection in the mirror and noted how terrible it
was. Her skin was pale, almost ash looking. Her
eyes were bloodshot and swollen and outlined in
circles of dark gray. Even a case of concealer
wouldn't help. Walking through the double doors
into the lobby, she expected to see Tom or even
Stephen, but there stood Kimberly. Tears filled
Kate's eyes as Kimberly threw her arms around her
and hugged tightly.

"Good thing I made you go out drinking with me sister," she said, "otherwise you'd have been at home sulking with no alibi for your whereabouts."

Kate look confused. "But I was at home alone at the time of her murder," she whispered.

Kimberly wrapped her arm around her and leaned in close, "I had to fudge a little on the time I picked you up to go out." She winked at Kate.

Kate bit her lip to hold back the smile. "Thank God for girlfriends," she thought.

They stepped outside the station and Kate never thought the sunlight on her face felt so good. She had only been in jail one night but it felt like an eternity. She breathed in deeply and exhaled slowly.

Once in Kimberly's car, Kate finally began to relax. She couldn't believe everything that had happened the past twenty-four hours. "Why don't you close your eyes and rest," encouraged Kimberly and Kate did just that. The warmth of the sun on her face, and the sheer exhaustion from a night of little sleep and questioning left her completely drained. She closed her eyes and within minutes she began to doze.

~

Stephen, Ernie and Tom signed in at the station desk and asked to see Kate and Officer Gordon. The Officer at the desk left momentarily and returned with Emily in tow. She smiled. "Kate has been released and all charges dropped," she explained.

Tom exhaled and let his shoulders slump over, "oh, thank God," he uttered. "Can I see her now?"

"You just missed her," Emily explained, "her friend Kimberly picked her up a few minutes ago."

Officer Gordon stepped into the lobby and stared at Tom with a glare Tom knew wasn't good. "Mr. Miller," he said, "I can either place you under arrest for the murder of Jeanette Carlen or you can agree to answer some tough questions truthfully." Tom stood speechless.

He knew the walls of that interrogation room all too well and he dreaded walking inside. It felt like a cement block was sitting on each shoulder as he followed Officer Gordon into the room, Stephen and Ernie in tow.

"Look," Dale blurted before they even had a chance to sit down, "I got a match on a murder weapon, and it's your gun." He was in Tom's face. "Your wife has an alibi for the time of death. She was out drinking with Kimberly and these two," he said, pointing to Stephen and Ernie. "Where were you?"

Tom stared blank. He knew where he was, but he couldn't tell Officer Gordon. "I didn't kill that woman," he said, his voice cracking and his hands shaking.

Dale kicked the chair against the wall. "Then tell me where you were!"

Tom sat silent, hiding his shaking hands beneath the table. Dale got down right in Tom's face. "What do you want to be Tom, a murderer or an adulterer? You tell me. Which of the Ten Commandments did you break?"

Tom smashed his fist onto the table, "I didn't kill anyone!"

Ernie interrupted with his usual calm, raspy tone, "Officer Gordon we can find the real killer if you help us get into the safe deposit box that fits this key."

Dale stared at Ernie as if he were nuts. Stephen added, "It's grandmother's box and I know the killer's identity is in it."

Dale shook his head. "Even if I wanted to I couldn't help you get into a safe deposit box."

Ernie intruded, "Yes you can."

Stephen added, "State and federal law enforcement can persuade the court to issue permission to open a safe deposit box if there is 'reasonable cause' to believe the contents are associated with a criminal act."

Dale stared at him, letting the thought process in his head.

Ernie jumped in, "we have 'reasonable cause'."

Dale poked his head outside and hollered for Emily, who entered within moments. "I'm going out for a couple hours," he explained, "he," Dale pointed at Tom, "stays here under suspicion for the murder of Jeanette Carlen."

"Wait a second," Tom yelled.

Dale whirled around and looked at him. "How 'bout I bring you in on a murder charge and an attempted murder charge?"

"Who did I attempt to murder?"

"Your wife."

"What!" Tom came out of his seat, arms flailing. "Are you fucking nuts?"

Dale yelled back with equal ferocity, "I suppose you have an alibi for your whereabouts when your wife was in her accident?" Dale used his fingers to quote the word accident, making it known Kate's collision was no accident at all.

Tom sank down in the chair and buried his face in his hands. He had no alibi. He was alone in his car reading Kate's journal, or alone in his car driving to their home or alone in their home reading Kate's writings. No matter what the exact time of the accident, Tom was alone with no alibi. He sank back down in the chair and buried his face in his palms. "Shit."

On his way out Stephen nudged Tom in the back, "hang tight, we'll get to the bottom of this, I promise."

~

Alisha couldn't stop the details Dale shared with her from replaying in her head. The whole thing haunted her. She sauntered to the kitchen to make coffee and noticed Dale forgot to grab his stack of files from the table as he ran out the door. That was very unusual. Dale never left case information lying around. Alisha couldn't resist the temptation to peek at the confidential folders.

Sitting down she opened the first file and saw the pictures of Jeanette Carlen, read the details of her shooting and the question of mistaken identity. She grimaced at the pictures of Jeanette's fingerprints burned off. The next file was the hit and run of John Doe. This was the case Dale had worked so hard on the past six months and never solved. Alisha studied the pictures of his car and frowned at the photographs of his crumpled body. His face, though coldly lifeless, seemed familiar. The third file was the report from the murder of Lou Miller. Photos of his body crumpled on the pavement made Alisha's stomach queasy. It wasn't the blood that bothered her, but the sheer hatefulness of the crime itself. The distortion made it hard to picture what Lou must have looked like, but when she put his picture next to John Doe there was a strange resemblance. It nagged at her but she couldn't place it.

Alisha read through the police report, describing the abandoned black pick-up truck found up the road. It had been set aflame so all evidence of matching hair, blood or skin fragments were rendered inconclusive. It made her shudder. She got up from the table to get coffee and stood across the kitchen looking at the picture from afar. Something felt oddly familiar.

NO EASY WAY                           S.R.CLARIDGE

**Chapter 18**

Dale was surprised at how quickly they
weaved through the red tape and a warrant to open
Madeline's safe deposit box was issued. "The
advantage of living in a smaller community," he
thought. Warrant in hand, he left the courthouse
with Stephen and Ernie.

"This better pan out," he said. "Or the
Captain is going to have my badge for breakfast."

"Don't worry," Ernie muttered, "you'll be the
hero."

They got into Dale's car, Stephen in the
passenger seat and Ernie in the back, and headed
toward Stillwell. Dale estimated it would take
approximately twenty-two minutes to get to the
bank.

"You know what's been bugging me,"
Stephen said, turning sideways so he could talk to
Ernie in the backseat, "is why would Arianna hire
an actress to tell Tom that story about Lou and the
affair?"

"It was a feel-out session." Ernie gruffed
without missing a beat.

"A what session?"

Dale interjected. "It's a technique we use
on the force. I tell you a version of truth to read
your reaction and find out how much you know of
the real truth."

"But if Arianna already killed Martin, then
she already knew she was going to have to kill
everyone else anyway, so why hire Jeanette at all?"

217

NO EASY WAY                    S.R.CLARIDGE

"Remember," Ernie pointed out, "Arianna didn't know who had the manila folder or even exactly what proof was inside it. She was probably disappointed to have killed Martin and not have found the folder in his possession."

"What bothers me is the burning of the fingertips." Dale grimaced. "Why go through the extra work?"

Ernie chuckled and shook his head. "You two are not thinking like a psychopathic killer."

"I think that's a good trait in a human being." Stephen noted.

"Not if you're trying to catch one," Ernie huffed. "Burning Martin's fingerprints shows her brilliance."

"How so?" Dale asked, squinting at Ernie in the rearview mirror.

"Martin had a police rap sheet a mile long and she probably knew it. Fingerprints would have identified him right away, a death certificate would have been issued to Tom, who would then have taken it to Madeline's attorney and the inheritance in the Will would be issued immediately."

"So?" Stephen interjected, "I thought that's what Arianna was after, the money promised her in the Will."

Ernie shook his head and exhaled extra-loud. "You disappoint me friend."

"Okay wise guy, then spell it out for me since I'm obviously not keeping up." Stephen rolled his eyes at Dale who cracked a grin.

"Arianna doesn't believe any money has been left for her in the Will."

Stephen jumped in, "but you said she and Madeline made a deal."

"Yes, but Arianna doesn't believe Madeline held up her end of the bargain. Why would she?

Why should she?" Ernie grinned, "She's had a better plan all along."

"Go on Superman," Dale spouted, "tell us her plan."

Ernie chuckled. "I'm more of a Batman than a Superman."

Stephen sighed, "Does that make me Robin because I always thought Robin was kind of a pussy."

Ernie laughed out loud. "Well, I didn't want to say anything."

Dale's voice of reason cut in. "The plan Batman?"

"Arianna isn't after just money. She wants everything and she has the ability to get it if all other living relatives are dead. Her daughter, Cindy, is Lou's biological daughter and the rightful, legal heir to his fortune."

"So the only question left," Stephen said, "is who is Arianna Borgman?"

"And how do we find her?" Dale added.

"Let's hope grandmother left us a picture in her safe deposit box." Ernie squirmed in the seat. "Are we getting close? I need a smoke."

~

Alisha showered and threw on a pair of Lucky low rider jeans and a black tank top. She pulled her hair into a pony tail and returned to the kitchen for a caffeine refill before her day of cleaning and studying began. Loading the dishwasher and scrubbing the sink took longer than usual because she kept stopping to glance over at the picture of the black pick-up truck that allegedly killed Lou Miller. There was something about it that lured her mind and drew her thoughts repeatedly closer. She dried her hands on a dishtowel and took a sip of coffee, all the while staring at the picture. She couldn't escape the feeling that truth was right in front of her face. She narrowed her eyes, as if she was struggling to birth a memory, and when she noticed the small dot on the very front of the hood, Alisha felt the memory flood her mind. With the picture clutched in her hand she ran to the desk drawer and dug around until she found a tiny magnifying glass. Placing it above the front of the truck, she saw something that made her stomach turn...the little white baseball sticker with a smiley face in the middle. She slumped into the office chair in shock.

Alisha was nine years old when she placed that sticker on the front of her dad's pick-up. Her softball team had just won their first little league tournament and the coach gave each girl a white baseball sticker with their trophy. Most of the players stuck their stickers on their glove or bat or even on their cheeks, but Alisha remembered saving hers until her father came to pick her up, then she proudly stuck it on the front of his truck. When her dad asked why she wanted to put it on the front of his truck Alisha proclaimed, "So everyone will know." Now, that statement took on a whole new meaning.

Alisha carried the picture back to the kitchen and sat down at the table. She dug through the Lou Miller file again, looking for another picture of the pick-up. Her mind calculated the odds of there being two identical black pick up trucks in Kansas during that time period, with the exact same baseball smiley face sticker on the hood. Even if the truck was the same, it didn't prove anything. Alisha knew her dad could never have killed anyone, not on purpose anyway. Anyone who met him would tell you Andrew Sutton was a drunk, but the sweetest, gentlest drunk you'd ever meet.  He couldn't squish a fly on a bad day.

Alisha felt the lump of past heartache rise in her throat as she thought back to the summer months she spent with her dad.  She only got to see him one month every summer and the rest of the time she lived out-of-state with her mom.  His excessive drinking was the reason the court allowed her mom to move out of state with her, and granted him no custody rights whatsoever.  It was her mother's compassion, not the judicial system, which allowed Alisha to see him every summer. Andrew's drinking is what made Alisha first realize she wanted to become a nurse and help people overcome addiction.

"Alisha," he stammered one night while she helped him off the floor and back into his easy chair, "one day I'm gonna kick this bottle and be the daddy my little girl deserves."  Tears filled her eyes as the memory replayed in her mind and stung her heart.

The one summer month at her dad's house was the only time Alisha ever saw her half-sister, Kimberly.  Alisha looked up to Kimberly.  She was older, had the coolest outfits, wore make-up and always had a boyfriend.  Kimberly was too busy to give Alisha the time of day.  Instead she would borrow dad's truck and go out with boys or friends while Alisha sat home and played pretend veterinary hospital on dad's three dogs.  She grimaced at the thought of what she put those poor dogs through.  Wrapped paws, taped tails and on the white Pointer she even drew some fake stitches with a big black magic marker.

Andrew Sutton was far from the ideal daddy for a little girl, but Alisha knew deep down he couldn't have killed anyone.  Besides, it didn't fit with Dale's theory that Lou Miller's killer was the same person who ran down John Doe six months ago and tried to kill Kate Miller this week. Alisha's dad committed suicide. He hated himself for his alcohol addiction and overdosed on sleeping pills the night before Alisha was coming for her summer visit. Kimberly found him dead in his easy chair. She never saw nor heard from Kimberly again, until they reconnected a year ago.

This mental trek down memory lane prompted Alisha to dig out her childhood photo album. It didn't consist of much. Sitting down on the couch in the family room she flipped through the pages. There were very few pictures of her dad. She wished she knew more about him or could remember the good things about him, but time eroded those memories. Three-quarters of the way through was a picture her father had taken. It was of Alisha and Kimberly and his black pick-up truck. Kimberly was laying across the top of the hood on her right side, propping herself up on her right elbow. Her left knee was bent up and her head tilted back. She was trying to look like a model. Alisha stood in front of the truck with her hair in pig tails and her baseball glove on her left hand. The longer she stared at the picture the more she began to remember that day. Kimberly was nagging at her to scoot over so the top of Alisha's head wouldn't block any of Kimberly's body. Typical Kimberly, always more concerned about her appearance than other people's feelings. Alisha looked closely at the photograph and there on the front of the hood was her baseball sticker. She looked down at the license plate on the truck; it was blue with white lettering and had golden Kansas wheat stalks on it. It had an S on top of an N over to the left and then the numbers 1919.

Alisha pulled the picture from the photo album and took it to the kitchen table to compare the plates, but the picture from the Lou Miller police file showed no plates.  There were notations in the file alluding to the fact that the black pick-up had been abandoned and stripped of the license plate. It also read that the VIN number from the vehicle was missing, and the pick-up truck had been set on fire.  By the time the police located the vehicle it was charred inside and out, rendering a positive match of blood or hair samples to either the driver or the victim, impossible.  It was speculated to be the vehicle that was used to murder Lou Miller, but the evidence read inconclusive.

Alisha couldn't believe her dad's truck was most likely the one used to kill Tom's grandfather. She wanted to call and tell Dale what she'd discovered but that would mean admitting to looking at his confidential files, and she knew he would be furious.  She also felt silly because her only proof it was her dad's truck was a smiley baseball sticker, and even she thought that sounded ridiculous. Besides, she told herself, knowing what truck was used didn't prove who killed Lou Miller.  Even if it was her dad's truck, it could have been stolen.  She wondered if maybe someone reported a vehicle stolen around that same time period.

Instead of phoning Dale she grabbed both pictures, threw on her converse tennis shoes, slung her purse over her shoulder and headed out. Since Kimberly was older, Alisha surmised she would have clearer memories about that summer and could possibly remember something that would help Dale tie the cases together.  She dialed Kimberly's cell as she drove but there was no answer.  It was too much to try to explain in a voicemail so she didn't leave a message, but decided she would just drop by Kimberly's house.

Kimberly wasn't home so Alisha used her spare key and let herself in. Ideally she wanted to talk to Kimberly about their dad and the truck, but since she wasn't there she thought she'd snoop around for some old pictures. She wasn't sure exactly what she was looking for, so she started with the giant book shelves that were inset in the family room walls. They were filled with books on all topics, but there were no personal photo albums on the shelves. She rummaged through Kimberly's desk, her file cabinet and every drawer in her bedroom dresser. Nothing. She searched Kimberly's closet, opening every drawer and looking inside every shoebox. Nothing. She walked through the house and for the first time noticed there were no pictures in it whatsoever. It was filled with artwork, but not one family or friend picture hung on a wall or sat on a shelf or was magnetically held on the refrigerator. Alisha couldn't believe she never noticed this before, how cold and model like the house felt. It didn't have the feel or scent of being lived in.

She walked out to the garage and turned on the light, which consisted of one light bulb to illuminate the entire garage. She hoped to find a stash of old picture boxes with high school yearbooks and childhood albums no one ever displays but everyone keeps hidden somewhere in their home. The garage was dim and dirty and she could tell this wasn't a place Kimberly frequented. There were shelves in one corner with a couple screw drivers, a flashlight, a hammer and a box of nails, but that was the extent of the tools she owned. The rest of the garage was empty. She was just about to give up and go back inside when a string hanging in the far corner caught her eye. She walked over and realized it was a pull down ladder to an attic. It was in the farthest corner from where the light bulb hung so the shadow made it virtually impossible to see. Had it not been for the tiny silver tip on the end of the string that caught the light just perfectly, Alisha would not have noticed it. The ladder pulled down with ease and Alisha grabbed the flashlight she found on the shelves across the garage, and climbed up.

It was dark, muggy and smelled musty. Alisha poked her head up and shone the light all around, before she climbed all the way up, making sure she stepped only on the support beams and not on the drywall in between. There were three medium sized boxes, none of them labeled. She sat on one board and stretched her legs across the other ones to keep her balance while she opened the first box. It was pictures. Tons and tons of pictures. There were photos of Kimberly in a hospital bed, holding a baby and pictures of her with a toddler and a little girl with long blonde hair and big blue eyes. Alisha sat stunned at the possibility that Kimberly had a daughter she never told Alisha about. Though, it was conceivable because she only saw Kimberly one month out of every year. Why would Kimberly never have mentioned her? Maybe she gave the child up for adoption? Maybe something awful happened and the child died? Alisha shivered at the possibilities. She filed through picture after picture until she came to one of Kimberly holding the baby and an older man with his arms around both of them. Alisha gasped when she studied the face of the older man. It was hard to say for sure, but he looked a lot like the picture of Lou Miller from the police file.

Her heart raced as she scooted over and opened another box. It was filled with letters and receipts and newspaper clippings. She skimmed several of the letters and realized they were love notes from Lou Miller, letters explaining how he cared for her. She opened every letter and noticed they all began with Dear Arianna. Alisha was confused. Who was Arianna? Why would Kimberly have love letters addressed to Arianna? Setting the letters aside she dug deeper in the box and pulled out a birth certificate. As she skimmed the page her chest tightened and a sick knowing filled her. She read and re-read the certificate as fear settled in her gut. It read:

> Birth Name: Arianna Kimberly Sutton
> Mother's Name: Amanda Borgman Sutton
> Father's Name: Andrew Sutton

Alisha's heart beat rapidly now as she dug through the rest of the box and found the birth certificate for Kimberly's daughter, Cindy Miller Borgman, listing the mother as Arianna Borgman and the father as Lou Miller. Her hands trembled as her mind completed the connection between Kimberly and Arianna. She made a pile of papers and pictures to take with her to show Dale, and then leaned a little further to reach the last box. Quickly opening it, she reached inside and her nails banged against something hard. She ran her fingers over the item, knowing exactly what it was before she even pulled it out. Finding the edge and lifting she beheld the blue Kansas license place with white lettering that read S above an N and the numbers 1919. Alisha thought she might vomit as panic started to take hold. She grabbed the pictures, birth certificates and the license plate and hurried back down the ladder. After closing the attic and turning off the garage light, Alisha bolted to her car. All of a sudden she found herself riddled with fear that Kimberly would come home and find her there. She sped out of the driveway and up the street, then pulled over and dug her

phone out of her purse. She was panting as she
dialed Dale's cell.

## Chapter 19

Dale, Stephen and Ernie were almost to the Bank of Stillwell when Alisha's call came through. She frantically ranted and Dale tried to calm her down, but nothing he said worked. "Alisha, I can't understand what you're saying," he told her, "you've got to slow down."

Alisha tried to breathe but the realization that her own half-sister was a murderer was more than she could emotionally process at the moment. She sobbed as she confessed to digging through Dale's confidential files, explaining how she compared pictures and found the baseball smiley face sticker. She told him how the license plate on her dad's truck matched the one she found in Kimberly's garage. She spoke at such speed she could barely keep up with her own words; much less expect Dale to follow along.

"Wait a minute," Dale interrupted, "how did you get my files?"

"You left them on the kitchen table."

Dale pulled the car to the side of the road. "Alisha, where are you right now?" His voice was direct and abrupt.

Stephen blurted, "Dale what are you doing? We're almost to the bank."

Dale u-turned, flipped on his sirens and began heading back the way they came. "Alisha, go straight home and wait for me." Dale ordered. Then he thought about it and changed his mind. "No, go straight to the station and talk to Emily and stay there."

"Okay," agreed Alisha, with tears streaming down her face.

"Take everything you took from Kimberly's and give it to Officer Emily, you understand?" Dale reiterated the importance of the evidence Alisha held.

"Okay," Alisha sputtered again, "okay."

"I'm on my way babe, it'll be okay," Dale tried to console her but he knew deep down there was nothing okay about the entire situation.

Dale hung up with Alisha and immediately dialed Emily, telling her to be on the look out for Alisha and to tag everything she brought in as evidence. "Tell Tom Miller he is free to go home," Dale added. "And start running a cross check on the names Arianna Kimberly Sutton, and Arianna Borgman."

"I'm on it," Emily replied, jotting down all the names he threw out.

"Another thing," Dale blurted, "our John Doe's name is Martin Miller."

"How do you know that?"

"With any luck we'll have a confession as soon as we pick up Kimberly or Arianna or whatever her real name is." Dale couldn't believe it, months of chasing John Doe's killer and the case was about to crack wide open. He filled Stephen and Ernie in on the details as they sped along the freeway.

Ernie slapped his fist on his knee, "I knew it!" He blurted excitedly.

Stephen sat quiet. "I think we should take a look at what's in that box," he explained, "it might have all the proof you need and more."

Dale shook his head, "there will be time for that later."

Ernie added, "He's right, the box isn't going anywhere."

As they drove Dale filled them in on all Alisha told him. Then they rode in silence, each letting the facts and the speculation seep into their minds and play out in various scenarios.

Suddenly Stephen jolted forward and grabbed the dash. "Kimberly picked up Kate from the station today," he gasped. Stephen's voice was loud and rang with an underlying horror that couldn't be ignored. They all knew what she was capable of.

~

Alisha gave everything she took from Kimberly's attic to Officer Emily and then sat down in the lobby to catch her breath and wait for Dale. She leaned forward on her elbows and chewed on her fingernails, a nervous habit she tried years to break. She was shocked when Tom came walking into the lobby area, but not nearly as surprised as he looked when he saw her. He did a double take and her eyes widen when they met his. She leapt to her feet as he rushed over to her, taking her by the arm and pulling her toward the glass doors.

"What are you doing here?" He asked.

"I'm waiting for my husband." She spoke in a hushed tone and wiggled her arm free from his grip. "It can't look like we know each other."

Alisha knew Tom could tell by the glassiness of her eyes she'd been crying. "He doesn't know about us, right?"

"Not yet," she said, "but he'll ask me about you later I'm sure."

Tom walked with her outside the station, onto the sidewalk. "Can you tell me what's going on exactly?" Alisha was silent and Tom studied her face. "Alisha," he begged, "you are my only alibi for the night Jeanette Carlen was killed." She looked up at him and nodded. "I can't go to jail. If it comes to that I'll have to confess I was with you."

Alisha shook her head, "it won't come to that. He already knows you didn't kill anyone."

"How do you know that? As of an hour ago he was getting ready to arrest me."

Alisha sat down on a bench adjacent to the front doors of the station and Tom joined her, careful not to sit too close. She took a deep breath and began to fill in all the blanks for him. When she got to the part about Kimberly, Tom leapt from the bench and took off running toward the parking lot, yelling over his shoulder, "Kimberly picked up my wife!" Alisha followed a couple strides behind until he came to an abrupt halt.

"Damn," he cursed, spewing obvious frustration and anger and fear all at once.

"What?" She grabbed hold of his arm and tried to make eye contact, but he was frantic. "What's the matter?"

"I don't have my car here. I rode with Stephen and Ernie." Tom paced in the lot, with anguish pouring from his face.

There was no time to worry how it may look or what Dale may think. Alisha tossed him her keys. "You drive."

Tom shook his head. "I can't take your car."

Alisha got in and slammed the passenger door shut. Tom cursed some more then slid in the driver's side. "We shouldn't be seen together." He said as he turned the ignition, backed out of the space and sped off the lot. His face was stern and Alisha could see the worry in his eyes.

"Just drive fast," she said flatly, knowing it was more important to get to his wife than to worry about how bad it would look if they arrived together.

Once again knots had formed in Tom's stomach. Every muscle in his body felt tense and his mind whirled with all the awful things that could be happening to Kate. Alisha held onto the handle above the passenger door as Tom sped around corners and floored the gas. "Let's get there alive," she belted after he skid around one turn so tight she feared the Isuzu rodeo would tip. Alisha grabbed Tom's cell and dialed Kate's number as Tom recited it. It went to voicemail. Alisha disconnected and dialed their home number. Again, voicemail. She threw his cell on the seat and grabbed hers, then dialed Dale. Voicemail. She grunted. "Why doesn't anyone answer their damn phone?"

Once on the freeway Tom weaved in and out of traffic but his speed was more fluid and he wasn't hitting the brake and revving the gas as often. Alisha wondered how much he knew about Arianna Borgman and the alleged crimes she committed. She wondered if he knew that the John Doe from six months ago was most likely his brother. She didn't want to be the one to tell him, at least not now, not while he was worried about his wife. She stared out the passenger window unable to believe all that was happening.

"So," Tom said, breaking the moment of silence in the car, "Kimberly killed my grandfather?" Alisha reached over and squeezed his knee, nodding her head. Tom's jaw tightened and Alisha could see the anger manifest in his clenched teeth.

"This other case your husband was working on," he asked, "you said it was connected, how?"

Alisha felt despair enter her voice as she tried to clear her throat and speak. He deserved to know but it broke her heart to have to be the one to tell him, especially now. "The hit and run from six months ago," she took a deep breath, "it was your brother Martin that was killed."

Tom's face drained of any last color he had and his hands shook against the steering wheel. He could barely contain the anger and hatred he felt erupting within. He swallowed hard several times to keep the knot of agony from showing itself. He had to focus on getting to Kate before it was too late. He had to hold it together for Kate before he lost everything.

~

When Dale pulled into the station parking lot, Stephen was the first to jump out in a mad dash for his car. Ernie hollered after him, "I'll get Tom. You pull the car around front." Stephen waved his arm in agreement as he sprinted to the car. Dale rushed inside to find Alisha. He was dying to get his hands on the evidence she pulled from Kimberly's attic. Dale did a quick scan of the lobby as he walked through, but no Alisha. He found Officer Emily right away, and though she began pouring over the evidence, Dale was distracted, moving quickly up and down the halls and peeking in rooms.

"Where is she?" He blurted, cutting Emily off mid sentence.

"Who?" Emily glared, obviously annoyed by the interruption.

"Alisha!" Dale yelled.

"Wasn't she in the lobby?" Emily asked. "That's where I left her."

Dale instructed Emily to check every ladies room in the building while he jetted back to the lobby to look one more time. There he ran into Ernie, who shared his frustration, as he couldn't locate Tom. Dale ran out the glass doors to the parking lot, scanning the rows of cars. He bent over and put his hands on his knees, hanging his head down and breathing heavy as the realization hit him. Alisha wasn't there and neither was Tom.

Stephen pulled his car around front and honked impatiently for Ernie and Tom. Finally, jumping out of the car, he made a dash for the station doors. Just as he was about to walk in Ernie came through the doors and shrugged, "he's not here," he said.

"Where is he?" Blurted Stephen. "He didn't have a car here."

Ernie shrugged his shoulders again. "Maybe somebody picked him up."

Dale jogged over from the parking lot, "or Alisha gave him a ride."

Stephen knew there was more to Dale's statement, and shot him a knowing glance, but there was no time to get into it. "Let's go," he belted, "we've got to get to Kate's house."

Ernie shook his head no.

"What?" Stephen exclaimed.

"She won't take Kate home."

"How do you know that?" Dale intruded.

Ernie shook his head at both of them. "You're not thinking like a killer. If she has any indication we're onto her she won't take Kate home."

Stephen was growing antsy. He slammed his hands on the top of his car. "If not Kate's house, then where?"

"Arianna's," Ernie muttered with a cigarette pursed between his lips.

Dale gawked at both of them, "where the hell is Arianna's? You mean Kimberly's house?"

Ernie shook his head, "nope, Arianna's apartment."

Dale looked shocked. He obviously didn't know there was an apartment registered in

Arianna Borgman's name. Ernie gave Dale the address and then hopped in the car, dropping his cigarette butt on the street.

Dale ran back inside the station and told Emily to send back up to the address Ernie gave him. "Send a car to Kimberly Sutton's residence as well," Dale grabbed his phone and saw Alisha called, but left no message. He dialed her back but it rang through to voicemail. "I'm heading to Kate Miller's house," he told Emily and jogged out the door.

Emily ran to catch him. "I'm sending a car to pick up Cindy Miller and bring her in."

Dale nodded, "good thinking, don't arrest her, just hold her for questioning and see if you can use her to find out where her mother is." Dale sprinted to his car.

~

Pulling onto their street, Tom stopped the Rodeo two houses up and turned off the engine. "That's Kimberly's car," he said, pointing at the Cadillac in the driveway. Alisha nodded. "You stay here," Tom said, "she can't see us together or she might get suspicious." Alisha started to argue, but Tom's jaw was set. He grabbed her hand, "please," he pleaded, "I don't want to risk Kimberly freaking out and doing something to Kate."

Alisha understood. He was scared. So was she. She squeezed his hand and nodded. Once Tom closed the door and headed to the house, Alisha grabbed her cell and text Dale. "At Miller house. Kimberly here." She then put her phone on mute and slid it into her front jean pocket. Alisha suddenly remembered her gun was still in her purse from Friday night when she had gone to Kimberly's to find Tom's phone. She pulled it out, made sure the safety was on, and shoved it into the back of her jeans. She waited and watched as she saw the front door open and Tom walk inside. Alisha took a deep breath, then reached back and tightened her pony tail. She nervously stepped out of the car, closed the passenger door quietly behind her and ran toward the back of the house.

Kimberly was sitting at the kitchen table when Kate walked back into the kitchen with Tom. "I'm surprised to see you here," Kimberly sarcastically grinned, "I mean, who was your alibi for Friday night?"

Tom tried to hide the disdain he thought for certain was oozing from his eyeballs. He wanted to strangle her right there in the kitchen. Kate saw the tension in his face and rubbed her hand across his back. "Come sit down Tom, she's just teasing you." She walked past him to the table and sat down next to Kimberly.

Tom could feel his whole body clench when Kate neared Kimberly. He tried to hide it but knew he was failing. "Geez Tom, a little tense are we?" Kimberly asked.

Tom ignored the question altogether and stared at Kate. "I need you to come with me right now," he said. "Right now Kate." Tom's voice elevated and Kimberly shot him a glance of both suspicion and insight.

"What's the matter with you," Kate questioned, "why are you acting so weird?"

"Yes Tom," Kimberly spewed. "Do tell us why you're acting weird."

Tom froze. His mouth was dry, his pulse raced and his stomach felt knotted beyond description. Fear crept into every thought and he just wanted to get Kate out of the house. He licked his lips and reminded himself to breathe. "Kate, can I talk to you in private for a minute?" He hoped at the very least he could get her alone and somehow signal her of the danger.

Before Kate could respond Kimberly pushed her chair back and stood up, "I have to use the bathroom anyway," she said. "So you two can stay right here and chat while I'm gone." Kimberly snatched her purse off the counter as she breezed by Tom.

Kate stared up at Tom with eyes of innocence and ignorance. "What is going on?" She narrowed her brow. "It's like you're going out of your way to be rude to her."

Tom leaned both hands on the table and put his lips against Kate's ear. His heart was pounding hard in his chest as he whispered, "Kimberly is Arianna Borgman."

"Kimberly is who?" Kate blurted.

Before Tom could speak, the answer came from behind him. "Arianna Borgman," Kimberly seethed. Tom turned to see Kimberly standing at the edge of the kitchen with a gun aimed at them. Tom stood up straight and moved his body to block Kate. Kimberly laughed at his noble endeavor. "Oh Tom," she gleaned, "it's a little late to try and take care of your wife now isn't it?"

"What are you doing?" Kate's tone was evidence she thought this was some kind of joke. Neither Tom nor Kimberly answered her but kept their eyes locked on each other. It wasn't until Kate noticed Tom's hand trembling that the reality of what was happening began to sink in. She reached up and touched Tom's arm. "How can she be Arianna Borgman? I thought you said that was the name of the woman you met with at Murrays," she shook her head in confusion, "the one who ended up dead?"

Tom never moved his glare from Kimberly and he barely moved his lips as he spoke with monotone speed. "Kimberly hired Jeanette Carlen to pretend to be Arianna Borgman and then killed her afterwards because she could identify her."

Kimberly smirked, "impressive, but I believe the gun used to kill that woman was yours."

"It is mine but you borrowed it to murder Jeanette Carlen and then brought it back so Kate would be framed for the murder." Tom scowled at her.

Kate stood up, "what's going on?"

"Sit down sweetie," Kimberly spewed, "you don't want to end up hurt." Kate sank back in her chair. Kimberly then pointed the gun directly at Tom, "you should take a seat too," she ordered. Tom didn't budge. He returned her piercing gaze with equal fervor. She grinned and uttered, "don't try to be a hero; you don't have the genes for it."

"I don't know what the hell my grandfather did to you, but that's over Kimberly. It's the past!" Tom's voice cracked with emotion, as fear and rage flooded his veins.

"You either sit down and shut up or I kill you right here." Kimberly cocked the gun and held her aim firm. Tom took one step back and sank into the chair across from Kate. Kate's face was terror stricken and Tom knew she was trying to process the fact that her best friend wasn't at all the person she thought. He reached across the table and gripped her hands, squeezing them tightly to let her know somehow they would get through this.

Kimberly pointed the gun at Kate and instructed her to go get grandmother's journal and bring it to her. "Don't even think about calling the police," she said, "I already removed the phone from your bedroom." Kimberly watched as Kate walked down the hall and entered the bedroom. She hollered down the hall, "you have ten seconds

to return with the journal or I kill your husband."
Then she looked at Tom, "I'm going to kill you
anyway but she doesn't need to know that yet."

Tom looked at Kimberly with a snide
squint, "it's not in the journal anymore," he told
her. She abruptly turned her head to look at him
and he could see the peaked interest on her face.
"The key," he explained, "it's already gone."

"Where is it?" Kimberly's face flushed,
telling Tom this tidbit of information foiled her
plans.

"You let Kate go and I'll tell you where it is."
Tom crossed his arms in front of him.

Kimberly shook her head, "how stupid do
you think I am Tom?" She peaked around the
corner and saw Kate coming down the hall with the
journal. As Kate neared her she instructed her to
set the journal on the floor, and return quickly to
her seat across from Tom at the table. Once Kate
was seated she and Tom immediately reached for
each other's hands.

After flipping hastily through its pages,
Kimberly threw grandmother's journal across the
kitchen in an angry rage. She turned the gun on
Tom, demanding to have the key.

"I don't have it," Tom yelled back. Kimberly
screamed at the top of her lungs with a piercing,
screeching tone that made every muscle in Kate's
body tense and shake.

Kate sobbed, "Why are you doing this
Kimberly? Why are you doing this?"

Kimberly stopped abruptly and looked at
Kate, "you want to know why?" Her tone sounded
almost amused by the question. "Because Lou
promised me an inheritance for my daughter."

Kate met Kimberly's eyes, "your daughter?"

"My daughter Cindy, you know Cindy, your
husband's assistant?" Tom hadn't made this

connection yet and he was floored. Kimberly looked at Tom, "you remember Tom, I recommended you hire her a year and half ago." She smirked, "I told you she came highly recommended." She gloated at the cleverness of her plan to infiltrate and gather information. Tom dropped his head.

"Why?" Kate asked again.

"Lou loved me but Tom's grandmother wouldn't let him leave." The anger rose in her voice as she continued, "that old bitch was strangling the life out of him." She paced back and forth in the kitchen, recalling her last conversation with Lou. "He told me he couldn't leave her but he'd make sure me and Cindy were in his Will and he'd leave us enough that we'd never have to worry about money again."

Kate studied Kimberly's face and felt compassion, still unable to fully view her best friend as a killer. "I'm sorry Grandpa Lou broke your heart," she said softly.

Kimberly whirled around toward Kate and burst into laughter. "Poor simple Kate," she spewed, "thinking life is like a romance novel, where everyone's in love and lives happily ever after." Kimberly's laugh faded off and a cold, harsh tone replaced it. "I never loved Lou. I wanted him for his money. Why do you think I got pregnant?"

Tom was putting it all together in his mind and interjected, "so you tried to trap Lou, wanting him to divorce Madeline and marry you." The pieces of the past were quickly fitting together in his head. "Lou saw thru you and refused to leave Madeline, so you ran him down."

Kimberly screamed, "Lou loved me!"

"Maybe," hollered Tom, "but you never loved him and he was wise enough to sense it."

Kimberly grinned. "But not wise enough to stay alive."

"So after you killed Grandpa Lou, you went after Madeline didn't you?" The anger was overwhelming Tom's heart and he fought to stay rational.

"No," Kimberly blurted, "your grandmother came after me."

"What?" Exclaimed Kate. She couldn't imagine Tom's grandmother having a violent bone in her body.

"She came to me and cut a deal. If I disappeared, left her and her family alone to die of old age, she promised to leave me the inheritance Lou promised me." Kimberly's eyes flashed with hatred.

"Otherwise she was going to turn you in," Tom finished the story. "She had proof you killed Lou didn't she?" Kimberly glared at Tom, unwilling or unable to answer that question. "She knew you'd try to kill all of us for the money."

"And I will," Kimberly spat flatly.

Tom ignored her and continued with the details of the story. If he could keep her talking, he could prolong the inevitable. "So you disappeared and re-emerged two years ago using your middle name of Kimberly."

"I always went by my middle name of Kimberly, except with Lou. He loved the name Arianna and he was the only one who called me that." Kimberly's eyes glazed over for a brief second, as if she were remembering him fondly.

"You re-emerged and waited for grandmother to die."

Kimberly's face hardened. "I kept my end of the deal until your brother started digging around. He threatened to turn me in and not to pay what was rightfully mine."

"But there has been no pay out," said Kate, confused. "Grandmother's Will has been held by the attorney this whole time because both Tom and Martin have to be present to sign."

Tom looked at Kate, "that isn't going to happen," he said quietly.

"Since Martin figured out who I was," Kimberly explained to Kate, "I had no choice but to help him meet with a terrible accident." Kimberly's tone lacked all remorse and Kate couldn't adjust to the fact that she could really be a cold hearted murderer.

Kate gasped, "You killed Martin?"

Kimberly rolled her eyes at Kate, "Get over it," she exhaled, "it's not like you really knew him."

Tom squeezed Kate's hand harder as the anger filled him and tears welled in Kate's eyes. That was his brother Kimberly was dismissing with icy aloofness. It was his brother. Tom fought the urge to allow tears, as he didn't want Kimberly to see any sign of weakness.

"If Martin is dead then no one will ever touch the Will." Kate looked at Tom. "Right?"

Kimberly laughed. "You just don't get it do you?"

Kate was starting to put the pieces together. She stared out the bay window and swallowed hard. Mustering up all the nerve she could find, Kate asked, "Did you try to kill me in an accident too?"

Kimberly grinned and shot a look to Tom, "Well, look who is finally catching onto things," she sarcastically spewed. Tom gave Kate's hand another tight squeeze but it didn't help, she already put her head on the table and started to cry.

"It's not personal Kate," Kimberly sighed, "I don't have another choice."

"What are you talking about?" Tom stammered.

Kimberly exhaled loudly, as if she were frustrated by the need to explain, "The only guarantee I have of getting what was rightfully promised to me now is to kill all of you, leaving only Lou's biological daughter, my Cindy, as heir to his inheritance." She walked toward the sink, spun on the ball of her foot and walked back toward the pantry, all the while keeping the gun pointed at Tom and Kate. "Why do you think I wanted Cindy working at LouLineCo? Duh. I needed her to learn the business since she'll be the owner soon."

Kate lifted her head up, "that's why Martin gave me the manila envelope with that birth certificate in it." Kate's eyes lit with knowing. "That's what he meant when he said it was a matter of life and death." Kate looked at Tom through teary eyes. "Martin was trying to protect us."

Kimberly chuckled, "well, that plan backfired." She tightened her grip on the gun and inched her way closer to the table. Kimberly then told the story of how Martin found her and stole the barrette, the picture and the birth certificate from her apartment. "He stole my proof," she seethed. "Proof I sat on for over eighteen years waiting for my payout." Kimberly kicked over one of the wooden stools that sat around the kitchen island. Kate jumped as it slammed to the floor. "That's when I knew Martin would never allow me to touch the money. So I followed him and after he left your house I ran him down."

Tears streamed down Kate's face.

"Now," Kimberly exhaled, "who wants to die first?" Kate and Tom squeezed each other's fingers until they were turning white, and their eyes locked in an embrace of desperation.

"You can have whatever inheritance money is in the Will," glared Tom, "it's all yours."

Kimberly laughed, "oh Tom, Tom, Tom," she scolded, "I don't need your charity. My daughter is biologically owed all the money and she will get it. That you can count on."

~

Alisha couldn't hear the whole conversation from outside, but she heard enough to know Kimberly was going to kill Tom and Kate. She pulled her phone from her pocket and quickly text Dale, "K has gun. Going to kill them." Her fingers were trembling as she pushed each letter and hit send. Surely Dale has back up on the way, she told herself, trying to calm down. But she feared they wouldn't get here in time. She crept closer to the kitchen window where she could see what was happening. She saw Tom and Kate at the round kitchen table, which sat directly in front of the bay window. Kimberly was ranting and pacing behind them, holding the gun and waving it as her voice elevated. Alisha reached back and pulled the gun from the back of her jeans, sliding the safety off and positioning herself where she had a shot at Kimberly if she needed it. She held the gun firm in her right hand and used her left hand to support her arm and hold her hand steady. She was trembling. Kimberly's voice rose to a screeching level and Alisha blinked. Everything felt like it was moving in slow motion. Kimberly's face turned deep red and Alisha swallowed hard, seeing her seethe obscenities at Tom and Kate and wave the gun in the air. Then all of a sudden Kimberly stopped and she stood perfectly still. Alisha could hear the loudness of her own breathing as she panted from the fear driven adrenaline rushing through her. Kimberly's expression went stone cold and Alisha watched as she lifted the gun toward Tom in one fluid motion.

Glass shattered everywhere and the sound of Kate's scream echoed through three rapid shots. Kate jumped up, shaking and sobbing uncontrollably. Alisha felt the damp ground seep through her jeans as she hit her knees and lowered her gun to the ground. She had fired twice and her ears were ringing. Tom reached his arm for Kate and gripped his left shoulder. He'd been hit. Kate rushed toward him just as Dale and three other officers burst into the house with guns drawn. Dale looked down at Kimberly, who had taken two bullets, one in the chest and the other straight through the forehead.

Dale and Tom locked eyes and Tom tilted his head toward the shattered window. "She's out there," he said, "she saved us."

Dale rushed out the front door, leaving the other officers to attend to Tom and Kate. He ran down the hill to where Alisha sat, still on her knees, gun still gripped tightly in her hand. Her body shook violently and tears poured down her cheeks. She couldn't take her eyes from the shattered window and the image of Kimberly. Dale knelt next to her and slowly reached forward, sliding the gun from her hand. He moved in front of her and pulled her close, embracing her as she crumbled in his arms.

~

By the time Stephen and Ernie arrived at the scene, Tom was in an ambulance and Kimberly's body had already been removed from the house. Alisha sat in Dale's car, and Kate stood next to the ambulance, giving her statement to an

Officer.  Ernie peeked in the ambulance and saw Tom sitting upright, "take a shot?"

Tom nodded, "straight through the shoulder."

Ernie grinned, "Lucky."

When Kate saw Stephen approaching, she rushed over and threw her arms around his neck. He hugged her tightly for a brief moment, as the relief that she was all right filled him. Suddenly aware of Tom's watchful eye from the back of the ambulance, he released his hold, pulling Kate's arms away from his neck.  There was an unspoken truth between them, a truth that confirmed things were different now.  Kate leaned forward and gave him a kiss on his cheek, allowing her lips to linger, and feel the warmth of his breath. There was so much to say, but it wasn't the right time or place.

"Thank you," she whispered, "for everything. I will never forget what you did for us. What you did for me."

"I played a small part."  Stephen looked down and shifted his weight from his left foot to his right.  He was uncomfortable by Toms scrutinizing eye, but more than that he was uneasy about the depth of his feelings for Kate.  He didn't want her to know how much he cared, how worried he had been or how hard it was to let her go.

"You played more than a small part to me." Kate grabbed his hand and let her finger tips momentarily interlock with his.  Stephen gave her hand a tiny squeeze, and quickly released it.  Then he backed away and turned his attention toward Officer Gordon.

Dale hung up his phone as Stephen approached.  "That was Emily at the station.  She interrogated your client, Cindy."

"And?"

"She had no idea her mother lead a double life. She knew her mom only as Kimberly Borgman Sutton. She was under the impression her mother traveled abroad a lot, which explained why she didn't see her often and never went to mom's house."

"Did she think her mom had the house close to the Miller family or the apartment across town?"

"The apartment. She thought her mom had apartments in various cities throughout the country."

"Wow," Stephen shook his head, "talk about living a life of lies."

"The only thing she knew was her mom told her she was owed an inheritance from Cindy's father, which is why she hired you to find him."

"I feel sorry for her."

"Yeah, me too."

Stephen nodded. "So, case closed then."

"Yep, case closed."

Stephen looked over at Alisha sitting in Dale's car, "is she going to be okay?"

"Eventually, yeah, she'll be fine."

Stephen shuffled his feet on the ground. "Are you going to be okay?" Dale's eyes darted from his car to Stephen with a knowing glare. He didn't say anything and Stephen surmised it was probably because a lump was permanently lodged in his throat, forcing him to hold back the emotion until he could be alone. "You know," Stephen spoke softly, "if it hadn't been for the awkward relationship between Tom and your wife, you'd be bagging up two innocent people and still have a killer on the loose."

Dale stared at the ground and nodded his head up and down. He swallowed hard. Stephen put his hand on Dale's shoulder, "even the bad stuff can be used for good sometimes," Stephen said.   Dale looked up and nodded.  Stephen reached in his pocket, pulled out the brass key from grandmother's journal and handed it to Dale. "Remember," he smiled, "forgiveness is key."

Dale grinned and took a deep breath.  "You and Ernie want to take a ride to the bank of Stillwell?"

Stephen grinned, "Whenever you're ready."

Dale shook his head, "not me.  You." Stephen looked puzzled. "Ernie still has his badge right?"  Stephen nodded.  Dale handed him back the key and the warrant.  "I'll call ahead and let them know I'm sending Deputy Ernie James to pick up the contents of the safe deposit box."  Dale knew how badly Stephen wanted to know what was in that box.  Stephen's face lit up like a kid at Christmas.

"Thanks man," he grinned.

Dale stretched out his hand and shook Stephen's.  Glancing back at Alisha and then to Stephen, his voice quaked as he uttered, "no man, thank you."

Ernie was as excited as Stephen to take the trip to Stillwell.  He took one last drag on his cigarette before mashing the butt into the ground and slipping into the passenger side of Stephen's car.  Ernie buckled his seatbelt and sighed, "Am I good or am I good?"

Stephen laughed, "Excuse me?  Wasn't it you who said, 'you're not thinking like a killer' and took us to the wrong place?"

Ernie shrugged, "oh, that, well, that doesn't count."

"It counts," said Stephen.

"Are you telling me that overall I didn't wow you?"  Ernie stared at Stephen with his eyebrows raised.

"You wowed me," Stephen conceded.

They drove in silence for a few moments then Ernie noted, "the whole thing is pretty ironic don't ya think?"

"How so?"

With his usual raspy flare Ernie explained, "It was the grandfather's girlfriend that started the whole mess and the grandson's girlfriend that ended it." He shrugged, "that's what I call balance."

Stephen let Ernie's words sink it. It was ironic. He smirked at Ernie, "deep man, really deep."

Ernie grinned with satisfaction, "Lookey there, I wowed you again."

## Chapter 20

Stephen walked into the waiting area and scanned the room for Kate. She had her head down and her face buried in grandmother's journal. He recognized the leather exterior. She didn't even look up as he walked across the room and sat down two seats away. He watched her for a moment, smiling to himself at how truly beautiful she was, inside and out. Finally, after she was oblivious to his presence, he over-dramatically cleared his throat, "Ahem." Stephen surmised that everyone else in the waiting room noticed him and looked up, but Kate did not. He moved to the seat right next to her and whispered, "Kate."

With that she jumped and shrieked with a shrill squeal that Stephen thought surely rendered any patient with a hearing aid, inoperable. He let out a belly laugh as she gripped her chest, "you scared me to death!"

In between chuckles he tried to contain himself enough to explain that he had a special delivery for her. "First," he said, "how is Tom?"

"He's in recovery now. The surgery went well and he will have full use and normal range of motion in his arm."

"That's wonderful," smiled Stephen. "I have something grandmother left for you."

Kate's eyes widened. "She left something specifically for me in the safe deposit box?"

"Funny story about that, it wasn't exactly in the safe deposit box."

"Where was it?"

Stephen grinned at the curiosity in her eyes. "You wouldn't believe me if I told you." Stephen went on to explain how he and Ernie opened the safe deposit box but found only a picture.

"A picture of who?" gasped Kate.

"Not who. What." Stephen reached into the inside pocket of his black sport coat and pulled out a photograph of the mouth of a creek just before it empties into a small lake, and a broken log. Chills bolted up Kate's arms and grew into shivers around her neck. Stephen studied her face and flipped the photograph over to show a copy of the poem from her journal. She had taped it on the back. "It seems Grandma knew you would know where this place was."

Kate nodded. "I broke that log a long time ago." She took the picture from Stephen and held it closer. "It looked a lot different then."

"Time has a way of changing things." Kate knew he was referring to the aging log but his sentence took on a deeper meaning. Time did have a way of changing things. Even love altered over the years, shedding layers and taking on various forms, but never leaving completely. Stephen studied her face, as if he were reading her thoughts. "It would have been nice to have you with us because Ernie and I traipsed all over that woods for about four hours before we finally found the right log." Stephen belly laughed as he recanted the story of Ernie up to his knees in mud, digging into every log they found as if searching for hidden treasure.

Kate smiled. "I'm not sure I could have found it any faster. I haven't been there in a long time."

"I learned something new about my friend Ernie."

"What's that?" Kate asked.

"Ernie's afraid of snakes." Kate giggled. It was hard to imagine big 'ol Ernie afraid of anything, much less a little snake. They laughed for a moment and then Stephen swallowed hard. He stood up and handed Kate an envelope.

"Do you want to stay and read it with me?"

Stephen shook his head. "It's for your eyes only. My work here is done." He leaned down, taking her hand and kissed it gently. "You are a remarkable woman Kate Miller, and Tom is a very lucky man."

Kate blinked slowly in gratitude, gave a slight nod of head and half-smiled. This was their final goodbye, and though she only knew him a matter of days, she felt like he was a long lost friend. As if he entered her life for the sole purpose of reminding her how to feel again. Stephen winked at her, and then vanished almost as fast as he appeared. Kate watched him leave, knowing she would never forget him and the uncanny way he made her heart flutter.

When he was out of site, she turned her attention to the envelope. Opening it up she saw grandmother's beautiful penmanship and she leaned back in her chair and began to absorb her words. *"My dearest Kate, if you are reading this letter you have indeed found out the truth about our family secret. In this box is all the proof you need for justice to be served. I always knew you were strong enough to carry the burden and protect us. Remember my dear, the Miller boys make mistakes and it is the God-given strength of the Miller women who cover those transgressions with love and forgiveness. Hold close to your heart God's promise in Romans 8:28, 'And we know that God causes all things to work together for good to those that love God, to those who are called according to His purpose.' ALL things Kate. God can take the worst seeds and turn them into the most beautiful flowers.*

*My Will was not to be issued unless the security of my living grandsons was evident in their signatures. If this is not the case, you can have the Will released by giving the attorney the code word engraved on the inside of your wedding band. As promised, special instructions have been left for the inheritance of Lou's daughter, Cindy Miller.*

*My lovely Kate, as you and Tom traverse the rugged terrain of life together, remember in marriage there are a million reasons to give up and walk away, but the key is in finding the one reason to stay. And then stay, even when there's no easy way."*

Kate finished reading and blinked through the tears that filled her eyes. She wished grandmother was here now so she could see the glow of wisdom on her face and the sparkle of inspiration and strength in her eyes. She wanted to fall into those boney arms and hug her tight.  Kate folded the letter and placed it back in the envelope, then twisted her wedding band until it slid off her finger. She angled it toward the light to read the engraving. "ILYWAMH" it read. Kate's face beamed as the irony overtook her. Grandmother used Tom's acronym from college, knowing to anyone else it was gibberish, but to Kate it meant the world.

The nurse emerged from behind the double doors and told Kate she could see Tom now. She grabbed her purse and grandmother's letter and followed the nurse down the hall, into the recovery room. There lay a groggy, medicated Tom, barely coherent. Kate stared at him, overwhelmed by the feeling that she almost lost him. A few inches to the left and the bullet would have ripped into his chest and lungs. Kate walked closer and rubbed her hand through his hair, then bent over and kissed his forehead.    There were so many things they needed to discuss. His relationship with Alisha. Her encounters with Stephen. Right now it all seemed trivial. He was here and that was all that mattered. She slowly climbed onto his bed and apologized as he winced from the movement. Laying her head on his good shoulder, she interlocked her fingers in his and squeezed. He squeezed back. "Tom," she sniffled, "I want us to stay." Her voice cracked with emotion, "Even when there's no easy way, I want us to stay. And stay. And stay."

Kate closed her eyes and listened to Tom's breathing. She thought he was falling asleep again when all of a sudden he whispered, "ILYWAMH."

Kate whispered back, "ILYWAMH."

Twisting her wedding band counter clockwise around her finger, she looked up at the ceiling and could sense grandmother gazing down with that ever present sparkle in her eye and an approving grin. Kate snuggled in and realized Grandmother was right, she did get the last laugh.

~

# ABOUT THE AUTHOR

S.R.Claridge, nominated for the 2010 Molly Award, 2013 Pushcart Prize and awarded the 2011 Rocky Mountain Fiction Writers Pen Award, writes full-time and lives in Colorado. She loves autumn, moonlight and Grey Goose martinis with bleu cheese or jalapeno stuffed olives. She believes Friday nights are for indulging in Mexican food and margaritas and Sunday mornings warrant an extra-spicy Bloody Mary. Growing up in St. Louis, Missouri and earning her BA in Psychology from the University of Missouri, Columbia, S.R.Claridge is a mixture of mid-western family values and western wild nights. She loves Jesus, believes in the power of prayer, in the freedom of forgiveness and that life is a gift that should be enjoyed to the fullest. With a background in theatre, S.R.Claridge creates characters with dramatic flair and is known for her intense plot twists and engaging humor. S.R.Claridge would rather walk dangerously where there's a view than sit in idle safety and let life pass her by. Her spirited outlook comes shining through in her novels, as she takes readers to the edge of their seats with bone-chilling suspense.

# BOOKS BY S.R.CLARIDGE

Tetterbaum's Truth *(book 1 in the Just Call Me Angel series)*

Traitors Among Us *(book 2 in the Just Call Me Angel series)*

Russian Uprising *(book 3 in the Just Call Me Angel series)*

Death Trap *(book 4 in the Just Call Me Angel series)*

Loose Ends *(book 5 in the Just Call Me Angel series)*

Divine Intervention *(book 6 in the Just Call Me Angel series)*

Petals of Blood *(short story; Pushcart Prize Nomination 2013)*

House of Lies *(Political cult suspense)*

No Easy Way *(debut novel; nominated for The Molly Award from the HODRW 2010)*

The Candy Shop *(Suspense Thriller)*

All S.R.Claridge novels are available in Ebook and Print at Amazon, Barnes & Noble, Smashwords and anywhere books are sold.